Yorkshire's Northern Stars

Ethel Fledd

First Published in Great Britain in 2016
By KP Publishing
71a Aston Lane,
Shardlow, Derbys DE72 2GX

ISBN: 978-1-911472-12-4

Love is not love
Which alters when it alteration finds,
Or bends with the remover to remove.
O no, it is an ever-fixed mark
That looks on tempests and is never shaken;
It is the star to every wand'ring bark,
Whose worth's unknown, although his height be taken.

Sonnet 116, William Shakespeare

Introduction

Yorkshire was a hard, but exciting, place to live in the 1720s. Its prosperous wool merchants exported their goods around the world and, from their hard-earned profits, built manor houses and mansions amongst the moors towns. The city of York too was well on its way to becoming the capital of the northern parts and evolved to replicate all the delights, but also the vices, of London.

And yet, co-existing with these forward looking people, there were some amongst them who saw change as an enemy. Some who harboured deep prejudices and who were implacably fixed on resisting all that was new or different.

This book, inspired by a true story, tells the story of sisters Aurora and Elizabeth Fairfax, the so-called Northern Stars of Yorkshire, and their struggle to challenge those who wanted to take Yorkshire back to the dark ages.

YORK

Grace Dieu Manor

TADCASTER

Vavasour Hall

Doncaster

Sheffield

MATLOCK BATH

Chapter 1

Secrets! Why is it that one half of the world can keep them but the other half cannot? A shameful secret, yes, all can keep; but a shocking one, or a happy one ..... is impossible to resist sharing. To know that what you have to say will astound and captivate your listener makes for a compelling and satisfying conversation and one need only add a small rider such as 'between you and me' or 'this must go no further' and the deed is done. The secret can be shared with impunity.

Aurora Fairfax had the most joyous secret of all, but it was one she'd promised faithfully to keep.

Her family, the Fairfaxes, had resided in Yorkshire for generations and a few had earned their place in the history books by commanding parliamentary forces in the English Civil War, being renowned for their great leadership.

Aurora's particular family resided in the small town of Tadcaster at Fairfax Manor, a dozen miles away from York where they lived comfortably and quietly. There were six in her family; parents Duke and Isabella; then married sister Catherine, engaged sister Elizabeth, brother Nathaniel, who was called Nathan to his friends or if anyone was cross with him, and then Aurora herself, the youngest.

In 1720 Aurora was 22 years old and approaching the right age to think of marriage. Her prospects in that regard were quite good because, although her family were not rich, her lawyer father was extremely well connected and all his daughters received life-time annuities from a prosperous Fairfax relation.

Aurora had the means therefore to attract a suitor and was quite pretty and slim. Not such a great beauty as her older sisters Elizabeth and Catherine, yet still she'd attracted interest from men in Tadcaster and York.

As the only unattached daughter in the family, however, certain duties now fell to her that she'd previously been free of. Her mother's health had been deteriorating for some time and so it now fell to Aurora to become of use. It was decided that she'd accompany her mother to Matlock Bath for the summer. Isabella Fairfax had suffered a variety of ailments, which no one could actually name, more a collection of random symptoms which she was well disposed to discuss with anyone who would listen.

On the advice of friends drawn over a considerable period of time, rather than doctors, Isabella had reached the conclusion that, since so many of her friends had undergone miraculous recoveries from visiting spas, that she would try one too. A visit to Matlock Bath in Derbyshire was just what she needed to recover her health and spirits.

Aurora, who'd passed through Derbyshire many times, had never actually stayed there and so it was a great adventure. She dutifully travelled with her mother to the spa town and, for the first few days, they both enjoyed the warm, thermal spring waters and visits to the bath house. Isabella was happy to idle away the hours conversing with other ladies of a similar age and station and made friends with a cluster of them.

For Aurora, however, there was hardly anyone there of her own age and she quickly tired of the daily routine once the novelty wore off. She knew it was essential to her mother's well-being but, now tired of the familiarity of the baths, she made excuses to leave her mother there for a few hours and return later to take her back to their lodgings. She thus managed to have several hours a day free to pursue her own interests and explore the town.

She began to seek out friends of her own age. This was easily achieved as there were plenty of opportunities to mix with others at the weekly assemblies held in town and she became acquainted with quite a few other young people, some being resident in the town and others, like her, being visitors for the summer. It was during one of these assemblies when one of her friends introduced her to Benjamin Vavasour. He too was from Yorkshire and was visiting friends in Matlock for the summer.

To her surprise, and perhaps to his also, the new friends developed a relationship, far beyond just being acquaintances, they began to develop feelings for each other and no longer sought the company of other friends, preferring to spend time together.

With plenty of time on her hands and, before she knew what was happening, Aurora began to feel herself falling in love with

Benjamin. He appeared in her life at the exact moment when she'd begun to feel she was ready to fall in love. She'd seen her eldest sister fall in love and marry, then her second sister was recently engaged and now it felt it was her turn. The time was right.

They began a dizzying, fast-moving relationship which Aurora delighted in. It seemed all the more special because it was necessary to conceal it from her mother. She knew one hint of anything untoward, no matter how innocent the relationship may have been at the start, and her mother would whisk her away from the spa town. And so what began as small evasion and a degree of creative fibbing to explain the hours she spent away from her mother, gradually expanded into falsehoods and bare face lies, as the occasion demanded.

It was necessary, she told herself, because she wished the relationship to continue but, at the same time, wished her mother to have complete peace of mind to recuperate. Considering she'd no real experience of deception, she was surprised to find it became easier with practice. It became quite a daily challenge for her; not just to create a fictitious account of how she spent her day, but to create one that was wholly believable, that was the hard part.

In later years, Aurora would look back at this time with a degree of detachment and see it for what it really was - the folly of youth. She was a young woman who had arrived at a point in her life where she *wanted* to fall in love and Benjamin Vavasour just happened to be in the right place at the right time. There'd been numerous preparations for this day, men she'd observed as handsome, men she'd even had a crush on but none, until that moment, had all the elements she wanted combined together. He did.

There was also something about the place. The sheer beauty of Matlock with its stunning enclosed landscape gave her an inspiration to reach for something … something greater than herself - and it seemed that her new friendship with Vavasour fulfilled that lifting of spirit. Matlock was so totally different to anywhere she'd seen in Yorkshire - it felt quite magical. They fell deeply in love and Aurora thought he was the only man she ever would, or could, love. It was her first experience of being in love and it overwhelmed her.

5

In the midst of this growing, pleasant turmoil of emotion, her unaware mother Isabella, whose health she believed had improved during the weeks, made the first mention of a possible return home and Aurora immediately took fright at the prospect of having to leave. A subsequent hurried conversation with Benjamin brought matters to a head and both, fearing separation, were prompted to speak freely about their feelings. Hour upon hour they conversed in private - their mutual desire to continue the relationship being the only topic of conversation - before Benjamin proposed a plan for them to marry before they left Matlock.

This was the moment when the normally rational Aurora should have backed away, sought her mother's advice, or consulted a friend for a dispassionate opinion. But she didn't, she couldn't. She was incapable of denying her own feelings and that made her incapable of refusing him - the source of those feelings. Like lovers in war-time, frantic at the thought of never seeing each other again, they took their vows in haste, with strangers for witnesses and before a minister neither knew.

In the event it was to be a further week before the Fairfaxes finally left Matlock Bath. But it was a week the likes of which can only be experienced in youth, where every moment was heightened, precious and significant.

Benjamin and Aurora spent every possible moment of that week together as if they were their last days on earth, greedily commanding every minute together. The marriage was consummated. Not in any wonderfully romantic, honeymoon-type setting but in a second rate lodging house and in a frantic haste.

By this time, returning to her mother later in the day with stories of what she'd been doing during her absent hours had been so well practiced that it was now an effortless skill. And it was easy in this ultimate test to appear absolutely normal to her mother. It was a great feat she carried out and with great restraint to disguise the tumult of her mind.

Benjamin had impressed on her that it was imperative that news of their marriage was kept secret until he told his father. As eldest son and heir to a great estate in Yorkshire, his Roman Catholic father had threatened to disinherit either of his sons who married against his wishes, or outside the faith and the Fairfaxes were Protestants. So their marriage had to remain a secret until after they had returned home and he found the right opportunity to tell his father.

This issue of religion was of no consequence to Aurora as she'd been brought up in tolerance but, clearly to Benjamin, it was a major obstacle and he wanted to manage the situation carefully. It was, she thought, a small price to pay and besides, her own family needed breaking into the idea of her being in a relationship slowly too.

The day arrived for their departure and when, at last, the coach started the journey back to Yorkshire, Aurora could feel herself welling up with tears.

'Oh come now dear' said her mother, sensing her distress, though not the true reason for it. 'We'll come here again some time. Maybe next year. I didn't realise you'd formed such an attachment for the place.'

Any conversation was difficult for Aurora now and so she gazed out of the window for hours as the winding River Derwent and majestic high cliffs of Matlock and peaks of Derbyshire slowly gave way to the familiar green hills and then the moors of Yorkshire. Every mile taking her further and further away from where she wanted to be, though she knew Benjamin too would soon return to Yorkshire. How and when they would meet again she didn't know, she only knew that they would.

Chapter 2

Back home at Fairfax Manor in Tadcaster, Aurora tried to settle into her old familiar routine of busying herself around the home but couldn't restrain her thoughts. She was plagued with anxieties about when she would see Benjamin again.

She felt different; she was different; she was a married woman and yet strove in every particular to tell no-one of her secret and allow nothing in her behaviour to appear different. Even so, she took great alarm when a visiting neighbour commented to Isabella 'Aye …. how grown up Aurora is looking these days. She's outgrown the days of skipping down the lane to see me!'

It would've been so much easier if she could have confided in *someone*! The urge to talk about Benjamin, the one person who completely dominated her thoughts, was overwhelming, and she fleetingly considered confiding in sister Elizabeth, but yet it was too great a secret to trust to anyone. Elizabeth was a feisty character, bolder than Aurora, and empowering her with knowledge of Aurora's secret could've been dangerous, so she thought better of it.

Her father, Duke (as in Marmaduke), was a lawyer who divided his time between York and London and, having one foot in the north and one in the south, kept him busy but also allowed him to maintain good connections; a necessity in 1720s England.

Within a week of Isabella and Aurora's return home, there was news that Duke's next planned visit to London was now to include the whole family. An unexpected invitation had been received for them all to attend Leicester House, home of the Prince of Wales, for a social evening and such an offer had, of course, to be accepted. Much of Duke's business depended on him taking opportunities to mix with those people who would be attending the Prince and who could be of value to him as potential clients.

So the journey was made in their crowded family coach where Aurora, Duke, Isabella and sister Elizabeth all jostled along together.

During the long journey, Aurora amused herself by thinking about how each of them would react if she'd told them of her secret marriage. She of course knew that sister Elizabeth would be excited and thrilled; her mother Isabella would be horrified and would probably never forgive her for the deception at Matlock. Her father's reaction worried her most because she knew he would be disappointed; stoical but gravely disappointed in her. Disappointing him would be far worse than all the hysterics in the world from her mother.

He would then want to know of what standing her husband was and what fortune he had. If his prospects were good enough, Duke would manage his disappointment.

Arriving at Leicester House later that evening, the Fairfax family met up with other relations. Brother Nathan was there and so too was Aurora's eldest sister Catherine and her husband John Mason. Her brother and Mason were Members of Parliament, jointly, for York and, like her father, divided their time between York and London. Another acquaintance they met there was William Knightley who was the fiancé of sister Elizabeth.

Aurora found herself engaged by Knightley in conversation:

'Who would not, for a very little effort, increase their fortune? For he that wants money, means and content is without three good friends.'

'Oh William' she said laughing, 'those are not your words, shame on you. I do believe I heard them in As you like it.'

'Indeed Shakespeare thought of so many words first, it hardly seems worthwhile trying to find new ones.' he said. 'Still, fortunes are being made daily, indeed by the hour, as money invested is being doubled overnight and in solid, government-backed stock. You simply cannot lose in this investment. The Spanish silver mines of Peru, profits of the Asiento, where could your money be more safely put to bring rich rewards?'

Since Knightley had become cashier of the South Seas Company, Aurora had heard his 'sales pitch' a thousand times to people eager to hear it. Everyone felt the allure and excitement of a promised quick profit. She herself had already agreed to make a small investment but Knightley was now appealing to her greed, a characteristic she thought herself bereft of but, with such a clamour for the stock by everyone, she felt herself caught up in the general excitement. Rich or poor, everyone wanted South Sea stock and Knightley was 'the' man who was steamrolling the issue. There were so many stories of vast fortunes being made within just a few days, that her only regret was that she dared not venture to invest more.

In a moment he was gone. Knightley was the most popular man in the room that night and it was clear that his presence there was business, not pleasure. He moved from person to person; all were eager to speak to him and, whether overtly or discretely, all eyes were upon him. He moved effortlessly from one engaging and intense conversation to another and he had about him an aura of importance that far exceeded that of his host, the Prince.

There had been few occasions when Aurora and her family had been present at formal court functions and, though the King was away in Hanover, her father had secured them an invite for a glittering night out amongst the 'great and the good'.

A recent serious rift between the King and his son had left the Prince of Wales keen to give his supporters a chance to do just that - show their support - and, for those attending, it was easy to give (or feign) support for the Prince in the sure knowledge that his father was safely out of the country.

A few yards away at the same ensemble, though blissfully unaware of how significant they would become to each other, was another group and they too were talking of money. Sir Richard Wortley, recently returned to government as the most senior minister, was talking to his old university friend Gervase Vavasour and they were remarking on the phenomenal success of John Law, a mutual acquaintance, who had travelled to France where his financial acumen had almost eradicated the French National Debt. What if, they pondered, the South Seas Company could do the same with the British government's debts. Wortley confessed he'd already made a fortune on the stock, though could have made more had he not cashed in early but, he thought, once the 'common man' became involved and wenches were investing their gin money, he thought it high time to get out.

Wortley, in a pause in the conversation, directed Vavasour's attention over to the other group and mentioned them being connected to William Knightley and their brother being MP for York.

'They (the three sisters) are called the Northern Stars at Court'
Wortley said. 'Fairfaxes, you must know them? Countrymen of
yours from Yorkshire'.

'Aye, well ...', said Vavasour disinterestedly, 'I've had dealings
with Knightley but not Fairfaxes. They're not *our* kind of people'.

Wortley pondered a moment until he took Vavasour's meaning
and began to grin in amusement... 'Oh really, I thought the Fairfax
name was an eminent one in Yorkshire. It certainly was
memorable in the Civil War years.'

'Aye' replied Vavasour 'and I durst say those gals are part o'
same clan. Our folks had nowt to do with 'em. Not then and not
now.'

'Live and let live Vavasour, that's what I think. Pretty things
though, and I dare say they're on the lookout for husbands'.

'So long as they keep out the way of my sons because I would
disown either of 'em if they courted a Fairfax, no mistake'.

The men were suddenly joined by another, 'Ah' said Vavasour,
'you know my son Pascal I believe?'.

'Yes, though it was some time ago' said Wortley.

'Good evening sir".

'Pascal has just returned from St Omers .... We sent him to the
Continent so he could've a *proper* education .....'

'Urgh ....' grunted Wortley gruffly. 'Very nice to meet you' he
said half-heartedly.

'It's an honour sir'.

Wortley nodded, begged to be excused and shuffled away.

Pascal told his father 'I don't think Sir Wortley approves of
our religious leanings. Oh, by the way, Benjamin is here, have you
seen him?'

'Seen him? Why would I want to see that drunkard, I'm
surprised he could prize himself away from the gaming tables long
enough to meet his Prince'.

'I wouldn't be surprised if there isn't a table or two here
somewhere!' Pascal muttered. 'He's your eldest son and heir
father, I thought you'd like to know'.

'He *was* my son - that's all. By the way Pascal ...' he said in
earnest 'beware some of the parading females here, 'beauty is a
witch' and the prettier the creature the bigger spell they cast.'

12

'Yes father' Pascal dutifully replied. His father moved away to talk to another guest but Pascal kept watching as his brother Benjamin moved in the direction of the Fairfaxes. He kept watching and became a looker-on for a while noticing first his brother's absorbed attention in the ladies and then saw that it was one in particular who Benjamin singled out.

Her face, Aurora's face, Pascal watched carefully and noticed it light up with surprise and pleasure as the couple talked. He guessed what it meant and he rejoiced in his brother's folly.

Chapter 3

The Fairfaxes returned to their home at Tadcaster in Yorkshire and, since it was approaching the Christmas period, there was a gathering of friends and relations.

The family's long residence in the area and Duke's involvement as a lawyer, particular when his business concerned local issues, meant most of Tadcaster's leading families were friends and clients who all knew each other intimately. It was very much a *circle* of friendship and kinship and the only variation was *where* they assembled together; whoever the Fairfaxes visited they would be sure to see the same group of people. Only when they ventured out of Tadcaster to York was there a chance of varied company; though even there the familiar circle with its wider acquaintances would be sure to be found.

The Vavasour family, although residing only a few miles away from Tadcaster, was not part of this circle. They were infinitely more wealthy than any of those residing in Tadcaster and, as such, had a more aristocratic circle of friends who were mostly Catholics, being from some of the oldest families in England.

Aurora, of course, hadn't been able to see Benjamin over the festive period and was longing for his company. She wondered at him being able to stay away from her so long and kept her spirits going by thinking to herself 'Perhaps he wants to wait until after Christmas to tell his father....... oh, but why is it taking so long ..... surely by now he could've found some way to tell his family the good news'. The questions kept plaguing her but she could only guess at the answers.

Still a house full of visitors came some way to providing a distraction for her. Still reflecting over their evening with the Prince of Wales, brother-in-law John Mason was deep in conversation with her father and brother:

'That was a fine evening we had at Leicester House.'

'It was indeed' replied Duke

'The Prince is setting up a rival court, I think'.

'It isn't good for the country' said Nathan. 'Such a schism at the top of the royal family will be exploited by some, you mark my words!'

'Indeed, that seems to be the way things are going' said Duke. 'Though I don't think the Prince was the centre of attention he expected to be, as our good "future son" William Knightley was the only man anyone was really interested in. Everywhere you go that's all you hear about ..... South Seas stock and the good Knightley over there' he said looking over to his right, 'is the man right at the heart of it all.'

'Of course, any man who can promise, nay guarantee, to make money for his friends will always have a good abundance of 'em' said Nathan and the men laughed.

'You hear such stories' continued Duke '..... I heard t'other day that the Countess of Leicester pawned her jewels so she could invest in shares. Other stories are abounding that men are mortgaging their estates - all on the promise of a quick profit. It seems the whole world has gone completely mad. It's incredible what avarice can do to men, even well educated and highly born men. It makes no difference'.

'Tis true,' said Mason. 'From Wortley to the Queen - by which I mean the King's mistress, the Duchess of Kendal - everyone wants the shares, everyone wants the profit and of course everyone wants their fortune.'

'I wonder' mused Nathan, ' how will life be if we *all* end up with great fortunes. Who'll tend the sheep, who'll wait on tables and where will landlords find tenants if everyone can buy their own land'. Loud laughter from across the room drew their attention to the man they were talking about. Knightley was smiling broadly and chattering to the ladies surrounding him.

Duke said: 'Of more immediate concern is what has all this attention done to Knightley? My daughter finds her fiancé greatly changed, not to mention frequently absent from her. He's in so deep with this venture that, should anything go wrong, I'm afeared for him. At least, I doubt he'll be ruined though, not if he has a modicum of sense. If I were in his shoes I'd have some safe funds stashed away in case of misfortune. No man can live constantly in the sunshine, there has to come a rainy day'.

Nathan seemed unperturbed. 'Well if you're rich enough, you can be master of your own fate and I durst say order the clouds away' he said laughing. 'I heard Wortley say t'other day that *every man has his price*' and this present scramble to make money is evidence to me that most men will sell their very souls for a quick profit. Speculation is spreading like a contagion, and an out of control one at that. You know ....' he said in a whisper, 'I've noticed that men are changed by money and power. Very few can keep their greed in check or resist the temptation to exploit their power. Knightley has power because he makes money!'

'Aye, and too much of both, is turning 'is head' warned Duke.

Nathan continued 'I say that Knightley is handling such large, incredibly large, sums of money that it would be very hard for him to come back down from that elevated pedestal he now rests on. He's offering his largesse to so many of his friends that there's bound to be resentment from those overlooked.'

'Not just that,' added Mason 'but there now exists an obligation to him from them that's benefitted. Including, of course, all of us!'

'Yes, and it gives him power over people which, as you know, can be a dangerous thing if not handled well. I fear 'twill end badly for him in some way .....' said Duke. 'Nearer the top o' tree, the greater the fall .....'.

'Ah' interrupted Mason, 'here's my brother George to join us.'

John's brother was General George Mason who had spent many years abroad serving in the army and, being unmarried and only his brother, he brought him along to the Fairfax household for Christmas. He was known to the family, having visited on previous occasions.

'Good evening sir' said George to Duke, 'thank you for inviting me to your home. A Happy Christmas to you all.'

'You're very welcome. I understand you've just returned from Spain?'

'Yes indeed. The army seems to think I've a particular liking for that part of the world, as they keep sending me back. This time, however, I was tossed from pillar to post, no sooner was I settled in Spain and I was off to Gibraltar, then back to Spain via Portugal. The army thinks it can look like its achieving something, you know ...... making progress ..... if regiments are marched

here, there and everywhere. I have to say though, I'm relieved to
be back in Yorkshire for Christmas and, in fact, through to the
New Year.'

'You've missed all the hullabaloo here about South Seas
stock, that's what we were all just talking about' said his brother
John.

'Oh no' said George smiling, 'I can assure you it's just as well
talked about overseas as here.'

'Wortley's friend, Princely Chandos is Paymaster-General to
the Forces Abroad .....' Nathan started to say.

'Exactly' said George emphatically. 'And ee's made more
money than everyone else put together.'

'If you've a patron who can protect you, all things are
possible' said Duke, 'and Chandos has his protectors'.

'Still .....' said George. 'There are rumours circulating about
him. I were invited to visit him last year at his Cannons home .....'

'Ah' said Nathan. 'John and I visited there some months ago.
Have you ever seen the like?'

'Aye' said John Mason. 'He's got more money than taste, I
should say. It's sheer opulence but completely devoid of style. I
hear he has 90 gardeners ...... imagine that .... 90 gardeners. I
doubt they've that many at royal palaces'.

'But where did his great fortune come from?' said George.
'He was a man of relatively modest means only a few years ago.
Now look at him!'

'So, you see .... with him as our paymaster, there's no getting
away from the subject' said George. 'Excuse me for a moment,'
he said abruptly 'there's someone I want to speak to .....' With that
George moved over in the direction of Aurora.

After he had moved away out of earshot, his brother
whispered to Duke, 'his fellow officers call him 'Gentle George
you know! A more placid, infuriatingly placid, man you'll never
find. Always polite, even tempered and courteous. I swear if you
put the very devil in front of him he'd call for tea with him and
make polite small talk.'

'I find him perfectly charming' said Duke.

'That's as maybe', continued John, though I have to say that if
I was going into battle and had George for a commander, happen I

wouldn't like it. I'd want someone who inspired the men, a leader of courage, not a mild mannered and serene diplomat.'

'Well it takes all sorts' said Nathan who rejoined the conversation. 'He'd probably have made a better politician than you, and you the better General.' Both men laughed heartily at each other.

'Gentle' George began talking to Aurora who had been standing with her sister Catherine, telling her, 'I haven't seen your mother, I was wanting to thank her for inviting me this evening.'

'Actually she's unwell' said Aurora. 'She's upstairs lying down, my sister Elizabeth's with her now'.

'I hope it's nothing serious?'

'No, I don't think so but we're planning a visit to York next week to the Assemblies. Good company and conversation might heal better than spa waters. Our recent long stay at Matlock Bath did help but I think a good gossip with friends might lift her spirits even more.'

'Aren't John and Nathan having a meeting at the Burgesses Hall in York next week?' said George.

'Yes. We thought we'd visit the Assemblies and, if mother's well enough, drop in at the political meeting whilst we're there. Not for long though, just long enough to show our faces and show the world we support our Members of Parliament. It's important the Corporation know that the family support them.'

'Oh, um, I couldn't agree more. Actually I was thinking of going there myself. As you, to support my brother and, of course yours. So I'll probably see you there.'

'Not for the assembly gossip though I presume?' said Catherine laughing.

George moved away and Aurora turned to face her sister.

'I think you might have an admirer there' said Catherine feverishly.

'Nay, not at all' was the dismissive response.

'Why not, he's quite handsome and good natured.'

'Yes that's the thing though, George is too mild for my liking. There's no spirit, no energy, no passion with men like that.'

'Oh my word' said Catherine astonished, 'and just when did you become an expert on men then?'

'Only from observation' said Aurora. 'Actually I wish I did find that sort of man attractive because he'll probably make someone a right good husband one day, but it won't be me. I'd be bored silly with such an insipid appeaser. No, when I marry it'll be to someone with more spirit! Look at your good husband over there. A Member of Parliament, a confident and well thought of man, successful businessman and, with friends like Wortley, the sky's the limit. He may have a good future ahead of him - I mean for both of you.'

'Well maybe...' said Catherine teasing, 'one day you might see men like George differently, perhaps when you're older!'

'Yes ...... if I should live that long' Aurora replied laughing.

Chapter 4

A few days later Aurora and her mother Isabella Fairfax arrived in York as arranged, staying at Crown and Anchor Inn next door to the Burgesses Hall. No sooner had they arrived and the landlord, Mr Wentworth, assaulted them with an 'Ow do' and the promise of gossip, with the energy and vigour of one who knows they impart news that couldn't have been heard from another source, and hence impeccably fresh.

'Well, well, there is such a fuss. It's all o'er town that your esteemed relations and Members of Parliament for York are to attend the political rally tomorrow night and, who do you think arrived in town a short while ago?' ... Not waiting for a reply because he knew there would be none, he continued... 'well, Stanhope and 'is men are here, put up at the Seven Stars round t'corner'.

'Who?' said Aurora looking puzzled.

Mr Wentworth looked crest-fallen as he clearly expected mention of the name Stanhope to be enough to impress.

'Stanhope ..... you know ..... the defeated candidate in the last election. Poor sod stood against your relations, I 'ere and, despite spending a fortune on bribing voters, he still lost out. And, he's bent on revenge.'

On getting no response from Isabella or her mother he continued .... 'Ee's brought a large group of men with him, probably paid 'em I dare say, and says he won't leave town till he's had a set-to with Mr Fairfax and Mr Mason. What a to-do!'.

'Mr Wentworth please!' urged Isabella 'less of the scaremongering, my mother is here to recover her good health and I don't think this is helping'.

'No, I'm alright' said Isabella. 'What's this, someone wants a fight with my son?'

'Mr Wentworth's exaggerating mother'. Aurora frowned and nodded at Mr Wentworth angrily. 'I'll take my mother upstairs now if that's alright with you .... and we'll talk about it later'.

The inn keeper looked suitably chastised and held his tongue whilst Isabella guided her mother out of the room and off to a comfortable room to settle in.

When Aurora came back downstairs alone some time later she found her brother Nathan and brother-in-law John Mason, who'd just arrived together at York, deep in conversation with Mr Wentworth. A conversation which was abruptly halted when she approached them.

'How's Mrs Fairfax?' asked Mr Wentworth, 'I didn't mean to alarm her, I didn't realise she was unwell.'

'Is it true Nathan?' Aurora asked, looking at both her brother and Mason, 'is there a group of men arrived in town bent on doing you both harm?'

'So we hear, yes' replied Nathan, but don't worry we'll find some way to resolve the matter and tell mother that Mr Wentworth was exaggerating ....'

'Aye I was ....' nodded Mr Wentworth enthusiastically, keen to please his guests.

'We don't want her worrying.'

'Of course she'll worry', said Aurora 'she heard what was said and, besides, we're planning to attend the meeting tomorrow to support you both'.

'And so you shall' said Mason, 'Catherine is coming along too, she'll be here tomorrow. She's bringing the children, Marmaduke and Margaret will be coming along and I can assure you I'd never put anyone in our family in harm's way. Stanhope's men will do nothing during the meeting as the full corporation will be there. They're businessmen as well as land owners and he won't want to provoke the most important dignitaries in town. He's not a complete fool. They'll wait until after the meeting, when we're leaving, to try and ambush us. But ..... we have cooked up a plan to divert them.'

That was all that was said on the matter and, though Aurora felt that she'd been fobbed off somewhat, she hoped rather than believed they were in earnest.

The following day Aurora took her mother to the Assemblies which, being mid-day, were attended mostly by ladies. Some husbands were to be seen but were mainly in the elderly age range and they sought each other's company out staying huddled together throughout.

Isabella was in her element chattering away enthusiastically to her friends and seeming to be perfectly happy. What parts of her conversation Aurora heard seemed to consist of her mother extolling the virtues of spa visits and, since most of her listeners were somewhat advanced in years and with various ailments, she found a ready audience. When one of the ladies happened to comment about the dreadful smell of some of the spring waters being like rotten eggs, this gave fresh gusto to Isabella. Oddly enough this one lady's brief negative comment seemed to do immense damage to the validity of the argument. No amount of further persuasion by Isabella could shift the newly entrenched and implacable general opinion against therapeutic waters. So the conversations, though fruitless, served their purposes in keeping everyone amused and the exertion took Isabella's mind off her own ailments for a while.

Later in the day Mr Wentworth, on seeing Aurora come down stairs at the inn after settling her mother back in her room for a rest, beckoned her over to speak. It was clear, once more, he was bursting with news and having trouble keeping the words inside. He began talking hurriedly before they'd even sat down.

'Mr Fairfax and Mason are gone out to make arrangements for this evening but ...' he whispered, though there was only two of them in the room 'I do know something of their plans.'

Aurora made no response, for she knew Mr Wentworth was going to divulge his information without any prompting. He continued, 'Last night they were discussing what to do this evening if they're confronted by Stanhope's men - some of 'em, by the way, tried to come on to my premises last night trying to find out which inn you were staying at, but I told 'em you were not 'ere'.

Wentworth looked directly at Aurora, as if waiting to be thanked for his protection, and so Aurora duly obliged by saying thank you.

'Although it was a crowded night, I was able to see 'em off without any trouble' he crowed proudly, 'they don't know you are staying 'ere' he emphatically repeated.

'And .... what do you know of their plans then?' she prompted him to continue.

'Well, since they refuse to cancel the meeting, their only choice was to either set about rounding up their own group of men to be a match for Stanhope's, or to manage their departure after the meeting so as to avoid a confrontation'.

'I don't think I can take mother to the meeting if there's going to be trouble ....' said Aurora.

'Oh, but you must' continued Mr Wentworth. 'I don't think our honoured Members of Parliament should be bullied or prevented from speaking in public. Perish the thought. We must support 'em and stand our ground'.

'We?' said Aurora. 'Are you coming too?'

'Well, no, I have this place to run, but I stand ready to assist. When the meeting breaks up I'll go outside and see you all guided back inside this comfortable inn where you'll be under *my* protection. No 'arm will come to you on *my* premises' he said proudly. 'I'm a public spirited man and, if I 'ave to rally all my customers to your assistance I will - though they might not all be clearly sober!'

Aurora was struggling to resist the urge to judge Mr Wentworth, believing him to be a buffoon, but also thought him an honest and decent type of man and so continued to hear him.

'Now, let me tell you what the plan is .... though tis a great secret,' he said excitedly. 'Mr Mason 'as business interests at Silk Mill in Derby, as you'll know, and he told me last night that on his last visit there, he saw something incredible. It was a great distraction and just what's needed at the end of the political meeting, so they can safely get away. It's called The Flying Rage.'

Aurora was bemused.

'Tis the most spectacular sight you can imagine. Flying ..... like a bird. You'll see men flying in the sky. Yes. ..... literally flying through the air! What they did at Derby was to tie a rope from the top of All Saints steeple, attached it to a nearby building at a much lower height; then, by means of a wooden pulley device, have men dangle from the rope and descend, as if they're flying, at the speed of lightning, they fly down through the air. At Derby it drew a huge crowd to watch and cheer the spectacle and, for added entertainment, the speeding men fired pistols into the air and blew trumpets'.

Aurora could restrain a laugh no longer.

'Well might ye laugh', said Mr Wentworth. 'Such a sight has ne'er been seen and they flew with such speed that rope burned leaving a trail of smoke following 'em down the line.'

'And this is the distraction that Mason and my brother have planned for tonight?' she asked.

'Yes' said Mr Wentworth enthusiastically. 'With so many people in town, good neighbourly people and families with children, it'll be difficult for Stanhope and his men to carry out their plan of forming a violent mob. They're out now making the preparations. It'll be the most astonishing spectacle anyone has ever seen.'

'If it's to be a great secret, then there won't be a crowd to attend it' Aurora pointed out.

'Well ..... you know ..... secret as to the true purpose, but I'm telling all my customers and anyone I meet, to be 'ere this evening at nine and there'll be a great crowd as word is spreading throughout the town. We shall 'ave all the good folks from hereabouts. So many of 'em, we'll drown Stanhope's lot out. They won't be able to move for the crowd.'

'And good trade for your establishment?
Wentworth shrugged his shoulders as if that thought had never crossed his mind.

Chapter 5

As the time for them to attend the political meeting approached, tension in the Inn was growing. Aurora paced back and forth in her room taking glances out of the window as she watched the growing crowd assemble outside. She examined the faces of those waiting, though she didn't know what Stanhope looked like, never having met him, nor any of his men, so she was looking for people, anyone, who looked suspicious. Anyone who looked like they were preparing for a fight rather than anticipated fun. Any groups of men, as opposed to families and she fancied, at numerous times, they were there. That Stanhope was amongst the crowd already.

A short while before they were due to leave, Aurora called Wentworth into her room and asked him to examine the faces in the crowd.

'Is Stanhope there?' she asked. 'I don't know what he looks like?'

Mr Wentworth obliged and spent some minutes looking at all the faces he could see before pronouncing that he couldn't see Stanhope anywhere, though one or two men looked suspiciously unfamiliar.

The noise of the crowd outside filtered into her room and her mother started asking what was going on. So, as it was now past the time for the meeting to start, Aurora asked Wentworth to take them over to the Burgesses Hall. He did as he was bid and them left them at the entrance way and returned to the inn.

As they entered the room, Aurora saw her sister Elizabeth and Gentle George seated together listening intently to the speeches; they'd all made their way separately to the Burgesses Hall. Catherine, who had been standing at the back of the room with her two young children, approached them from their left side.

'I didn't want to sit down amongst the audience' she whispered, 'in case the children get tired and start playing up and getting noisy.'

'I'm surprised you brought the children' whispered Isabella. 'Hasn't John told you there might be trouble with that crowd outside?'

'I know' said Catherine, 'he's told me about it. But I insisted we wouldn't be dissuaded from being here. It's important not to be seen to give way to bullies like Stanhope'.

'But the children?' said Isabella in despair.

'There are lots of children in the crowd outside' said Aurora. 'I think Nathan's right to persevere and there's such a crush of people outside, I don't see how a gang of thugs could get through'.

'The crowd might be what's hiding them' said Isabella. 'I think I should go back to the Inn and take the children with me'.

'No mother, I insist we all stay' said Catherine.

Aurora and Isabella remained standing at the back of the hall and took care to keep the young children entertained and quiet. Aurora had heard her brother and Mason make the same speeches many times and so spent much of the time rolling her eyes over the assembled audience who numbered about 80 persons, nearly all being men. Aurora had no knowledge of, or interest in, politics and the only highlight of the meeting for her, was an unfortunate moment when strange noises were heard emanating from behind the stage. The solemnity of the meeting was in stark contrast to the cursing and thumping noises distinctly heard above the speakers and there was a soft murmur from the audience who were struggling to suppress laughter. The worse and louder the cursing got, the harder it was to listen attentively or keep a straight face.

Those on the small raised stage looked increasingly uncomfortable as time progressed and, whether the speeches were intended to end at that precise moment, or it was felt dignity would be lost if they carried on, it's hard to say, but the meeting drew to a rapid, possibly premature close and, like an actor given her cue to enter stage, Isabella Fairfax sprang into hostess mode.

Marching straight to the front of the room she embraced the Mayor and, smiling broadly made sure everyone of importance knew her entire family was present. She could be heard repeating over and over how incredibly proud she was that her son and son-in-law represented York and how she knew they would move mountains for the good people of the city. Her daughters were presented and, she positively beamed, to introduce her young grand-children to the important dignitaries.

'I 'ear you've just returned from Matlock Spa', said the Mayor 'I hope you can be prevailed upon to sample those at Harrogate one day?' said he.

'Oh I already plan to', said Isabella lying, 'I've heard such good reports and shall recommend them to all my friends'. It was such a convincing lie that Aurora looked at her mother in astonishment. She sincerely hoped it was a jest because the idea of spending another summer taking her mother to and from spa baths wasn't too appealing.

'If you come this way' the Mayor said, 'you can all get a good view of the entertainment that's about to start'. He gestured and they all followed him out via a rear door into a small courtyard. The Mayor had been made aware of the threat from Stanhope and had given Nathan and Mason his personal guarantee that the family would be given safe passage.

'Don't worry', he told Isabella. 'At the first sign of trouble from Stanhope's men I've arranged with the burgesses that the church bell will be rung. Townsfolk have never let us down before and, if there's any trouble, we can call on 'em for help. Although' he said looking out at the mass of faces, 'I think most of the town's already here for the entertainment!'

He stood close to them, as if shielding them with his civic office. Moving them out into the streets, his gold mayoral chain hung proudly round his neck and his long flowing gown all seemed extraordinarily out of place and a magnet for all eyes. The Mayor seemed to revel in his distinction and paraded his magnificence like a great brute of conceit. The symbol shouted 'No one, but no one, accosts those in the protection of the Mayor'. And, indeed, no one did.

He guided them to a place he considered safe. And then, knowing the eyes of the crowd were on him, he waved his arms to clear a path in a large, exaggerated manner and then gave himself a smile of satisfaction knowing that his important guests were indebted to him. Isabella flattered and thanked him and seemed excessively pleased at the distinction her family were receiving.

Then, one by one, faces tilted up, as if to worship the moon and, moments later, all eyes had focused on the skyline, where a dirty thick rope had been strewn from the Burgesses Hall roof in the direction of nearby houses. It quickly became apparent where the strange noises in the meeting room had emanated from when, from way above the gathered crowd, brute honking sounds were heard from a distressed donkey.

'I couldn't get a man to do it at short notice' John Mason said apologetically, 'so we've got an ass ....'.

'What?' said Elizabeth.

'Keep watching' said Mason. 'Cos it'll be over in a flash'.

In the next moment the poor creature, braying through the whole ordeal, flew - accelerated by its great weight - down the rope. It's dark figure swooped over the crowd and watchers of a more nervous disposition ran for cover in case it fell on them.

The donkey's rapid descent came to a premature end 20 feet short of the intended destination when its weight bowed the rope to such an extent that it brought the creature down to ground level too soon. It crashed into the crowd, thereby giving it a softer landing that might have been expected. For those in its way, there were cries of pain and general excitement and confusion, though the animal itself was unscathed and walked off dazed but with barely a scratch.

The great force of the so-called Flight of Rage and the jolt on the rope had the effect of toppling a house chimney around which the rope had been strung and isolated bricks crashed to the ground as the remaining chimney bricks wobbled.

This was the moment of distraction desired and the group moved, unseen, away from the Burgesses Hall back to the inn where Mr Wentworth followed them in, breathless with excitement from the spectacle he had just seen.

'Flying! Flying!' he said, expelling the words out loudly in the hope of encouraging a response. No one responded but some listeners smiled and nodded their heads eagerly. 'Did you ever see the like?'

He then urged the party to go into a backroom he had prepared especially for them with a roaring fire and well lit with candles.

'I hope no one was hurt' said Catherine to her husband 'the poor creature was knocking people down like skittles'.

'Not seriously' he said, 'though I am a little surprised the ass stayed on the rope. Do you know it took eight men to get the mule up on the roof in the first place and as many to strap it up there. I think it was probably sheer terror that stopped it wriggling loose and falling out'.

'I don't think an ass is meant to fly, nor men. We should leave that to the birds?' Elizabeth said laughing. Then, turning to Aurora, she said 'Isn't that Benjamin Vavasour over there?' She pointed. Aurora nodded as if she expected him to be there. Elizabeth added, 'that man seems to follow us wherever we go?'

Gentle George, appearing as if from nowhere, moved over to speak to Aurora but Benjamin Vavasour arrived at the exact same moment. Aurora looked startled and tried to address them both.

'Do you know each other?' she said, but the demur murmurings suggested that they didn't.

She looked at Benjamin and introduced George as her brother-in-law's brother, an army general, and then introduced Benjamin, rather sheepishly as he was not so easy to introduce, as a friend she'd met at Leicester House recently.

'Vavasour?' said George, yes I know the family name.

'It's a very old one ....'

'And distinguished' said George, 'yes, are you related to Gervase Vavasour of Vavasour Hall?'

'Indeed I am. I am his son and heir. The whole thing will be mine one day for my sins' replied George indiscreetly 'though my father wishes I weren't acquainted with him I think'.

'Oh I'm sure that's not true' said Gentle George.

'I can assure you it is was the reply, 'told me so himself'.

Aurora didn't like the direction the conversation was going in and so intervened to change the subject, 'And how did you like your brother's speech this evening George?'

'Well enough, he lives in the county at least half the year and means what he says that he wants to improve life for people'.

'Huh' said Benjamin, 'I don't know why our wonderful Members of Parliament bother to court local support when all they have to do is "pay" the right people. A few bribes here and there ...'

'This isn't Old Sarem with naught but two houses and yet having two Members of Parliament', said Gentle George 'my brother and Nathaniel's election was fair and by due process'.

Benjamin listened but rolled his eyes in despair, 'Really? Such an extraordinarily large county has just two MPs and both from the same family? Goodness' he said drolly, 'what an incredible coincidence'.

'The Corporation "invited" them to stand' said Aurora, that's why we're here to thank them and show them we support their choice'.

'As you say' said Benjamin, 'I cannot disagree with a lady ... even if she's wrong!' He smiled wryly.

Elizabeth joined the group and asked: 'Benjamin, we meet again! What brings you to York this evening?'

'I'm passing through on my way to the racecourse for a meeting tomorrow. Meeting up with some friends there. My good friend Charles Stanhope has a horse running .....'

'Not the same Stanhope who stood against Nathaniel and Mason for this seat? asked Elizabeth.

'I believe so' said Benjamin, 'and he weren't too pleased to lose it either'. It occurred to Aurora that Benjamin would have been in a position to tell Stanhope where the family were staying that night. Either he didn't tell him, or perhaps had told him not to cause trouble.

'If he's such a good friend of yours' said Elizabeth, 'then you must know he's in town tonight?'

'Yes he is' said Benjamin. 'I am aware of that'.

'And are you aware of his reason for being here tonight?' persisted Elizabeth.

'To ...... prepare for tomorrow's race I should imagine' he responded.

'Really! Benjamin ..... now you *do* surprise me. I'm all astonishment' said Elizabeth with unconcealed sarcasm. 'So you must be .... Now let me see the *only* person in the entire county who hasn't heard that Stanhope was spoiling for a fight tonight with my brother and Mason?'

'Nah' said Benjamin. 'I've heard no such thing. As far as I'm concerned he's only here for the race. I think you might have been misinformed!'

'I'm only surprised you didn't .... at least not yet so far as I can tell ... inform him where we are staying here in York'. As she finished her words, Elizabeth brushed past Benjamin, moving away and not giving him an opportunity to respond.

After she'd moved away out of earshot, Benjamin said 'now why would I do that?' he said looking directly at Aurora.

The mention of Stanhope was noted by the Fairfaxes but, other than Elizabeth's conversation with Benjamin, it was deemed too impolite to pursue the matter further.

Conversation continued between Gentle George and Benjamin Vavasour and, if George was offended by Vavasour's tone and manner of speaking, he gave no hint of disapproval, maintaining a calm politeness throughout.

Moving behind the group, Elizabeth re-appeared to whisper to Aurora ,'This is no coincidence. What's going on with Vavasour?'

'Not now Elizabeth' was the only reply she got.

Chapter 6

With the New Year well advanced, the winter days at Fairfax Manor in Tadcaster slipped by quickly. For several weeks there was barely a single visitor to their isolated house, the roads being impassable, until gradually the hours of daylight began to lengthen and the daffodils bloomed, heralding the coming of an optimistic spring.

The cold easterly wind which had persisted finally relented in the face of southerlies and a crop of new lambs and the last of the frosts signalled the start of the new growing season in earnest. The earth was coming back to life and there were stirrings within Aurora too which were a portent of major change to come.

One particularly fine day, one of those bright, sunny good-to-be-alive-days, Catherine (who was staying with her family for a few days), Elizabeth and Aurora had just returned home from paying a courtesy call to a neighbour to find their father pacing up and down looking deep in thought. It seemed he was only waiting for his daughters' return to give voice to what was troubling him. Duke grew grave as his mood darkened. He beckoned his daughters to listen as he had bad news for them.

'I have something to tell you' he said anxiously, 'which simply cannot wait'.

'What's wrong father?' asked Elizabeth as she tried to calm him down and make him sit. 'Are you unwell?'

'No, of course not, I'm perfectly fine, only worried for you all.'

His thoughtful tone produced the desired effect of subduing the ladies who, without knowing why, sank their spirits to match his, judging that was what he wanted. A couple of moments of silent anticipation and held breaths was all that was necessary to induce their father to believe now was the moment for him to speak.....

'It's serious. It concerns Mary!' he started to say.

'Oh God!' exclaimed Elizabeth, 'Is she dead?'

'No. No. Nothing like that!' he replied.

'Well …. it's just that you seemed so serious'.

'Aye well, perhaps this is worse than her being dead.' Duke continued. 'As you know, my cousin Mary, Duchess of Buckingham, who I have had the privilege of working for these many years, granted an annuity to all my daughters for the full term of their lives and you have, hitherto, all benefited from her generosity. Truly' said Duke, 'there is not a kinder and more generous woman in the world and her lack of children has made her exceedingly considerate of her closest relations.'

'Yes father' said Catherine smiling, 'I'm sure my portion went some way to encourage my husband to take me off your hands …'

'Just so' her father replied emphatically. 'So now that's my point … we now have a problem as her circumstances have markedly deteriorated. I've just returned from York where there are court papers calling for her bankruptcy to be declared.'

'Oh dear, poor Mary…' said Aurora.

'But her estate has always been in a bad way father, we all know that. That scoundrel of a husband of hers ruined it some years back. What has changed?' asked Elizabeth.

Duke explained how Mary had indeed been left in a financial mess after her husband's mishandling of her estate and his subsequent death but that death duties and poor investments had been followed by years and years of selling off what assets were left.

Duke had persuaded Mary to sell her father's substantial residence to pay off her debts - as she lived elsewhere and had rented the house out - but the current Lord Fairfax, her uncle, had intervened. Despite the Duchess finding a prospective buyer for her estate, Lord Fairfax's lawyers found a loophole with which to halt the sale. It was clearly Lord Fairfax's desire to defer a sale until the Duchess died and, being childless, he would become heir to her estate. His savvy lawyers had found a way to 'sour the milk' and the buyer backed off from the purchase.

Duke continued, 'The creditors have now taken fright at this turn of events and Mary's assets have been seized by the courts.'

'And … that includes our annuities?' asked Aurora.

'Yes. There is insufficient money in the estate to fund any annuities and the whole matter is now in the hands of the courts'.

'What will happen to us?' asked Aurora plaintively. 'Come to think of it, what will happen to you and your work for the Duchess?'

'Well, although there is still work for me to do, collecting her rents and leasing out what properties she has, I shall have to scale it back in case the courts suddenly decide that there is insufficient funds to pay me for my time. I do have other clients though, thank goodness and I shall have to think on myself first now. But it's you girls that I am worried about'.

'There's no need to worry about me' said Elizabeth half joking, 'my fiancé has already abandoned me in search of Plutus, the god of wealth .... even with an annuity I wasn't rich enough for him..... now he'll have the perfect excuse to abandon me completely.'

'This ain't no laughing matter' said Duke, 'Catherine .... I don't know what John will say, he may consider himself duped as to your marriage settlement. Oh, for sure, I know he's got good business interests, as does Nathan, but still .... he may think I've deliberately misled him as to your prospects.'

'Is there no chance .... absolutely no chance whatever that the annuities could be salvaged father?' Catherine pleaded.

'No', said Duke glumly, 'I suppose with hindsight it's surprising that they continued so long. The Duchess could, I dare say, have intervened many years ago to suspend the payments but wanted her closest cousins to have some security. Nathan of course was never part of the annuity arrangement as Mary felt it incumbent on him as a man to make his own way in the world and he manages well enough with his parliamentary salary and other investments. But Elizabeth and Aurora, I fear the impact will be the greatest for you because you're yet unmarried and, I'm very sorry to say, likely to remain so with no portion to induce a suitor'.

'Father' said Elizabeth indignantly, 'I'd like to think I could attract a husband without having to line his pockets first!'

'Well, that's a fine idea' he said sadly, 'but in the real world it just doesn't happen that way.'

Seeing her sister Catherine's growing distress, Aurora said 'Hush now your husband is madly in love with you, that's plain for all to see. Father 's painted too gloomy a picture, John has solid business investments in Derby that will support you. You know that.'

'I know' said Catherine looked downcast 'but that was money of mine, my own. Now I'll have to look for him for everything!' Catherine looked worried and fearful for her own future. She was distracted and wanted to be on her own. She left the room saying she'd check in on mother before leaving.

'Elizabeth' said Duke now turning his attention to the eldest remaining daughter. 'I'm compelled to ask you ….. what really is the situation with you and Knightley? Is there owt that can be done to speed up your marriage?'

'Do you want me to go?' asked Elizabeth, thinking they'd want privacy.

'No' said Elizabeth. 'This is all known to you already. You know I've had no word from William since Christmas, not a single letter …..'

Duke pressed on ….. 'You'd not be needing an annuity with him as a husband. He's one of the wealthiest men in England now and I have to say that your marriage to him could be the salvation of this family.'

'I would gladly oblige you father' said Elizabeth, 'but fear the remedy isn't in my hands. Perhaps this development will bring matters to a head. I've no objection if you wish to speak to him on the matter but, I have to say, that my own feelings are very changed regarding him.'

'How so?' Duke asked.

'Well, I've been thinking for some time now that I'd rather bring the engagement to an end. It should be plain for all the world to see that he's much occupied with other matters and, from what I've heard, he is not *acting* as a man who's engaged to be married.'

'He's a busy man, I know that ….'

'No, it's not just that he's busy Father. I believe he truly prefers to spend more time in London and enjoys what he's doing. I see less and less of him. I think it just needs someone to let him know he's released from his obligation to me and that'll put an end to it'.

'But ….' said Duke, 'my dear ….. with no annuity, no marriage portion, where are we going to find you a husband ….. there'll never be another who has a fraction of the money he has. Is that not worth ..... a little inconvenience child?'

'I'd rather have a husband who was poor but who I could spend my life with, than one whose immensely rich, never home and who acts like I'm an encumbrance'.

'Think what you're doing now. There's nothing noble about being poor, I can assure you. Ask anyone who's without means and they'd gladly change places with you' said duke. 'You may yet live to regret letting this opportunity slip through your fingers. Can I prevail on you .... please Elizabeth .... to reconsider your position. You could have a very comfortable life with Knightley and ..... yes .... I have to say .... t'would bring some security to the rest of your family too.'

'I know it' said Elizabeth. 'But yet I feel it's out of my power to control. I wish it were different. I wish I could meet him, privately and face to face, with no others around him. I wish we could fight it out. I would relish disputing the matter with him, finding out how I stand ... but he seems to prefer to torture me by neglect. No sooner were we engaged to be married and he stopped calling on me. I've seen him .... what twice .... in the last six months and both times in company with the family. Now, I may not know much about married life, or even how engaged people should be, but that can't be right. I've written to him .... and ...... I get no reply.'

'Oh my dear' said her father sympathetically, 'I thought it was so, but I needed to hear it from you directly. I had to ask .....'

'I cannot ..... will not ..... go chasing after him' said Elizabeth.

'Well, that's that then' said Duke.

'Yes Father, but it's not *because* of the annuity being ended, this was happening before I can assure you.'

'Yes I know' he said, 'I have observed it myself, but I just thought in the changed circumstances that you might wish to try to catch him while you can, *before* he hears of it ......'

'No Father. Besides, I wouldn't want him to marry me .... what, out of pity? No, that won't do at all. Besides, I believe I was so caught up with the *idea* of being engaged, I'm not sure I was ever really in love with him. I was flattered by his attention but, when the attention vanished, I found there was little else to commend him. He's outrageously ambitious and I do believe there's little inducement to him to settle down at this time. He has been married before …. and widowed. I don't think the *idea* of being married was such an exciting adventure to him as it might have been for me ……'

'Then there's no more to be said about it' said Duke. The only silver lining in the heavy clouds is that we did at least make some money through Knightley's South Seas stock, so we're not completely destitute.'

'We both' said Elizabeth indicating Aurora 'had our last annuities doubled in value' said Elizabeth so there's no immediate concern.'

'Yes, you Aurora …..' said Duke 'will now also find the world altered. Young men who may have shown interest in you in the past will now have none. Word will spread quickly among our friends and soon everyone will know.'

Her father looked so depressed at having to tell his daughters of their altered finances that Aurora felt pity for him. She was moved by his distress to the point where she felt it was the right time for her to tell him her secret …. that she was already married ….. and that she was married to the heir of a great estate.

'Father?' said Aurora meekly 'there's something I have to tell you and I think Elizabeth should hear it too. I know this'll disappoint you …..' she said, taking a deep breath. 'Since we are now discussing such serious matters, there is something I've been meaning to talk to you about for some time. I've been concealing something'.

'Go on' Duke said nervously.

'I'm not quite sure how to begin' she stumbled. No one came to her aid as her father and sister were in trepidation of what she was about to say, so she briefly paused and then continued.

'A few months ago you will recall I was in Matlock…..'

'I recall perfectly, yes'.

'Well, whilst there I met someone …. a man who became very dear to me. *Is* very dear to me. So dear to me that I couldn't imagine my life without him.'

Duke murmured a noise which couldn't be interpreted as a good or a bad sign, it was just a noisy acknowledgement that he heard the words. 'And ….?'

'Well, now this is the thing I've to tell you and which is very difficult. I was persuaded of the necessity to keep our relationship an absolute secret.'

'Relationship? Why? Secret from your own family?' he asked.

'Secret from everyone'.

'And who is the man?'

'Oh ... I think I can guess' said Elizabeth.

Ignoring his question, Aurora continued, 'Mother knew absolutely nothing about it I promise. Which, incidentally, I'm right sorry for.'

'And ...?' persisted her father.

'Oh, there's no easy way I can say this to you, but say it I must as time is moving on. I've been secretly married since that time, last autumn. We were both of full age ... and .... and ... it was straight forward, and ..... that is what I have to tell you. I am truly and legally married and I'll be expecting a child in a few months.'

The words said, in somewhat of a rush, Aurora paused. Although she knew her father wasn't a man given to explosions of anger, she instinctively paused after the words, wanting to see a reaction - "any" reaction in preference to silence.

Elizabeth's eyes widened and she looked startled at Aurora but stayed silent waiting for her father's reaction too. When it came, however, it wasn't fury, it was a sadness that added to the despondency he was already suffering.

Then a flood of questions came .... 'Why the secrecy? Who's the man? What's his name? What manner of person is it you have connected yourself to?..... How could you do this to your family?'

Seeing no way of avoiding answering all of his questions, Aurora cut to the main point and said the words slowly ... 'Benjamin Vavasour'.

Chapter 7

The rest of that day passed slowly, as if there'd been a dreadful bereavement in the house. There were hushed tones and occasional words from the inmates but, otherwise, a subdued atmosphere prevailed. Only the passage of time would permit normal life to resume and a single day wasn't enough to adjust to this shocking news.

The following day, with such great matters on everyone's minds, an aura of heavy confusion existed within the family. Isabella had received news of her daughter's changed status with astonishment and disbelief which, within the hour, had turned to acceptance and resignation, as was her way. The much used phrase 'it's no good crying over spilt milk' was bandied about freely for a while until the practicalities of Aurora's situation began to dawn on her. Then there began conciliatory comments about having saved them the cost of another daughter's wedding and, then finally Isabella arrived at a point in her thinking cycle where she could see a positive outcome - the Vavasours at least were a wealthy family and Benjamin appeared to be the heir to his father's estate. It could've been much, much worse.

Duke, however, went through no such evolution of thoughts and feelings. His thoughts remained dogmatically where they had been when he first heard Aurora utter the words. Without having answers to most of his questions, Duke emerged after many hours of solitary contemplation in his library with a determination to tackle head on what he now deemed a crisis.

The hopes he had for Elizabeth being the salvation for his daughters' financial future, now turned to Aurora but her situation in living separately from her husband was unsatisfactory and what he wanted, above all else, was clarity.

Decisive action was to be taken and Duke ordered the coach which was to take him, Isabella and Aurora straight to Vavasour Hall. As a lawyer, Duke instinctively disliked unfinished business and unanswered questions and Aurora couldn't satisfy him properly on any score and so he designed to settle the matter man-to-man with Benjamin Vavasour in person.

Isabella, who'd rallied her spirits that day, had insisted on accompanying her husband as this was a crisis involving her daughter. Duke dismissed out of hand Aurora's continued pleadings that absolute secrecy was still essential and that they should, on no account, visit Benjamin's home.

On an emotional level Duke was shocked and disappointed in his daughter who he'd always thought knew right from wrong. Of his three daughters, Aurora was the one he could least have imagined behaving wildly; Elizabeth he could more easily have believed this action of, but not his youngest daughter.

No amount of vehement objections from Aurora could prevent the planned journey taking place that day and the apprehension she felt during the coach journey was unbearable. Small talk between the family was impossible and unnecessary and so most of the journey was spent in silence except from small noises her mother would make every now and then.

Aurora knew what the situation was with her mother to whom long emotion-filled silences were as unwelcome as the news itself. She knew the groans reflected every bump and jolt of the carriage on the poor uneven roads and that they jarred with her mother's joints. Isabella tolerated the discomfort far better than she normally would, because there was in progress a far nobler cause. She was suffering *for* her daughter and therefore complaining was inappropriate when engaged on a journey of martyrdom. Indeed the experience of pain enhanced her tribute to her daughter's cause, but the little wimps and soft noises she made were solely to remind those who knew her disposition that she was silently suffering.

The shock of yesterday's news had abated now and transformed itself to a dull resignation of Aurora's predicament, exacerbated by the news of her failed annuity. Each person was absorbed in private musings; with Duke rehearsing in his mind, the conversation he would have with Benjamin and, for Aurora, her thoughts were full of trepidation of Benjamin's reaction.

The coachman indicated that they were nearing their destination and, as they traversed the long, winding drive up to the house, it was impossible for at least some of the Fairfaxes not to look, to absorb how extensive the estate was and to inwardly gasp at the first sight of the enormous mansion in its stately glory.

The coach at last pulled up at Vavasour Hall and they all stepped out into a dull, drizzly day to be admitted into the Hall by the butler. Aurora could see, from the corner of her eye, her mother perusing the large estate and knew what was running through her mind. Her father may have been bracing himself for a hard negotiation but her mother was counting rooms, eyeing tapestries, evaluating furniture and imagining what income Aurora might expect as mistress of Vavasour Hall.

They were shown into a grand, but cold and lifeless room which seemed little used to receiving company where they were told to wait whilst Mr Vavasour was told they wanted to see him. Some half hour passed before they were led across the hall and into a library where two men were seated by the fire.

Duke glanced at Aurora to see if she would indicate if the younger man was her husband, but she wouldn't return his look. Then recognising the elder of the two men he spoke:

'Good day Mr Vavasour' Duke said, 'I believe we saw each other a few months ago at Leicester House, I am Duke and this is my wife Isabella Fairfax and daughter Aurora'.

'Yes', said the elder of the two men, 'I am Gervase and this is my son Pascal. What can we do for you?'

'Actually it's your son Benjamin we've come to see, but also wish to speak to you'.

'Go fetch him' barked the old man to Pascal, who left the room straight away.

'What's this about' he asked.

'Well, I think we should wait until Benjamin is here if you don't mind'.

'Oh?' said the old man, appearing to be unused to anyone disobliging him, but still he persisted, 'What's he been up to now? Gambling debts no doubt? If you're a creditor of my son's then I want nothing to do with you. I've an agent who deals with that kind of thing.' Gervase moved closer to the fire as if wishing the Fairfaxes were gone and seemed disinclined to make further conversation with them.

'No, sir,' started Duke, 'It's nothing of the kind.'

At that moment the door opened and Benjamin and Pascal appeared in the room.

'What's this about?' Gervase directed at Benjamin.

Benjamin was startled and what little colour he had in his face quickly drained away when he saw Aurora. He must have guessed at the purpose of the visit. He was clearly flustered and alarmed by her presence and remained standing, unsure of how he should act. Duke and Isabella looked him over, noticing his discomfiture at their presence, and more particularly by Aurora's, and curious as to how he would react to their impending challenge.

'Benjamin' said Duke to the young man.

'Yes sir' was the instant response.

'I believe you know why we are here?'

After a moment's hesitation he responded 'I do know your family sir yes, of course. I was at Leicester House and York when your family was there. But …. erm …. I'm not specifically sure why you're here today, no sir.'

Seeing that talking around the subject wasn't yielding results, Duke spoke directly, 'Benjamin, my daughter tells me that a few months ago in Matlock you went through a marriage ceremony with her'.

'Sir?' said Benjamin, clearly stalling for time to think.

'You did *what*?' laughed Pascal.

'Is that not true?' Duke asked Aurora.

'Yes Father' said Aurora in a faltering voice, 'I was married to Benjamin in Matlock Bath ….. before God ….. the minister and witnesses. Several months ago'.

'Have you nothing to say young man?' asked Duke. 'From what I've been told you appear to have married my daughter, sworn her to secrecy, and it would appear from our reception here today that you've told no one in your family.'

'Urm ...' was the only audible sound from Benjamin who then, most inappropriately, broke out into a smile, gave a laugh fraught with nervous tension and muttered something that not one soul in the room could hear.

'Well, what have you to say?' asked his father. 'Did you marry this girl, or not?'

'I …. erm …… we …….. we met in Matlock ...'.

46

'Oh yes …..' said Pascal realising the significance, 'you *were* in Matlock a while back staying with James Onslow - his family have a house there..... I do recall .....'

'So you've put her up to this have you?' said Gervase to Benjamin. Then talking directly to Aurora, said 'Did he' looking at Benjamin 'tell you to come here today with this ridiculous tale? Has he promised you money to invent this story?'

Not waiting for a reply, he turned to Benjamin and angrily said, 'You know I won't give you any money, so you've got this girl to pretend there was a marriage in the hope that I will take pity. Let me guess' he added after a brief pause, 'she's an actress? Pick her up on your last trip to London did you? If I attended the theatre more often I'd probably be able to recognise her. As it is, this farce is at an end.'

Turning to Isabella, Gervase said 'And I suppose you're bit-part players too'.

'Sir' interrupted Duke who was affronted, 'you know full well who we are. You've seen me before and you know my son is MP for York - your allegations are ridiculous, rude and, I may say, extraordinary.'

'I say what I will in my own home' he snapped back. 'So, that's the end of the matter' Gervase said decisively. 'I believe that concludes our business. Good day.' Turning away from the visitors, Gervase picked up a document, to show his irritation at the intrusion and to make the point he had more important matters to deal with than this.

'Not so fast' said Duke before fixing a fierce look on Benjamin. 'Are you denying that you married my daughter, a daughter who, until she met you, has never deceived anyone in her entire life?'

Gervase, irritated that the conversation was continuing, interrupted with a condescending comment, 'I say begone with you all. There was no such marriage, you have no claim on my son, nor on my family and you should take your tricks away with you. I have heard of such schemes which are commonplace. Only the other day I heard of an Earl's son who, on visiting York, was plied with drink to the point where he could barely stand, some rogues forced him through a sham marriage ceremony and then the not so demure bride then hotfooted it over to his family's seat demanding maintenance. If it isn't a marriage trick then it's gaming debts; get a young heir to his family's fortune incapacitated, encourage him to run up notes, then make demands on the family who, for honour's sake, are bound to oblige. It happens all the time. I say begone with you and take your parlour trick down the road and try it elsewhere. Get rid of them' he shouted to Pascal who immediately rose to his feet and moved towards Duke.

'Have you *nothing* to say?' Duke implored Benjamin.

There was silence.

'We shall return' Duke said to Benjamin 'with the witnesses and even the Minister to prove the marriage took place. And' he said emphatically to Benjamin 'when my daughter's child is born in a few months' time we shall hire fifty town criers to announce to the world who the father is. That is, of course after we have it blazoned across every newspaper in the country' he said angrily.

'Will you indeed, by gad' shouted Gervase Vavasour. 'Then my lawyer will have your guts for garters'.

As the Fairfaxes moved to depart, Benjamin finally, but too late, looked tenderly at Aurora and tried to hold her hand but she recoiled from him, disgusted that he hadn't spoken out.

'A baby?' he said to Aurora. She didn't reply but kept walking away.

'Yes ..... alright ...... yes I did marry Aurora' Benjamin finally was heard to say to Gervase, 'it's so ...... I did marry Aurora ....'

'I don't believe it' said Gervase whose blood was up. 'All of you, get out'.

Duke, Isabella and Aurora left the room in silence but Benjamin chased after them, begging Aurora's forgiveness and promised that matters would be sorted out. 'You see why I wanted the marriage to be a secret?' he pleaded, 'my father is not a reasonable man and has it in his power to leave me destitute'.

Aurora pulled away from him and followed her family out of the house. If their home hadn't been so far away Aurora would have insisted on walking as she'd absolutely no desire to be confined in such a small space as a carriage with her family at this time. As it was, she dutifully stepped inside and sat down resolutely determined to engage in no conversation.

Inside the coach, however, as they drove away from Vavasour Hall, Isabella was unable to let the silence continue. Her good breeding and hostess qualities prevented her from seeing the necessity for calm after a storm.

'What a terrible man,' she exclaimed. 'His sons looked frightened of him.'

'He *shall* know the marriage took place' said Duke defiantly. 'We shall get proof and force Benjamin to face his responsibilities, to take care of Aurora. And ..... and' he said angrily, 'that worthless old man will pay maintenance for the child when it arrives. He will, if it's the last thing I do. I've never felt so humiliated'.

'Father' said Aurora humbly, 'I did beg you not to visit the Vavasours. Benjamin wanted to keep the marriage a secret from his father because he knew he would disapprove, because I'm not a Catholic.'

'Oh?' said Duke incredulous. 'Aurora! Did you hear one word about your faith in that room just now? Because I didn't. Is that what that fool of a boy told you, to stop you telling anyone about your marriage? I don't know who's the bigger fool here, the cantankerous father, the pathetic son or you ..... you for going through with it!'

Aurora made no response because she knew it would further aggravate the situation. Yet again Isabella broached the ensuing silence with words of support for her husband, 'What could've possessed you Aurora. Not to tell your father and me you had married'. On getting no response she continued 'I can't understand it. You've never been deceitful before. I should never have taken you to Matlock if I had suspected for one moment that you would get into such mischief. You have cruelly deceived me. To have a relationship behind my back, to marry? And to lie to me about how you had passed your time. I never thought you capable of such deception.'

'I'm sorry mother' said Aurora. 'Truly I am'.

'Never rains but it pours' Isabella continued. The annuity's gone, my youngest secretly married and having the baby of a father who hasn't the backbone to stand up to his father and Elizabeth ... well what an almighty mess. That so-called fiancé of hers is soaring high like an eagle at the moment, barely time to spend one evening with her, so full of himself. He's plotting and scheming to make himself rich with so many others hanging on his coat tail that it's bound to end badly. She never sees the man he's in such demand. Building new houses and I don't know what. He's making so much money he hasn't got time to spend it.'

Aurora by now was so tired of the journey she was counting the miles in silence, desperate for it to end. It felt like the longest journey she'd made in her entire life. It was pointless repeating what had already been said, so she let her mother prattle on. Even her father was politely ignoring her.

Back home at Fairfax Manor she went straight to her room; the only place she could be sure her private thoughts wouldn't be intruded on. She knew she'd been rash in marrying Benjamin Vavasour at Matlock on so short an acquaintance but had been certain in her own mind that he was the only man she could possibly be happy with. Now, seeing him in his own home for the first time and meeting his family in such confrontational circumstances, left her doubting herself and her judgement.

She'd been persuaded by Benjamin that his father, being a leading Roman Catholic in the area, would never accept the marriage of his eldest son and heir to a Protestant and that, at least for a while, it would be better to be discrete about their union. Aurora had agreed with him, and no one had twisted her arm. She knew full well what she was doing and her instincts, which had served her so well in the past, told her it was for the best.

Benjamin told her that the Vavasour Hall estate was entailed on him as the eldest male son' as stipulated in his grandfather Dionysus Vavasour's will, and his father was powerless to prevent that inheritance. However, Benjamin had no means of supporting himself, let alone a family, without his father's assistance and, since he had been brought up as a gentleman expected to run a vast estate, he had no occupation or career to support him and feared upsetting his father who had the power to stop his income.

All this she'd freely accepted and agreed to. But, as a young woman, completely in love for the first time Aurora felt powerless to refuse Benjamin anything. His argument was so convincing to her that she agreed, though reluctantly, that they would return from Matlock to their respective homes and keep the marriage a complete secret. There was always the possibility that Gervase

Vavasour would die as he wasn't in good health and then, Benjamin told her, there was no need to trouble him with their news. It would all be well if they just took some time and were discreet.

Keeping such a big secret from her parents, however, had been too great a burden for Aurora. Her sister Elizabeth had begun to guess that a relationship had formed between the pair and had urged caution but, caught up in her romance, Aurora hadn't wished to hear words of reason.

The realisation that she was expecting a baby, however, changed the dynamics. The issue had forced itself into the open and there was then a fixed period of time in which matters had to be urgently dealt with. That was what had prompted her to tell her father. Now, her difficulties were compounded with the news of the cessation of her annuity. Her prospects seemed bleak indeed.

The afternoon's exchange had rankled Duke profoundly, not just because there was no acknowledgement of his daughter's status, or that there was no solution to her predicament but for other reasons. He brooded resentfully over the words of Gervase Vavasour 'So, he'll have my "guts for garters" will he? We'll see about that'.

Ethel Fledd

Chapter 8

The Fairfax family's visit, it was later discovered, had quite an impact on the inhabitants of Vavasour Hall, even if it didn't seem so at the time. Benjamin's marriage, so richly and vehemently denied by his father, was privately conceded as a probable fact though it would be a long time before this was publicly acknowledged.

Although Benjamin had failed to disclose his marriage to his family of his own accord, the unexpected visit which revealed news of the event, had the effect of relieving him from the burden of having to tell his father himself. And his father's response was every bit as bad as he had anticipated.

Meanwhile, the injury done to the Fairfaxes had to be resolved. So in the weeks that followed and, realising he had to redeem himself with the Fairfaxes, Benjamin embarked on a major charm offensive with the family beginning with boundless apologies for their dreadful reception.
He began openly visiting Aurora and, amongst all their acquaintances, it quickly became known publicly that there was a relationship between Benjamin and Aurora.

It took time to break through the barrier of wariness that existed and lack of respect he detected from Duke. It was, however, a relentless and sweeping effort that delighted Aurora as it made her feel special and reminded her *precisely* why she'd developed feelings for him in the first place. She delighted that others could see him, as she initially had, so full of charm and ease of manners. He flattered her mother, spoke sensibly and seriously to her father and beguiled everyone with his affection for Aurora and tender care of her.

He had promised to set up a home for the couple and even took care to plant a rumour that they were, in fact, already married, so no eyebrows were raised when a lease was taken on a substantial house, Grace Dieu Manor, a short distance away from her family's home.

For those who had troubled to contemplate on the matter, the sudden arrival of Aurora's child so soon after marriage rumours had started, there probably was a knowing nod and a wink exchanged on the baby's rapid arrival. For Aurora herself, she was too busy with baby preparations, adjusting to marriage and running her own household to care about such gossip. Her father Duke, meanwhile, though acquiescent in the face of his son-in-law's energetic platitudes, which he tolerated for the sake of others, still nurtured a deep rooted resentment to Vavasour senior - unfinished business, a score to be settled. He nursed an injury which he had no desire to see healed and, but for his daughter being married into the family, it would've been easier to plot revenge, but for his daughter's sake, he suffered Benjamin's presence with all the equanimity he could muster. Meanwhile, the only satisfaction he could remotely find, was to concentrate on getting proof that the marriage had occurred.

After the loss of annuities to his three daughters, Duke decided that, despite the rising and rising value of his South Seas stock, he must sell whatever remaining stock he had at once. His daughters, who held more modest investments, also decided to cash in theirs too. He made contact with Knightley, in writing, and instructed the sale, though was particularly careful to make the letter strictly business-like, with no personal comments at all as felt it safer to conclude the financial business before raising the issue of how things stood between Knightley and Elizabeth. It was, he judged, probably unnecessary to give any explanations.

It was a hard thing to do; to swim against the tide when no one else was selling and hoards of people were still clamouring for shares, he was forced to sell up. 'A bird in the hand is worth two in the bush' he told himself to justify his action. He would provide for his daughters now and later reinvest if the stock would still be climbing.

In the fullness of time, he would come to bless the day he made this decision when, some months later and in desperate times, the money-making 'bubble' spectacularly burst.

On her father's instructions Elizabeth travelled to Matlock Bath to try to find the witnesses to Aurora's wedding, but she discovered the witnesses had unfortunately moved out of the county and couldn't now be traced. She had better luck with the Minister, an elderly gentleman named Rev Reginald Jarvice, who was found and was happy to do all he could to help. He took an extract from the parish register, wrote a covering letter addressed to Gervase Vavasour assuring him of the fact that the event had taken place and confirmed that he had personally conducted the service.

Elizabeth returned after visiting him armed with the letters and documents and presented them to her father. 'This should confound Gervase Vavasour out of his complacency' Duke thought to himself. That, he thought, was the closest he could get to bringing him to book whilst still supporting his daughter.

For Aurora, her life was all changed. Benjamin had acquired a house for them and …. she loved it. It was almost as large as Fairfax Manor and ….. it was all theirs. It felt as if she'd made the transition from being a girl to a woman - as if womanhood was a tangible threshold she was now crossing. She was so excited to be having her own home, just in time for her baby's arrival, that everything seemed to be coming together nicely at the right time.

Grace Dieu Manor and was but a short distance from her family's home. Everything was in place awaiting the arrival of her baby.

Getting used to sharing her life with Benjamin was another 'first' too. He was, at least initially, full of the utmost attention. Anything …. everything …. Aurora wanted, he was able to procure. Nothing was too much trouble. But …. the devoted attention …… as quickly as it had arrived …. began to wane and it waned long, long before the baby's eventual arrival.

These were major adjustments for her to make and difficulties soon began to surface. All such difficulties, however, were easily dismissed as mere trifles. All would be well once the baby arrived. The baby would make their new family complete …… and all the worrying signs of her new husband's erratic behaviour she'd begun to notice ….. would fade away. She lived in a state of perpetual expectation and belief that, no matter what vexations existed now, *after* the birth ….. a state of utopia would exist. She knew how it would be …. every spring, since she could remember, she'd been excited to help her farmer neighbour carry new-born lambs to shelter. There could be nothing more natural than to bring forth a new life.

The arrival of a daughter, to be called Stella, in the early summer was the beginning of a new chapter in Aurora's life as a mother and the baby absorbed all of her attention. She was happily engaged in doing another's bidding now as she, being the youngest in her family, had never before had someone other than herself to think about, and that thought motivated her.

From morn till night, she fussed, she fretted, she ran back and forth helping - to the point that the nurse who'd been engaged to care for the baby was exasperated with her meddling.

Benjamin had tried to maintain his care and affection for Aurora until the birth and had joined in the pleasantries of setting up home. He greeted his daughter's arrival with affection, but showed thinly disguised disappointment that it wasn't a boy.

'There'll be more, God willing' he said.

'Not just yet' urged Aurora. 'There's no hurry'.

But not long after the baby's arrival, his old inclinations began to surface. The difficulties, which had begun to manifest themselves almost as soon as the couple began living together, became much more manifest after the baby's arrival.

Benjamin was - it has to be said - immature for his age and, passionate though he had been about Aurora, he still wanted his singleton life of drinking and gambling to continue. The moment the novelty of the baby's arrival began to wane, he seemed to quickly tire of their new life together. He began going out in the evenings, and staying out until the early hours of the morning, but offered no explanation for where he went, other than vaguely referring to visiting friends, friends he never called by name.

One thing that Aurora did quickly notice was that no one from Benjamin's family had visited Grace Dieu Manor. Aurora wasn't too surprised by this, given the reception the Fairfaxes had received at Vavasour Hall, but thought it strange that no-one, not even a distant relation or anyone from the wider Vavasour family, aunts, uncles, cousins etc had called on them. She began to wonder if her husband had even told his family where he was, or where they were living.

But these were just random thoughts, Aurora was too busy and tired to initially notice her 'jobless' gentleman of a husband was not adjusting as well as she to their new life. As his behaviour became more and more restless, however, she hoped rather than believed that he could settle.

Busy weeks passed by and autumn approached, with days shortening again. The approach of winter seemed to exacerbate Benjamin's restlessness. He was, she thought, at times rather like caged animal living a life that wasn't natural to him. He became irritable, short-tempered and drank every day in the home, which Aurora hadn't anticipated. He drank regularly and to great excess which not only made her fear for her infant's safety but hampered any further close relations between the couple. Her move into a separate bedroom passed without a single comment from Benjamin.

He was, however, always apologetic. Whatever drunken condition he was in towards evening time, after a few hours sleep he would wake and be back to his normal self again. So, without thinking, Aurora developed a routine of avoiding him later in the day.

They had no mutual friends, beyond those they had met whilst at Matlock Bath and, but for the visits of her family members, Aurora wouldn't have received any visitors at all. When she'd tried to invite her own friends over to the Manor, she'd felt embarrassed by Benjamin's behaviour. Drunk or sober he seemed bent on not encouraging her friends there and so she gradually stopped inviting anyone. It began to feel that, but for their daughter, the couple had nothing to share, no common interests, no common friends and no meeting of minds.

Family, however, was different. The Fairfaxes already knew her husband's ways and no misbehaviour on his part deterred them from coming. She relished a visit from her father Duke, mother Isabella and brother Nathan who came to Grace Dieu Manor where Benjamin, although at home, was elsewhere in the house and had made no initial effort to greet her guests.

'Darling' said her mother 'cooing at baby Stella who Aurora presented to her. 'Isn't she just beautiful?' The question required no answer, of course, as naturally all babies, no matter how severely crumpled and lacking any pleasing appearance, are beautiful to their grandparents.

'Benjamin is at home' said Aurora, conscious of his absence and added 'and he'll be here shortly. I'm sure', she hoped rather than knew.

Her brother Nathan, who'd been the last to discover Aurora's unexpected marriage commented, 'I have yet to meet your spouse dear sister, at least not formally, except I did see him briefly at York. Father has given me chapter and verse on the family you've married into.'

'Yes, I can imagine' said Aurora dryly.

'I certainly do know of them, as big landowners in Yorkshire and have been at many functions where Gervase was present, though I little imagined we'd be related one day. What's the situation with him now?' he asked.

'I don't know' replied Aurora, 'I've had no contact with that family and, to my knowledge, neither has Benjamin.'

Isabella moved closer to Aurora, as if to confide a secret, and said, in a whisper, 'your brother's heard, from his friends, that Benjamin was thrown out by his father after our visit.'

Aurora was astonished to hear that but didn't wish to show it. She struggled against giving any outward sign that this was news.

Isabella continued 'there was an almighty argument and his father said if he had indeed married against his wishes that he wouldn't have him in the house, that he'd disown him'.

'Benjamin's told me that his father is a staunch Roman Catholic and insisted that he married within the faith. That me being a Protestant is the problem.'

'Strange that he chose you for a wife then?' said Duke. 'Singular.'

'There's nothing wrong with our daughter' Isabella said defensively.

Aurora was thoughtfully quiet for a moment. It was a pregnant pause, full of a single thought which occurred to them all but no one quite had the courage to voice it. So she felt compelled to give the thought a sound ... 'And' ... she gingerly suggested .... 'you're thinking that may have been the motivation behind Benjamin's sudden leasing of this house. The need for somewhere to live for himself as well as us?'

No one said yes, but their silence affirmed the consensus. Aurora sighed in despair, but this was not the first time she'd detected disappointment from her family about her choice of husband. She saw his faults, she wasn't blind to his weak character but felt powerless to join in their opinions. He had a hold, a grip on her feelings that bound her to him. The love she felt that drew her to him and to marriage was too strong to overcome and so gradually, day by day, as each new disappointment came to the surface she found herself excusing them. So he drank ... but he was a young man, so he was irritable ... but he had no employment to fill his time, so he argued with his family ... but he was heir to a great estate, and so on. Anything he did, her mind found some way to explain away. She'd made her bed and must lie on it, was a thought she frequently had. And who is without fault?

The sudden arrival of Benjamin into the room at that moment necessitated not just a change of topic but also a raising of spirits. After all the usual greetings were exchanged, it became obvious from his excessive and unnatural warmth and animation that he'd been drinking.

Duke, battled on regardless with the purpose of their visit which was to present the couple with the letters from Reverend Jarvice which gave proof of their wedding having taken place. 'Reverend Jarvice will be passing through Yorkshire in a few days time and has said he will call at Vavasour Hall. But if we can get his letters to your father in the meantime, then he'll be prepared and can hear affirmation from the Minister's own lips.'

'Thank you sir' said Benjamin. 'I can see you having the makings of a first-class father-in-law' he said stupidly grinning.

The Fairfaxes stayed about half an hour and Benjamin seemed to sober up as the time passed. He talked pleasantly to each of them and told Isabella how thrilled he was to be a father. He told everyone, basically, exactly what he thought they wanted to hear.

'This must only be a flying visit. We shall have to be going now' said Isabella 'as Nathaniel has an appointment in town, but you know' she said looking at Aurora, 'you know your father and brother will do everything in their power to help you'.

'I know, thank you father' she replied, and with that they were gone.

Benjamin and Aurora were left in the room while their guests were escorted to the front door. But then, just as they were leaving the house and entering their coach, they passed a figure waiting to come inside. The figure watched silently for a moment and then spoke:

'Well, well, if it isn't the Honourable Nathaniel Fairfax, Member of His Majesty's Parliament representing the historic city of York, Esquire' he added sarcastically.

'Stanhope?' said Nathaniel.

'The same.'

'Wish I could say it was a pleasure to see you, but it ain'.' Nathan said moving towards the coach.

'I was sorry to miss you at York. Weren't for lack of trying I assure you, but some fool sent an ass flying through the air and, in the general confusion, you ... the most Honourable Fairfax ... slipped the net'.

'Well?' said Nathan standing his ground, 'I'm here now, so what do you want to do?' He spoke calmly and with measure, staring the man directly in the eyes. It was a small challenge which his opponent seemed not willing to take up.

'If I weren't here for a merry evening with my friend, I'd know exactly what to do. But I'm looking forward to a sociable evening playing cards.'

'Not so brave on your own are you' said Nathan, to which his opponent responded with anger.

'Perhaps I'll have your sister wait table for me' Stanhope sneered threateningly.

'Lay one finger on my sister and I'll ....' said Nathan angrily but at that moment Duke leant out the carriage and interrupted the tension by urging Nathaniel to join them.

'I know your game' Stanhope whispered in his ear as Nathan turned to face his father. 'Been taking bribes from the Sword Blade Company, heh? Got yourself wealthy on a parliamentary seat that was mine. Got Knightley in your pocket and been making money that should've been mine. That seat's been in our family for decades.'

'If you'd been wanted by the corporation, and the burgesses, you could've got yourself elected ......'

'Nathaniel' shouted Isabella. 'Come on, we have to go'.

Nathan climbed in the coach but was unhappy. Was Aurora going to be safe with Stanhope in the house? He couldn't be sure, but he felt unable to voice his concerns as he knew it would alarm his mother. The coach pulled away and Nathan resolved that 'something' must be done for his sister.

A random thought occurred to him. Could Stanhope have engineered the imprudent match Vavasour made with his sister? Clearly Stanhope had a personal vendetta against him and felt he'd been cheated out of, not just a parliamentary seat, but opportunity for making his fortune. Almost immediately the thought occurred to him, he dismissed it as too absurd. Or was it? The thought wouldn't go away.

He felt like turning the coach around and taking his sister away from the house, but she wouldn't have come. He knew, at least for his sister's part, the marriage was based on genuine affection. Yet, something *must* be done.

Chapter 9

Aurora watched her family's departure from the library window at Vavasour Hall as the coach pulled away. It was still a novelty to her to have visitors to her own establishment and she felt immensely proud of her baby daughter Stella, so peacefully sleeping.

That evening, for the first time, Benjamin had invited guests to the house. Knowing of her family's visit too, he arranged the visit to fall after their likely departure which, Aurora thought, was sensible. The arrival of those friends, however, wasn't quite what Aurora had been expecting. She'd thought it a good sign, to bring any of his friends into their home, that he was putting down roots and introducing her to his friends. Up to that point he'd contented himself with spending most of his days within the house and many evenings without.

The friends who arrived, however, were only young single men wanting to play cards. Aurora would have preferred it if there'd been some couples to include females, but that wasn't to be. After Stanhope, three others arrived and, although she initially went to greet the guests, it quickly became apparent to her that her presence wasn't desirable; that there was a male banter and camaraderie between the men that rendered female company out of place, so she withdrew and left them to it.

Aurora took herself off to a room which was far enough away from the gathered friends to protect the baby, and herself, from the growing crescendo of noise and, once more, made excuses to herself. Well, at least if he's here no harm can come to him, she told herself ….. if he got drunk it would be in private ….. and men together are always more raucous without the presence of ladies.

On arrival, the names of the friends wasn't disclosed to her beyond their Christian names. For certain, if she'd heard the name Stanhope, it would most certainly have raised her alarm, but it wasn't until much later that she heard it.

For a long while, probably the best part of the next two hours, Aurora passed the time watching over her infant who was breathing lightly and sleeping in contentment, seeming not to hear the growing rowdiness coming from down the corridor. The friends, now playing at cards and sounding drunk, were in high spirits with their own banter and, at that point, nothing in the world could have induced Aurora to look in on them again.

Then, at that moment, there was the noise of growing footsteps outside her door and she hoped it was Benjamin popping in to check on her, a prospect she welcomed, but the figure that stepped inside the room was not he. A tall, gaunt figure moved towards her in an ungainly manner seeming to chuckle to himself and speak under his breath.

'Sir ....' Aurora started to speak, 'the baby .....'

'Ohhhh ...... shhhhhh .....' the figure whispered 'sleep little one'. Then looking at Aurora he said in slurred speech 'I just wanted to say thank you for a most enjoyable evening. Really! I have been friends with Benjamin for many years and ..... and ..... you're the best little ..... wife he's ever had!' The man laughed loudly but immediately checked himself 'shhhhh .... the baby sleeps.'

'Would you leave us please' whispered Aurora, 'I don't want the baby waking'.

'Of course, of course' the man said frowning. 'Night-night little one.' Then added, with a tightly clenched scowling and menacing face 'There's a new life in the world .... A filthy, filthy little Fairfax .... one day you'll grow up to be the queen of the sluts .....'

'Sir!' Aurora said astonished, 'you're drunk, get out'.

'No, no, I'm not drunk' the man insisted. 'I'm.....'

At that moment Benjamin appeared in the doorway and snapped 'Stanhope! What are you doing here'.

'Stanhope?' said Aurora.

'Come here, man' insisted Benjamin. 'Don't annoy my wife ..... come back to the table'.

'Stanhope?' Aurora thought to herself after they'd gone, 'filthy Fairfax!' Who was that man? There was no one there to give her answers, so she swiftly walked over to the door and turned the key. Answers would have to wait and, in the meantime, she would protect herself and her baby.

More hours passed and Aurora felt sleep beckon. Surely they must be going soon, she hoped but the merriment still echoed around the house. Then, to her horror, there was a small knock on the door. She made no attempt to respond but sat silently, as if no one was in the room. 'He shall not bother us again' she thought to herself while resuming her watch over her infant daughter.

Then, a few moments later, she heard a voice, a female's at the door, saying 'Aurora? Are you there?'

She immediately knew it was her sister Elizabeth and admitted her to the room, though remembering to relock the door again.

'Are you alright?' asked Elizabeth in a concerned whisper.

'Yes, of course' she said instinctively. 'What are you doing here at this time of night, it must be, what ..... after midnight?'

'Nathan sent me to look after you. He was concerned. He saw Stanhope at the door ......'.

'Stanhope! Yes, I heard there was someone here called Stanhope?' said Aurora.

'Yes. Nathan was most unhappy to see that man arriving as they left tonight and was worried about you. He came straight to me and told me to come and stay with you, that I mustn't leave you in the house alone.'

'Oh?' said Aurora looking perplexed. 'Is this Stanhope the same one that hired a mob in York and was hoping to beat Nathan's brains out .....'

'The same and Nathan said he's here tonight. I went passed them as I came in here but they were too engrossed in their game to notice me' she said. 'I didn't come alone either, Nathan has instructed the coachman to stay close. He's parked a few yards away and, at the first sign of trouble, we're to take you away with us.'

'Oh really Elizabeth' her sister said. 'That's just too dramatic. My husband would never allow any harm to come to me!'

'Well we don't know that for sure do we and Nathan was sufficiently alarmed that he'd take no risk. Mother doesn't know, we didn't want to alarm her, if she thought you were in danger she'd probably have come herself ...'.

'But I'm not' insisted Aurora.

'Right. So, why was this door locked, I'm sure you don't usually barricade yourself in rooms in your own home'.

'Well' Aurora said reluctantly. 'I did have a visitor. The one called Stanhope came in here, when just Stella and myself were here, and I was …. sort of uneasy'.

'Why, what did he do?'

'Nothing really, but he was drunk. Looked into the baby's crib and then the strangest thing …. he called her a filthy, filthy, Fairfax who'd grow up to be the queen of the sluts'.

Elizabeth looked shocked. 'That's it! We're leaving' she cried and jumped to her feet.

'No, no' insisted Aurora. 'Goodness I've heard worse than that when Benjamin's drunk'.

'Have you?'

'He once threatened me with pistols when he was under the influence. Didn't remember a think about it the next day. Drink gives words wings' said Aurora, 'and half the time he doesn't know what he's saying. I am learning, the hard way, never to try and talk to Benjamin when he's …. well, when he isn't sober. He talks and talks, round in circles and then in the morning, he's forgotten everything he said.'

'Pistols? Good God. This is too much, Nathan was right to be worried,' said Elizabeth getting distressed.

'It is … what it is' said Aurora philosophically. 'If I ever thought Stella was really at risk, I can assure you I'd not tolerate it'.

'Was he drunk when he talked you into marrying him?' asked Elizabeth bluntly.

The words were so cutting Aurora flashed an angry look at her sister but was too tired to get into an argument so she simply said, 'Oh now, that's not fair.'

'This is serious' said her sister, 'you have this little girl to care for, if Benjamin is going to invite such people into your home then it may not be safe. *He* may not be safe'.

'You'll see' replied Aurora. 'Tomorrow he'll be himself again and all will be well.

Elizabeth sat stony faced and no amount of reassurance by her sister calmed her fears.

'So, you're staying here with us?' asked Aurora.

'Yes I must, Nathan insisted on it. If he asks, you're to tell Benjamin that I'm unwell and, what with mother not being well herself, that I had nowhere else to go'.

As they were talking, a loud bang was heard coming from the end of the corridor and then the sound of a carriage pulling away. They fell silent to listen. Aurora said 'that was the front door, they may have gone'. Aurora went into the corridor and returned a few moments later to say 'yes, they've gone, all gone, even Benjamin.'

'Where could they be going at this time of night?' asked Elizabeth.

'I don't know' said Aurora angrily 'but I can't leave the front door unlocked. It's time for bed. So wherever they've gone they can stay there till morning'.

She picked up her infant daughter and the women went upstairs to retire for the night.

Despite her words of defiance that Benjamin would have to stay out all night, Aurora slept fitfully, constantly listening for sounds of Benjamin returning, ready at a moment's notice to run downstairs and admit him, but no sound came, no one returned to the house and she lay awake hour after hour wondering where he had gone to. What was he doing? Why could he not have told her where he was going? He *must* have known she would worry.

At some point in the early hours, sleep had finally came but as soon as she woke early in the morning Aurora rose, thinking she'd missed something. She checked on the baby and then went from room to room seeing if Benjamin was at home but there was no sign of him. Elizabeth woke a little later and went through the same process, asking if the baby was alright and then asking where Benjamin was.

'I don't know' said Aurora, 'but, look ... the letters to his father are still here. He certainly hasn't gone to see his family.'

'I should hope not' said Elizabeth 'he was the worse for wear last night. In no fit state to visit family. I'll go and ask the coachman, if he's still there, if he saw anything'.

Returning a few minutes later Elizabeth said 'apparently the men all went off to York last night in Stanhope's coach.'

'York?' said Aurora sadly. 'Whatever for?'

'More of the same I should imagine' offered Elizabeth.

'Well, I suppose this means you don't need to stay Elizabeth, I should ask the coachman to take you back home. I can hardly be in any danger if I'm here on my own.'

'I have a better plan' said Elizabeth, 'I think we should ask the coachman to take us all to Vavasour Hall'.

'What for?' asked Aurora alarmed.

'I think we should .... all .... go there. Present your father-in-law with these letters .... and ... let him see his grand-daughter.'

'All?' said Aurora, 'you mean you, me and baby Stella?'

'You can hand over the evidence to Gervase Vavasour in person proving your marriage and, at the same time, introduce him to his grand-daughter.'

'No, absolutely not' said Aurora. 'No, no, a thousand times no. I shall do no such thing'.

Chapter 10

Later that day, very much against her better judgement and after hours of her sister's insistence, Aurora found herself seated in a coach heading towards Vavasour Hall. For the second time, at her family's bidding, she was making the journey, though this time in company with daughter Stella who was wide awake in the care of her nurse who had joined them.

Their journey *felt* wrong to Aurora. It wasn't usual for young women on their own to conduct such matters, but Elizabeth was a force to be reckoned with and, whilst Aurora would never admit to obeying her sister, she did instinctively look to her for guidance. She was a little older, prettier and infinitely more confident. She was also impossible to say no to, once she made her mind up on something.

The ladies arrived at the hall mid afternoon on a dim Autumn day where the wind had drifted up the russet leaves so high that they nearly disguised the steps into the house.

Aurora had such dread and foreboding about visiting this place again but reasoned to herself that if Benjamin didn't care to sort relations out with his father then someone must. The evidence of their marriage should have been taken straight to Gervase Vavasour and any further delay might prompt her own father to intervene again and she didn't want him to have to do that again. She knew he suffered ignominy last time and would have him spared it a second time. If things went badly she wouldn't tell her father about the visit. If things went well ... she probably still wouldn't tell him. He would find the idea of a party of women, with no male protection, visiting the Vavasours mortifying.

Out of the coach, Elizabeth took the lead and told the servant who emerged to greet them at the door to announce them as William Knightley of the South Seas Company. The servant, looking a little bemused at a group of ladies calling themselves such, nonetheless did as he was bid. 'That should at least get us a foot in the door' said Elizabeth.

This time there was no long wait in an outer room but, within minutes, the ladies were politely guided into the same library Aurora had visited with her parents months earlier. There sitting, in exactly the same positions as before by a roaring fire, was Gervase Vavasour and his son Pascal.

'What's this?' Gervase asked on seeing three ladies and an infant enter the room but no William Knightley. 'What have we here?'

Elizabeth grabbed the letters out of Aurora's hands and presented them to Gervase who instinctively took them.

'What's going on' he said looking annoyed. 'Why did you use William Knightley's name to gain entry to my house?'

Elizabeth answered, 'I am the fiancé of William Knightley'.

Pascal sniggered but refrained from speaking.

'I know of you' said Gervase, 'and I certainly would have been surprised if your *fiancé* as you call him was paying me a call. That's why I allowed you in, purely out of curiously. No one knows where that criminal is at the moment, unless you're hiding him madam'.

Aurora looked nervously at her sister, not knowing what Gervase was hinting at. She made a mental note to ask her sister later.

Taking command of the situation again, Elizabeth still standing as they all were, because no one had invited the ladies to sit, addressed Gervase saying, 'You have in your hand two letters from Reverend Reginald Jarvice of Matlock Bath; one contains a document extracted from the parish registers of that place showing the marriage of your son Benjamin to Aurora' she said indicating to her sister. 'The other is from the Minister himself, confirming to you that it was he, in person, who conducted the service and that your son is lawfully married to my sister here.'

Pascal snatched the papers out of his father's hands and threw them onto the fire. The ladies reacted with a collective gasp of horror but Elizabeth coolly added, 'It's of no matter. Tis an easy business to obtain copies. And besides the minister will be calling on you in a few days. He's travelling through Yorkshire and has undertaken to visit you in person and tell you, from his own lips, that he conducted the service, and to answer any questions you may have.'

Gervase said 'I recognise no such marriage has taken place. And why are *you* here? .... Surely this business concerns Benjamin? Yet he's conspicuous by his absence. Huh' he said looking at Pascal 'sending women to do his bidding now'.

Elizabeth soldiered on '... And, sir, this infant here, Stella, is your grand-daughter'.

'She could only be my grand-daughter if I had a son' Gervase Vavasour said defiantly. 'Pascal here is the only son I now have and the only one I recognise. And if this ....' he said pointing at Aurora 'scheming woman thinks to turn up on my doorstep - for the second time I might add - and expect money from me then she'll be disappointed. Is the bairn borrowed? Did you think I would take your word that it was related to me?'

'I want nothing from you ...' Aurora started to say.

'I dare say the marriage, *if* there was one, came long after the baby ..... and ..... listen to this young lady ..... I have disinherited the man you've ensnared and he'll get nothing. I shall leave everything to Pascal here. Now, what have you to say to that? He is worth nothing and, if you wish to take him under those circumstances, then you're welcome to him. Please do take him off my hands.'

Elizabeth was about to respond but her sister pleaded with her, 'Elizabeth please may we go, this is doing no good'.

'One moment' said Pascal before the ladies had chance to move, 'you may take this with you', he said as he went through papers on the desk. He handed an envelope over but wouldn't give it to Elizabeth, he insisted it went to Aurora. Then mockingly he said 'two of the northern stars! When you wish upon a star ..... this evening ..... may all your dreams come true'. Laughing, he showed them to the door and they all departed solemnly. The only sound coming from Stella who was gurgling happily.

On entering the coach for the return journey, Elizabeth said 'Aurora, whatever is in that envelope isn't going to be good news. He was sneering like an adolescent schoolboy over it, so brace yourself'. Aurora opened it and immediately saw it was a writ. She said, 'It's addressed to Benjamin and myself and it's a legal action for debt.'

'Whose debt?' asked Elizabeth as the coach pulled away.

'For debts incurred jointly by Gervase and Benjamin where property at Vavasour Hall was put up as security. Gervase has had the debt called in and Benjamin will be required to settle his half. I knew it was a mistake to go there' said Aurora.

'Maybe' said Elizabeth 'but the papers would have been served on you or Benjamin in a few days anyway, so it's only brought the process on a few days, that's all'.

'But what shall l do?' said Aurora, 'I feel so tired'.

'Father's a lawyer, we'll call in on him when we get home and ask for his advice'.

'Interesting' said Elizabeth pensively. 'The action is addressed to both of you. That means the old man knows full well that you're Benjamin's legal spouse, this is as good as an admission'.

'So the throwing of our papers on his fire ....'

'... Was all for *show* my dear'.

Chapter 11

When they were back at Grace Dieu Manor and infant Stella had been taken off to bed, the sisters were by themselves as there was still no sign of William. Aurora asked,

'About William? What did Vavasour mean? He called him a criminal and said he was in hiding.'

'Yes' said Elizabeth tentatively. 'I .... er .... as you know William is so busy at the moment and he's away so often....'

'But a criminal .... in hiding?'

'Yes, there are allegations that he's absconded with large sums of money.'

'What? Stolen money?' said Aurora.

' I don't know whether it's true, but everyone believes it to be'.

'But where? Where's he absconded to?'

'To the Continent' Elizabeth said, 'beyond the jurisdiction of the English Courts and Parliament.'

'Whose money?' Aurora asked.

'Sword Blade Company .... the South Seas stock. The price has crashed and he's apparently one of the main people to blame for it'.

'I did hear about that, indeed who can avoid hearing about it, it's all people are talking about these days. And ..... I did wonder if it affected you, but you seemed not to be concerned. I didn't notice you being distressed! Oh Elizabeth, I'm so sorry. Here we are fretting about my problems and yours are just as bad! Nay worse.'

'Hardly worse' said Elizabeth 'at least I didn't marry him. He hasn't really injured me ..... other than my pride. That is, my pride and self esteem. He has exposed me to comments from others though, for which I cannot forgive him.'

'Do you really care about other people's opinions? asked Aurora.

'Not in general, no. But my engagement to him is well known amongst our friends and, for quite some time, I've felt myself the object of gossip and stares. Such things can be quite hurtful, especially when it involves people who you thought were good friends. But …. that's money for you. Friendships, even strong ones, can be as fragile as gossamer when money's involved'.

'You weren't the one engaged on South Seas Company business, he was!'

'Yes, but my mere association with Knightley seems to have brought me to suffer censure'.

'You should write to William and tell him what a predicament he's left you in'.

'Write? Where to?' said Elizabeth. 'He's hardly likely to tell me where he is, or anyone else. Besides ….. even if I knew, I wouldn't write.'

Elizabeth sat looking pensive for a while and said, 'I suppose I fancied myself in love with Knightley. At least to begin with. But I don't think I could have been …. In love, I mean … because I don't think it's supposed to change that quickly. It's so hard to know whether you're *really* in love or not, don't you think?'

'I don't think I'm any better a judge than you are' said Aurora.

'I certainly liked him, I was dazzled by the romance of it all, the people he knew and the promise of having everything I ever wanted. I admit the lure of money played some part in his attraction' she laughed. 'But somehow it all changed. It was like he grew tired of me …. and, how quickly! One minute we were talking of marriage, the next minute he was gone out of my life, without a word.'

'I hope you aren't thinking of running off to the Continent to track him down ….' said Aurora.

'What …. chase after him?' said Elizabeth indignantly, 'no, never. He had abandoned me before he ever left this country so what would be the point in following him around now like a lost puppy!'

'What will you do?' asked Aurora.

'Well, for a start' she replied, 'this engagement ring is coming off my finger. I shall ask father to sell it for me and with the proceeds, which should be considerable because it a large, rare pink diamond, I should have enough to buy myself a small house.'

'Won't he want it back?' said Aurora.

'Let him come and get it!' said Elizabeth. 'I dare him. He'd be arrested if he set foot in this country'.

'We have both chosen men, I think,' said Aurora, 'who were exciting, perhaps even a little dangerous.'

'Those are the ones who attract us when we're young' said Elizabeth.

'But …..' continued Aurora, 'perhaps not the best ones to live with …..'

'No' said Elizabeth. 'I think maybe …… just perhaps …… you too are regretting your choice now?'

'Not regretting exactly' said Aurora, 'but yes with hindsight I shouldn't have allowed myself to be so easily persuaded that I was in love. But I don't believe I could have stopped myself from going through with marriage to Benjamin, I was totally convinced he was the only man I could ever be in love with …..'

'Was?…..' said Elizabeth.

'It's different for me' said Aurora. 'I have Stella now and that I cannot regret. If only Benjamin could have stayed on good terms with his father, if only he would try to mend the fences. If only he didn't drink …..'

'He's still a boy' said Elizabeth. 'Fatherhood hasn't matured him, he still wants to party at the hellfire club, gamble, drink and be one of the boys.'

'He may yet change' said Aurora.

'Or he may not!' replied Elizabeth

Chapter 12

As the days went on Aurora grew increasingly worried about Benjamin's absence. Clearly he hadn't returned to his family's home and no one knew where he was. Duke had been told of their visit to Vavasour Hall and was unsurprised at the reception they had. Aurora asked for his help with the writ that had been served on her and he promised to look into the matter for her.

A few days later Duke called in on his daughters to explain his thoughts on their respective positions. His enquiries to them about Benjamin's whereabouts were met with blank uncertainty, Aurora telling him she thought him in York but hadn't heard further.

'I fear my good daughters haven't used sound judgement in seeking husbands' he said looking at them both. 'I should have chosen for you, I'm sure I would have made a better job of it! Catherine comes to visit us tomorrow, I just hope she brings no crisis of marital strife with her as I shall be unable to manage another problem.' If his comments were aimed at humour they found no one willing to accommodate it and his daughters looked on him glumly.

'Now' he said with a heavy sigh, 'to business. Aurora I am attending the quarter sessions in York in a few days' time and if Benjamin hasn't returned home by then I shall send my scouts out to find what has become of him. I know the kind of clubs Stanhope frequents and, if we can find one of the friends, I'm sure the others won't be far away'.

'Do you want us to come with you father?' Aurora asked.

'Good God, no.' he said emphatically. 'This isn't a pleasure trip I can assure you and we may have to scour some pretty seedy establishments to track him down.'

Then Duke added, 'As to this legal action directed at Benjamin for debt, I really need to speak to him about it. I know nothing of loans, bonds or terms of debts, nor details of the estate entail and, until I do, can advise you no further. So be patient until we find him.'

'Can I get you a drink father?' asked Elizabeth.

'No dear,' he said 'I cannot stay long. By the way Reverend
Jarvice wrote to me to say that he visited Vavasour Hall but was
denied a visitation with Gervase. His offer to return later that day
was met with incivility and he thinks he can do no more than he
already has. For myself, I believe the issue of whether or not you
can prove your marriage is now a secondary one as we have
established that the documentation is there and easily obtained, so
he is being churlish in continuing to deny it.'

'We were trying to save you from such trouble when we
visited Vavasour Hall ....' Aurora started to say.

'I know you meant well child' Duke replied, 'but I'm not
entirely sure Gervase Vavasour is a sane man capable of being
reasoned with. He sees the worse in every situation and is cruelly
vindictive. Which brings me to the next bit of news .... well, not
really news, but information I picked up in town..... I learned
yesterday that Vavasour has been putting pressure on anyone who
has dealings with Benjamin. Including, I'm sorry to say, the owner
of this house'.

'What?' exclaimed Elizabeth, 'who is the owner?'

'A man called Paul Sampson leased Grace Dieu Manor to
Benjamin at favourable terms, knowing he was the son of Gervase.
Now that Gervase has told Sampson that Benjamin is estranged
from his family, Sampson has been told, in no uncertain terms, to
evict you from this place.'

'Evict? Surely he cannot do that' begged Aurora. 'Would he
do that to his own son, his own grand-daughter?'

'What little I know of the man' said Duke 'I imagine he
would. Sampson fears the consequences of disobliging him.
Gervase Vavasour is a big land owner and has such influence right
across the county that businessmen fear their ruin if they cross him.
Sampson came to me in the hope that I could persuade you to leave
here as he wants a peaceable resolution that pacifies Gervase but
also wants to give you fair warning to make other arrangements.'

Aurora could feel the anger welling up inside her. The
injustice of her treatment at Vavasour's hands was feeding a
growing inner rage. 'I know this is distressing' Duke said 'but you
may as well hear the rest of it.'

'There's more' she asked tentatively?

'Vavasour, actually I believe it was Pascal, made enquiries of where you obtained your supplies from - food, wood, coal and other necessities - and those who are tenants of the Vavasour estate, which includes most of the town, have been given notice to quit'.

'What?' said Elizabeth in disbelief. 'That's outrageous'.

'Anyone who has had dealings with you and Benjamin has had their leases terminated and will be thrown out of their homes. And that includes families who have lived in this town for many generations!'

Aurora, at last, gave way to tears. 'Is this all because we married without his consent, without his knowledge, or is it because I'm not a Catholic. Great God I'll convert to Catholicism if it means he'll leave us alone'.

'No, you will not' said Duke. 'The man is a tyrant and a bully, used to getting his own way and is treating you the same way he would treat anyone, a neighbour let's say, who got in his way.'

'He's a wicked man' said Aurora drying her tears.

'Yes that maybe so but' he said winking at her, trying to cheer her up 'you are in the fortunate position of having a lawyer for a father and a loving family around you. Gervase Vavasour will have to deal with all of us collectively. And .... together .... we are *invincible.*'

'It's no wonder Benjamin drinks!' she said half jokingly, 'I only wonder that he hasn't throttled his father by now'.

Duke paused for a moment, gave her a disapproving look but then turned his gaze on his other daughter:

'As for you Elizabeth, 'I'm afraid there's nothing I can do for your situation. The whole country has been buying those South Sea shares, including myself, and many are completely ruined now the share price has plunged.'

'Are you father?' asked Elizabeth, 'ruined?'

'No, I'm not' he replied. 'I have made a healthy profit which I mostly cashed in some months ago, I've only a small quantity left which I can stand to lose. Others, however, have lost everything and your fiancé, as you know, being the Cashier of the company is the man everyone wants to hate at the moment.'

'What should I do father?' asked Elizabeth.

'Do nothing' he replied, 'stay with your sister and when the fuss dies down, we'll see how you are placed. Your can be in no danger, some may fear you were privy to William's 'little green book' and know more than you probably do.'

'I've never seen a little book at all' she said, 'green or otherwise'.

'We'll let it be known that your engagement has been over for some time and you have no involvement with his affairs'.

'I would like my ring sold…..' said Elizabeth.

'Not so hasty' said Duke. 'Removing the ring is sufficient for now …..'

Chapter 13

The days rolled by and still there was no sign of Benjamin, nor any word about him. Aurora and Elizabeth settled into a domestic routine which was eased considerably by the absence of a man in the house. Infant Stella, quite rightly, regained the centre ground of attention and, to her surprise, Aurora found herself thinking less and less of Benjamin the longer he stayed away. The manner of him leaving the house hadn't been accidental, he'd walked out without a single word to anyone, which made Aurora feel less inclined to fret over his whereabouts.

By the week's end, a note arrived from her father telling her that he'd managed to find Benjamin in York and was bringing him home with him. But not to Grace Dieu Manor. He was taking him to Tadcaster, to Fairfax Manor and gave instructions that Aurora, Elizabeth, Stella and the nurse were to go there immediately as Grace Dieu Manor was to be vacated. The letter gave no detail and so Aurora was ignorant as to any circumstances, save that her husband had been found and was returning.

As instructed Grace Dieu was vacated but the short journey back to Fairfax manor felt like a defeat for Aurora. Only a few months earlier she'd left in such high spirits and with such joy at the prospect of beginning a new life in her own home, that returning to her family home felt like a comprehensive failure.

It was also a return with an entourage of Elizabeth, Stella and the nurse; in addition to her soon to arrive husband Benjamin. Her mother Isabella, however, saw things very differently and was excited at the prospect of having her grand-daughter in the house and she looked on the event as a cause for celebration. She made it her job to make them welcome by a bright, cheerful atmosphere.

Aurora wondered what circumstances had led to her father deciding to bring Benjamin to Tadcaster and how Benjamin would react to their living at Fairfax Manor. The Fairfax home was far more modest than Vavasour Hall, though slightly bigger than Grace Dieu. She wondered how he could possibly like the new surroundings. Would he be happy for them all to be in her family home? Yet what was the alternative? In his absence, however, and with the dreadful developments of legal action and the threat of eviction, something had to be done. What choice did she have?

Grace Dieu had already been furnished when they took up occupancy, yet still the volume of possessions that had been accumulated in a few short months was considerable and it took several days to make removal arrangements.

Once the bustle of settling in subsided, Aurora found, as the appointed time for Benjamin to arrive grew nearer, that she was experiencing a growing sense of dread. Deep down she knew that his absence could hardly have been for good reasons, that there would be a story to it and, worse of all, that she probably would not like it when heard. Soon the coach pulled up and her father came out first, holding the door open behind him.

'Stella's nurse will have her hands full' he shouted to his daughters, and then slowly Benjamin emerged from the darkness. Aurora was shocked to see her husband's once-fresh and handsome features look so altered and his physique so lean and weakened.

'Nurse' Elizabeth shouted indoors, 'come and help us please' she called. Benjamin struggled to make the few steps into the house and needed support.

'Father' Aurora pleaded, 'Is he ill, what's wrong?'

'In a moment' was the reply and, with that, the group moved indoors where Benjamin was taken into a side room and Aurora was told to let the nurse settle him.

Duke threw himself into a chair as Isabella brought him a whisky but, with so many eyes on him waiting for news, he drew on his inner strength and summoned the words they all wanted to hear.

'As you can see he's in a poor state. It took me several days to track him down ..... but, eventually, with the help of my friends he was found at the Two Blue Pots public house in town where he'd been abandoned by his friends. Drunk, passed out and sick, he was left to die and I dare say if we hadn't found him, that's exactly what would have happened.'

'What's he been doing?' Aurora asked.

'Too much excess of living' Duke said, 'it brings men low, drains them of life. I understand, from my agent's man who located him, that he lost all his money gambling and, when that ran out, so too did the friends. They left him to fend for himself. And ... he kept drinking to the point where he passed out. I cannot find out from him how long he lay there alone, he doesn't seem to know. He'd probably still be in that flophouse if we hadn't found him.'

'What can be done for him?' asked Isabella.

'The nurse will know what to do. She can care for him. I fear he's been living to excess for too many years. Most young men get drunk, some get drunk often and fully recover, but this .....' he said frowning 'is of a different order. I fear he'll cut his life short if he cannot control it'.

'What should we do about his family?' Aurora asked. 'They should be told'.

'Perhaps if it was any other family I would say so' said Duke, 'who knows, perhaps news of his illness may make his father think again about suing him! But my feeling is that we've had enough dealings with Vavasour Hall and, since his father threw him out, then he's hardly going to care tu'ppence if he lives or dies.'

'Oh dear' said Isabella. 'How did it come to this. I had no problems with Nathan that way.'

'I don't think anyone should, under any circumstances, tell him about his family suing him, we should keep that sort of thing from him for now. No point in kicking a poor man when he's already down is there. Now Aurora, you've not to worry. I shall see him again tomorrow and see how he is and, if he's fit enough, I will ask him to sign over his power of attorney to us so we may sort his affairs out.'

'Is that necessary?' asked Aurora.

'Do you think he will be willing to?' asked Elizabeth.

'I think he's in no fit state to manage himself, and with chancery cases now going to take place, someone has to have authority to act. We cannot risk him doing this again. But I need to wait until he's out of danger, if he does pull through, or it'll seem that I'm taking advantage of his reduced health.'

It was several days later before Benjamin began to rally, most of which he had spent sleeping. As he became more coherent, his appetite returned and, with Isabella and her two daughters and a nurse in the house, he had constant attention and fuss. He seemed pleased with his surroundings and maintained a better mood than anyone had seen before. When he finally asked to see his daughter Stella, Aurora knew that he was coming out of danger. This was the moment that her father Duke conferred with him and emerged to tell Aurora that he had secured his power of attorney. If Benjamin should absent himself again, Duke had the power to act for him.

'I've told him about the legal action his father has brought and that my advice to you both is to respond by bringing a counter-suit. Benjamin has a right to sue for maintenance, especially now he has dependants and he has provided me with some details. I've every reason to think it will succeed. And you' he said holding Aurora's hand, 'must go through these proceedings to protect your daughter's future. She's too young to care for herself, so you must be her guardian, you must be strong for both of you and do what's best for her.'

There was one more piece of information Duke had to impart to his daughter and he picked a moment when they were alone to do so.

'Aurora, there were a few details about the conditions we found Benjamin in which I didn't think fit to mention before your mother. Still, I do believe you should know.'

'Oh?' she asked.

'Yes, I'd prefer to spare you from this, but h's your husband and I think it wrong to withhold information from you, especially in the circumstances. So, I have to tell you that the place we found Benjamin in ..... was a brothel. And' he said sadly, 'the very worst kind of brothel. You need to have a care. Talk to the nurse .... Oh ..... but then perhaps not ..... she's likely to gossip. Just ... have a care' he said of yourself, he may have contracted some disease there'.

Chapter 14

Aurora took the news of her husband having been in a brothel very badly. The revelation was greeted by grim silence from her but, in the weeks that followed, it preyed heavily on her mind. It robbed her of peace of mind. It profoundly changed her.

Just one small word ..... brothel ..... that's all it had taken for her to hear, one little word that set her imagination racing and made her feel she'd aged ten years overnight. In weak moments she tried even to excuse this, thinking to herself that his companions may have drawn him there, may have put Benjamin there ... perhaps even without his knowledge! But, no, this time the excuses she invented in weak moments wouldn't pacify her.

Men visiting brothels wasn't a shock, neither was husbands visiting brothels a shock, but this was entirely different because this was "her" husband and Stella's father. It was a subliminal turning point and she could now never feel the same about Benjamin. How apt the bard's words, "For sweetest things turn sourest by their deeds, lilies that fester smell far worse than weeds'.

As time passed and life settled into a routine at Fairfax Manor, Benjamin seemed to be improving daily. There was, of course, never any discussion about where he'd been found. In pursuit of seeing his health improve, there was no conversation of a distressing kind whatever, only a polite formality in his presence. The whole family were convinced that his health was nearly restored - if only they could keep him on the right track.

The occasion of Catherine's birthday brought a little excitement when arrangements were made for her to visit and dine with the family. She brought along husband John Mason and her two infant children. To the Fairfaxes, Catherine's visit was a day predestined to be enjoyable. It had been many months since the whole family had been assembled together and Isabella, more than anyone else, was thrilled to be submerged in the preparations.

Whilst everyone else was happy in the full knowledge that an enjoyable day would occur, for Benjamin it was not so ..... as for him it was of no particular interest and would necessitate him feigning interest in family relations he barely knew, but he was obliged to join in.

Most of the excitement actually lay in the enjoyment of the planning in the days beforehand, as the day itself passed by happily enough, culminating in a sumptuous meal for the whole family.

Towards the end of the meal Catherine's husband John Mason said:

'I hope Benjamin won't taken offence Aurora if I say your marriage came as a disappointment to my brother George. I think he had hopes in your direction .....'

'Ahh, Gentle George ......' said Elizabeth.

'Don't let him hear you call him that' said Mason.

'George Mason is a General in the army' Isabella told Benjamin, 'should be coming back from Spain soon.'

'Yes, he's resigned his commission now' said Mason. 'Or, I should say he's sold it. I dare say he'll do what many former soldiers do and try to get into Parliament'.

'Should we be worried?' said Nathan. 'Do you think he'll be after our seats?'

'No' laughed Mason, 'actually I don't really see him wanting to go into Parliament. Our parents are both dead and, being the eldest, he has inherited their property, so he is a man of some means now. I think he will be able to live a gentleman's life.'

'You know, of course, that's the house we live in' said Catherine. 'When John isn't in London, we reside there ..... I suppose you could say we're George's tenants'.

'Actually I've met him' said Benjamin, 'at York. What ... almost a year ago. Very amiable man! And how should you have like been married to an army general?' asked Benjamin looking at Aurora.

'No thank you' she replied 'I like my present husband well enough, thank you. I'm looking for no other'.

'Nathaniel?' said Duke. 'How did you get on with the business I asked about.'

'Not too well, I'm afraid. When I spoke to Wortley he said he couldn't get involved. It's all to do with William Knightley and, now that Wortley is charged with sorting out the mess of the South

Seas 'bubble' he cannot be seen to be involved in helping any family members connected with the Knightleys.'

'That's a shame' said Duke, 'because I felt sure he could exert influence on Vavasour for us'.

'I hope everyone knows I had no involvement in Knightley's financial transactions?' stated Elizabeth. 'In fact I'm not sure there *is* any connection between the Fairfaxes and Knightley any more'.

'Well, only you know the answer to that' replied her brother, 'but the trouble is people have such long memories where money's concerned. There's such an outpouring of anger over the collapse of that company; there's barely a person I meet who hasn't been damaged by the business. Private individuals, banks and even the Royal African Company will have to restructure itself due to the collapse. It's a truly terrible mess.'

'I heard that Chandos has lost hundreds of thousands' said Mason.

'There's plenty of tragic stories but, at the end of the day, greed got the better of many men ..... and women.'

'Thank God I sold out when I did' said Duke.

Realising that reference to Knightley was subduing his sister, Nathaniel changed the subject. 'Oh, I do have some brighter news for your business Benjamin, I've heard that your case for a claim for maintenance from your father is to be heard by the Archbishop of York.'

'Really? Why him?' asked Benjamin.

'He's successfully arbitrated on family disputes before and, provided you both agree in advance to abide by his decision, it could make for a speedy resolution.'

'I'd be happy with that' said Benjamin, 'especially if it can save on lawyer's fees and, besides, my father won't be able to bribe or influence the Archbishop in his favour.'

'Exactly' said Nathaniel enthusiastically.

'That's good news' Duke added. 'I wonder though if Gervase will *want* a bishop of the Church of England .... he may see the bishop as partisan?'

'Huh' said Nathan. 'This is *the* Archbishop of York we're talking about. He is of the highest integrity. Not even Gervase Vavasour could dispute that!'

'Yes he could' muttered Benjamin under his breath.

'He couldn't decline the Archbishop's offer to intercede without defaming his character' said Mason. 'And I don't think he'll dare do that. Besides, I know that the Archbishop has recently overseen a similar case - in fact, where he found in favour of a Catholic family, so there's no history of bias there. I'm confident it'll proceed and, hopefully be to everyone's advantage'.

'Well done'. Duke congratulated his son and son-in-law for their efforts.

A little later in the evening, when both Benjamin and Aurora were out of earshot, Nathaniel asked his father about the legal action Gervase was bringing against Benjamin and Aurora.

'Any progress there?' he asked.

'It ain't looking good at all I'm afraid. Seems that Benjamin incurred large debts from gambling whilst he was living at home and his father, rather than see his son go to jail, set up a bond in both their names. It was set against the estate, Benjamin's future inheritance, but now that Gervase has called it in, Benjamin is left exposed but with no assets to pay it off. It's a poor state of affairs when a father turns so completely against his own son. I don't think there's anything Vavasour wouldn't do to injure his son. The man is quite insane.'

'And how might this affect Aurora?' asked Nathan.

'Well ..... she wasn't part of the bond when it was set up and, in effect, her name shouldn't be a party to his law suit. But I do fear for her, to have tied herself to such a worthless young man....'

'Perhaps he is a reformed character now? I've observed him here these last few weeks and he's been a model of sobriety and good humour' said Nathan hopefully.

'Yes, well ... you didn't see what a pitiful state he was found him in at York. He was at the Two Blue Pots ......'

'Oh!' said Nathan immediately looking a little surprised, 'one of the less salubrious whorehouses!'

'Are there any good ones?' said Duke.

'I think the only possible answer I can give to that question is .... I don't know, father. Never having frequented one! God ..... does Aurora know this?'

'She does ..... I did tell her, yes I felt obliged to tell her in what state we found him.'

'She will find that hard to handle I think' said Nathan.

'It's a shame Nathan and I can't be here more' said Mason, 'we'd soon have Benjamin sorted out. His problem is he doesn't have an older brother to box his ears.'

'He needs employment. Men *need* careers, they need to channel their energies into something useful' said Duke.

'Oh I don't know' said Mason, 'the Prince of Wales seem to manage well enough without lifting a finger'.

'Vavasour is no Prince!' said Duke, 'I suspect his father's tried to beat sense in to him over the years and that's what led him on the path he's on now' said Duke. 'And, unfortunately, as sure as night follows day, he'll revert to character when the inclination takes him again'.

'The Vavasours are a hardy clan of tyrants, I have heard many complaints of cruel treatment from their tenants' said Mason.

'They are bullies' confirmed Duke 'but Benjamin I fear has behaved like many an errant young pup. He knows that Vavasour Hall will be his one day, as per his grandfather's will and he knows that will cannot be broken by his father, the father knows it too and is resentful and this business about him being furious that Benjamin married out of the faith is nothing but a smokescreen.'

'How so?' asked Nathan.

'To elicit sympathy' continued Duke. 'Benjamin is no fool, he knows that if he tells everyone that his father is angry with him because he was foolish enough to gamble money away, no one will have any truck with him, but to tell the world that his Papist father is trying to cut him off because he has dared to marry a Protestant - now that's a different matter. It portrays him as the victim.'

'Are you now more sympathetic to Gervase Vavasour? said Nathan in astonishment.

'No, not at all. I think he's behaving abominably to his son, but maybe, just maybe, it's six of one and half a dozen of the other.'

'And Aurora' said Nathan 'is naught but a pawn.....'

'No, surely not ....' implored Mason.

'Well, to a degree' said Duke. 'I'm sure she has been persuaded to believe that it's her faith that has caused the friction between father and son, but I will not have her change it, not for a king's ransom and young Stella will be free to choose her own faith and follow her own path.'

'So, she's been duped! ..... and Benjamin cannot be disinherited?' asked Nathan.

'No, come what may he will inherit Vavasour Hall .....'

'But' mused Mason, 'Gervase could do great harm in the mean time ....'

'You do hear of such cases' said Nathan. 'It's very easy to devalue an estate if you have a mind to'.

'Yes, that's already begun' said Duke. 'I've heard that there's much felling of trees at the hall and neglect of essential maintenance. A resentful owner can ruin his estate very easily if he's determined enough. If the trees are not managed properly and replaced with new, then there'll be insufficient woodland to support the house in later years. He's selling off the wood for a quick profit and giving the money to his son Pascal, devaluing the entailed estate to Benjamin's detriment.'

'And so ...... ultimately then that'll be to young Stella's detriment' said Nathan.

'Yes, that's why we have to involve ourselves in the matter. I should like nothing better than to pack Benjamin off to his father, or wherever else he wishes to spend his time and be done with him. But there's Aurora and Stella to consider now and I won't let that foolish young man's reckless behaviour be a blight on their lives. Frankly I don't care what he does with his own life, but if Stella will one day become the owner of Vavasour Hall then I won't shirk involvement in a fight with Gervase to make that happen.'

'We'll help' said Mason, pointing to Nathan 'anything we can do to help further just ask'.

'You've already helped' said Duke.

'Actually, there is another matter I've heard a whisper about but I didn't like to mention in front of Elizabeth,' said Mason. 'I was at a party the other night and bumped into the Duchess of Kendall who told me that William Knightley's been found, that's he's been incarcerated at Antwerp.'

'Should we tell Elizabeth father?' asked Nathan.

'Heavens, no. She's managed this long without him in her life, why disturb her peace by telling her he's in jail. His friends may secure his release and then she'll have been alarmed for no good reason'.

'I get the impression Elizabeth considers their engagement over?' said Nathan. 'She's removed her ring'.

'Yes, but I don't want her to hear about him. She might take pity and I don't want her to join him on the Continent in his flight of shame. The man has abandoned her and I don't want to risk her making a spectacle of herself by chasing after him - let him go to the devil. He took no care to provide for her, she has only secured herself financially by her own means, not his goodwill, so I say let him stay right where he is.'

'Jail or no .... he has little reason to come back to England' said Mason.

'If he does get the opportunity, I'm sure .... one day .... he'll try and come back. A life in exile may be a hardship and severe punishment for him' said Duke.

'He is ... or rather was .... a man of some achievements. Though I have never before encountered a man of such ambition - to be sure he's possessed of exceptional abilities - but, like Thomas Dudley in the court of Edward VI, he just didn't know when to stop. Unconstrained ambition was his undoing and a complete and utter lack of scruple' said Mason.

'I hope' said Duke, 'with the passage of enough time, Elizabeth will have nothing to do with him - wherever he should be. He's spared her no consideration, even before his exile he was too busy chasing money.

'The Duchess .....' continued Mason, 'has been trying to get Wortley to persuade the Austrian government to release him.'

'Really?' said Duke.

'And the ambassador has been sent to make the arrangements'.

'Use your influence then' said Duke

'Anything Father' said Nathan.

'Ask Chief Minister Wortley to keep him in exile.'

Chapter 15

The following month, just a few weeks before Christmas, the day arrived for Benjamin Vavasour to meet with the Archbishop of York. Accompanied by his solicitor Mr Longshaft, Ben was joined by Duke and Aurora, and the four had their meeting. They presented their case with all the particulars to the bishop who seemed both understanding and sympathetic. He'd already met the Vavasours and so was well acquainted with both sides of the argument and promised a speedy decision. They left York hopeful but with no indication how the matter might be resolved.

Returning back to Tadcaster after a tiring day, Elizabeth greeted them with some news.

'Nathan has been here whilst you were out and told me of a development concerning the legal action your father is taking against you over the bond' she said to Benjamin. 'It's apparently been halted'.

'Really?' said Benjamin astonished. 'Well now that is good news. Wonder what's got into the old plague master'.

'Does he know why?' asked Duke.

'Well Nathan and John Mason made it known that they were considering raising the matter in Parliament. They started a rumour knowing full well that it would reach Vavasour's ears and, it would seem, that the prospect of having his personal affairs the subject of gossip at Westminster made Gervase hesitate.'

'Yes' said Duke wryly. 'That and also no doubt the fact that his son has not the means to pay the bond off in the first place and that would have made him look like the aggressor. A judge wouldn't have been sympathetic to him I think'.

'Thank goodness' said Aurora, 'one less battle to fight. What say you, Benjamin? Now if we can only get the Archbishop to get your father to agree to some maintenance, then we can perhaps get on with our lives.'

'Let's all hope for that' said Duke. 'We've given him every scrap of information, there's nothing more we could have presented to him, so we'll just have to wait.'

'Where one battle ends, another one's waiting in the wings'
Ben muttered under his breath.

A week later, the Archbishop's decision was confirmed to
them and it was in their favour. A sum of £200 per year had been
decided on, meaning Gervase Vavasour was compelled to support
his son and his family. The news was received with joy by the
Fairfaxes, but not unbridled joy by Benjamin who was far from
being satisfied. He was uneasy that the sum was too small to
support them.

With Ben's recovery in health, the cessation of his father's
pursuit of the bond and now the good news of the maintenance
being granted to them, Aurora judged - amongst so much good
news - that this was the time to tell her husband that her annuity
had been stopped and there was no chance of it ever being
reinstated. She hadn't anticipated that it would be of any great
importance to him and so, when he reacted badly to the news, she
was surprised.

'So now I've your livelihood to provide for …. and Stella's
….. as well as mine own' he said dismally.

'But you have a maintenance now …..' said Aurora, 'we are
all provided for'.

'Hah' said Ben, 'is that so? And just how far do you think
such a sum will go ……'

'Tis better than nothing' she said plaintively.

'And that's if my father deigns to pay it!'

'But he must …. The Archbishop ……'

'You don't know what my father is like' said Ben as he
stormed out of the room in anger.

To everyone's surprise then, within a few days of the
Archbishop's decision, a letter arrived from Pascal Vavasour
informing Benjamin that his father was ready to hand over the sum
of money, as directed by the Archbishop. It would not, however,
be put it into Benjamin's hands, rather it was stipulated that Aurora
was to take receipt of it. Duke thought the explanation for this was
that Gervase didn't trust his son with money and that, by handing
to Aurora, emphasis was being given to the fact that the money
was for infant Stella's maintenance rather than Benjamin's.

As arranged, Aurora travelled to the White Hart Inn, a short
distance from Fairfax Manor, the meeting place for the exchange

of money to take place. She was accompanied by her father and sister, and all three entered the inn where Pascal was already seated and waiting. He was grim-faced, sullen and clearly not happy to be designated the job.

'You're to check the amount and sign for it here' he said, rudely dispensing with any pleasantries.

Aurora wasn't surprised by his manner and, defiantly, seated herself and purposely took her time, knowing full well that Pascal wanted the matter over and done with quickly.

'Goodness, it's a cold evening' she said to Elizabeth, rubbing her hands and warming them by the fire. 'It was very considerate of you to set up this meeting near our home, so saving us a long journey'.

'My father doesn't want you in his house again' said Pascal.

'Oh dear' said Aurora, feigning concern. She was fighting within herself to restrain the urge for sarcasm but abjectly failing. She took the packet Pascal had dropped on the table and handed it to her father who began counting the contents.

'There' Aurora said, when satisfied the correct sum was there.

'Sign here' he pointed. She duly signed and held the receipt tightly in her hand.

Pascal leaned forward to whisper in her ear 'Much good will it do you. You obviously don't know the extent of Benjamin's debts. I can assure you this will never support him, let alone you and your infant - if it's yours. Or indeed, if it's his!

'That's enough' intervened Duke, 'our business is done'.

Pascal raised his voice so that everyone could hear. 'He's a pathetic gambler. My father had to mortgage part of our estate because of it and you .....' he said with a disgusted look 'are just another one of his tricks to extract more from us'. Everyone in the inn was now listening and staring.

Aurora listened but gave no reaction to him. Pascal wanted to disconcert her and she'd no intention of giving him that satisfaction. She stood up to make her leave and saw her father in the doorway, who was still observing them. She said nothing more to Pascal but moved towards the fire into which she threw the papers that Pascal had demanded she sign.

He started with surprise, but Duke moved towards him and prevented his approaching Aurora. It was a small act of defiance which didn't spring from a fit of pique or anger. What Aurora felt was more like quiet resolve which she applauded in herself. Pascal started to react with anger but checked himself on catching sight of the burly figure of the landlord approaching with concern that they should keep the peace. The Fairfaxes left him in the room cursing under his breath.

Back at the coach and seated ready to depart, Pascal came rushing out of the inn and over to the coach to approach Aurora but Duke, seated opposite her, filled the frame of the window and obscured Pascal's vision and stopped him in his tracks.

'My father has changed his will' he shouted with an ugly face glaring at Aurora. 'You'll get nothing, bitch'.

'Be off with you' said Duke, 'our business is concluded'. The two coachmen turned to face Pascal to show that they too were ready to defend their passengers and Pascal faded away, returning back inside the inn.

'Thank goodness you didn't come alone' Duke said.

Chapter 16

A few days later, it was the day before Christmas Eve and Tadcaster's Saturday market was bustling with people. The Fairfax ladies had been busy doing their last minute shopping for gifts and other necessities until fatigue forced them to retreat back home and declare their Christmas preparations were almost finished.

Their carriage took Isabella, Elizabeth and Aurora back to Fairfax Manor where, to their surprise as they approached, there was a large crowd of people gathered. So many people, in fact, were there they could scarcely manoeuvre the coach around them.

'What's going on? Who are all these people' asked Elizabeth leaning out the carriage window. 'Dozens of … tradesmen …. by the looks of it. Has father forgotten to pay the bills?' she asked her mother laughing.

'I've no idea' said Isabella. 'Is that ….. yes, I can see your father, he's among them talking. There's shouting …. and waving. They look hostile …. I think we should slip inside, round the back, while they're distracted.' The coach drove straight round to the back of the house, so the ladies could alight unobserved and then they walked around the side of the house where they could enter. Immediately inside the door, they met the nurse who was in the doorway cradling Stella.

'What's going on?' Isabella asked the nurse who looked distressed.

'There's been a crowd outside for most of this morning' she said breathlessly. 'I've heard that they're Master Benjamin's creditors from town.'

'Creditors?' said Isabella in disbelief.

'Mr Fairfax' the nurse continued, 'says that Pascal Vavasour has been round the townsfolk telling 'em that Master Benjamin's in funds and that they should reclaim their money from him. Told 'em where to find him. They've been arriving from all over. You can't get in or out of the house for 'em. They keep banging on the door, waking the bairn, and she can get no rest.'

At that moment Duke came into the house looking flustered and annoyed and tried to start explaining to them what had happened, but, within a few moments there was the sound of knocking on the front door, incessant knocking.

'Those Vavasours will stop at nothing' said Elizabeth in exasperation.

'Yes, but if Benjamin didn't have so many damned debts they would have no ammunition to use against him' said Duke furiously. 'I've just been out to pacify the tradesmen once, I shall have to go again'.

'Where's Benjamin?' asked Aurora.

'Ee's out' said the nurse. 'Soon as the crowd came, ee slipped away!'

'This is intolerable' said Isabella. 'What's to be done? My nerves can't stand this'.

'Come on ma' said Aurora, 'you go upstairs and rest. Use Elizabeth's room at the back of the house, it'll be quieter.'

Elizabeth, meanwhile, having watched her father's attempt to reason with the tradesmen, could see that the crowd was growing further and couldn't abide to see her family in distress. She went into her father's study where she knew there was a pair of pistols, grabbed both and marched out the front door before anyone could stop her, arms outstretched and holding both pistols at eye level. The crowd immediately silenced and, like a flock of birds in unison, swooned back, leaving her father the sole figure in front of her. With his back to the house, he alone hadn't observed her.

Elizabeth shouted as loud as she could, 'You have all been cruelly misinformed' shouted Elizabeth. 'You cannot have satisfaction for your debts here, only at Vavasour Hall. Present your claims to Gervase Vavasour in person.'

'We've already done that' shouted one man. 'Aye' they all echoed.

'Then pursue him in the courts' she retorted. 'We too are owed money by the Vavasours. There's no money here for you and you are wasting your time. And ... she said lowering her voice .... if you are still all here in one hour's time ... if I find *any* of you still here, I will shoot the first person I see.'

With that she turned on her heels and went back in the house. Duke stood fixed to the spot for a moment and found it was no longer necessary for him to assuage the crowd. They were furiously talking amongst themselves and, with much nodding and mean glances towards the house, one by one they began to disperse.

Back indoors, Aurora, who was looking out the window, shouted 'they're going Father'.

'Elizabeth!' said Duke. 'Those are my pistols. Were you going to shoot me in the back?'

'Yes ... I mean no ... of course I wouldn't have .....' she said, 'goodness my hands are shaking. Even my legs are shaking ..... I never knew legs could shake like this!'

'You do know that they're not loaded?' he said.

'I didn't know, no. But I shall thank you to load them for me in an hour's time if there is anyone left standing outside the house. Goodness they're heavy!

'I don't think you're meant to hold them both at once' said Duke. 'Besides, you can't go waving guns around at people!' he insisted, suppressing a small laugh.

'Well I'm glad she did' said Aurora, 'most of the crowd have moved away now. That was a fright.'

'This was Pascal's doing' said Duke. 'By the way where is Benjamin?'

No one knew where Benjamin had gone off to until later in the evening when he returned looking dishevelled, bloodied and bruised. He told them that he had been to Vavasour Hall, found out Pascal and had given him a beating.

Ethel Fledd

Chapter 17

The next morning, Christmas Eve, Benjamin rose early and told
Aurora that he was going to York on urgent business. He offered
no further explanation and her entreaties for him not to go failed.
Since her father had already gone out earlier and Benjamin was
resolved on leaving the house, she was unable to prevent him.

Elizabeth, although hearing the exchange between the couple,
resisted the temptation to intervene and so kept her silence whilst
Benjamin made his preparations and left.

'At least he told us he was going this time' she said at last.

'No, this isn't the same thing' said Aurora.

'I notice' said Elizabeth after he'd gone 'that father's pistols
have been moved'.

Aurora smiled and chuckled, 'I think he's learned his lessons
about having them displayed on the wall, I imagine they are now
securely locked in a trunk, somewhere you cannot get tempted to
make use of them again'.

'I shouldn't have actually fired them' said Elizabeth coolly,
'besides which I wouldn't know how to, but none of those
tradesmen knew that for sure' she said laughing.

'I don't know where you got the courage from' said Aurora, 'I
couldn't have done what you did yesterday'.

'It's surprising what you can do if you have to.' After a brief
pause she continued 'so then .... Benjamin has gone to York?'

'Yes' said Aurora, 'father won't be happy at that news, I know
he won't.'

'I think living here' said Elizabeth 'amongst a family such as
ours hasn't been too easy for Benjamin. He's been used to a very
different life at Vavasour Hall'.

'Much of his life has been spent away at school, or being
fostered out to relations' said Aurora.

'Perhaps then' said Elizabeth, 'this disharmony with his father
may have been of a long standing'.

'I suspect' said Aurora 'it intensified after his mother Celine
Vavasour died. She passed away a few years ago and, since then,

Gervase seemed to turn away from Benjamin in favour of Pascal.
At least, so Benjamin told me. And that is when he spent more and
more time with his friends, away from home.'

'Where he could indulge himself' said Elizabeth thoughtfully.

'Yes, I think all these weeks Benjamin has been here my
father has been expecting an eruption from him as he doesn't
believe he can change. So many weeks he has been well behaved,
I've been prodigiously proud of him.'

'But' said Elizabeth sympathetically 'we all know it cannot
be. It only takes one occasion for things to get out of hand.
Remember how did I find you, in that locked room, fearful for
your child's safety.'

'Of course.'

'A drunken card game going on whilst Stella slept .... what
will Benjamin be doing now in York?'

'It's only a trip on business Elizabeth. We can't keep him
confined to this house, can we? He won't do it again. Not after all
we've done for him: we've looked after him, nursed him, got
involved in defending him against his father's law suit. We've
even got him a maintenance. He would never throw all that away.
Besides, what are we supposed to do when he actually has money
in his hands? Lock him up?'

'Of course not' said Elizabeth. 'Besides, who am I to
comment? My former fiancé abandoned me, ran off with other
people's money and is exiled abroad. I didn't do a very good job
of guiding him, did I?'

'You're not responsible for Knightley .... and you know it.
You cannot guide someone when they are hell bent on doing harm.
Men live by their own counsel and we ....'

'Are their chattels' Elizabeth finished. 'Oh look' she suddenly
said seeing something out the window 'mother and father are come
home. I shall arrange some tea to cheer them'.

Once inside the house, Duke looked sombre and asked
Elizabeth to take her mother for a lie down as she was feeling
unwell. He stood by the fire with his hands in his pocket of his
long coat, fingering coins nervously. When they were gone, he told
Aurora to fetch Benjamin as he had something to tell them. 'I was
at the quarter sessions today when I heard a messenger relaying
information that Benjamin must know immediately' he said.

'He's gone out' said Aurora, 'this morning he left for York'.

Duke stared in anger and cold fury. 'And you let him go? Could you not stop him?'

'How can I stop him if he wants to? He isn't a prisoner, is he? He said he'd business to attend to in York' she pleaded.

'Where *exactly* has he gone?. For how long?' Duke asked.

'I don't know father. He wouldn't tell me any more'.

'Damn and blast it! he said angrily. 'Business ..... you say ..... in York? I wonder, he *might* have gone to his solicitor. I *wonder* if he's heard the news already? Who is Benjamin's solicitor?'

'Oh .... Um ... Mr Longshaft, Obadiah Longshaft.....'

'Ah, I know him, I know him. I'll send a messenger to him...... ah but no, it's Christmas Eve ...... and it's Sunday. No he hasn't gone there'.

Duke looked pensive, 'this is terrible news. I shall have to think how to act.'

'What is so urgent?' asked Elizabeth. 'I'm sure he'll be back soon ..... at least I imagine he will .....'

'That's not good enough' said Duke, lost in thought. 'There's something he needs to know straight away ..... I overheard the news that Gervase Vavasour is dead!'

Chapter 18

Aurora was unmoved by the news. She'd no feelings for Gervase Vavasour, her father-in-law, other than profound dislike. She didn't know, however, how Benjamin might react to the news and so was concerned for him.

'Oh heavens. How can we find Benjamin to tell him' she said.

Duke was distracted, full of busy thoughts. What to do? What would be the consequences of delay? How might other parties act? He was alarmed at the news of Benjamin's absence and was breathlessly weighing up his actions.

'Benjamin's not the priority at the moment. Elizabeth!' he shouted after a few more moments.

'Yes father' she said running downstairs as his tone sounded urgent.

'Run outside and get that carriage back here. Be quick about it'.

Elizabeth did as she was bid and Duke, looking at Aurora, said 'Don't you move from that spot'. And, with that, he disappeared off into his study, returning momentarily with a piece of paper in his hand. 'We have to act swiftly, there's not a moment to lose. Damn that boy for not being here' he said angrily.

Elizabeth came back inside and assured her father that the coach was outside, standing ready for him.

'Right, now. We must go.' he said to Elizabeth.

'Where?'

'Vavasour Hall. Right now.'

'Who?' asked Aurora.

'You, Elizabeth and me' he replied. Grabbing a coat and saying 'possession is nine tenths of the law' he ushered both Aurora and Elizabeth into the coach, shouting to wife Isabella to 'send Benjamin to Vavasour Hall if he returns'.

'Take care of Stella for me!' Aurora shouted to the nurse as the coach pulled away. And with that they were gone in great haste.

On the journey, a brief stop was made as Duke collected another passenger who joined their party and filled the coach; he was, they subsequently learned, the local bailiff.

By the time they arrived at the hall, Duke had explained to his daughters the necessity of action. Benjamin's absence, extremely ill timed as it was, necessitated him using his power of attorney to act on his behalf. 'We must act as if Benjamin is here amongst us', he told Aurora, 'the death of Gervase Vavasour means that Benjamin, as his eldest son and heir is now the rightful owner of Vavasour Hall. You must claim it on his behalf' he told a bedazzled Aurora who couldn't believe that, for a third time, her family were rushing her over to Vavasour Hall against her will.

Moments later, Duke was standing in the doorway at the Hall and, before his daughters had alighted the carriage, there was a booming thud as the door which had been opened quietly was then quickly shut in his face.

'What's happening?' Elizabeth asked.

'Clearly we have been denied access' said her father with a sanguine look.

'Father' said Aurora gingerly, 'Is this not disrespectful to arrive so soon after a death, demanding possession? Has the death not only just occurred? I don't like coming here without Benjamin's knowledge. Indeed without Benjamin.'

'If the wretched boy hadn't vanished we wouldn't have to be here at all' he snapped.

Some minutes passed and Aurora and Elizabeth sat patiently in the carriage listening to the muffled thud of raindrops falling all around them. Duke gave every indication that he wanted no assistance from his daughters and so they sat patiently awaiting further instructions. Aurora wanted to be away from that place; a house she'd never entered but to meet with distress and alarm.

It took a full five minutes or more for Duke and the bailiff to secure their entrance to the house but, then finally at long last, they were able to go inside.

As they entered, the household servants made themselves disappear, clearly not approving of the morning's activities. And so, with no one to direct them, Aurora led the way to the one room she was already acquainted with - the library, where they found the last vestiges of a fire glowing in the grate. It was a bitterly cold

Christmas Eve - too cold for snow - but the journey and sitting outside for so long had chilled them all to the bone. Duke and Elizabeth followed her into the room and, for a few minutes, they all huddled around the meagre source of warmth to recover from the frantic journey.

The bailiff, who'd been alerted to the likelihood of Pascal Vavasour's arrival and likely attempt to seize the estate, hovered like a sentry at the front door.

Aurora asked her father again 'was it really necessary for us to come here so quickly?'

'Yes' he replied, 'it would have been far more difficult for you to get possession later. Trust me.'

'What of Pascal?' asked Elizabeth. 'Is Aurora to share a house with him? Is he already here?'

'No, he's out of town until tonight and does not yet know of his father's death. So we have some time. I've been able to find out that he has a residence on the estate so hasn't actually been living here but I dare say he'll be here as soon as he hears the news. So I need to make haste. I shall leave you both here while I go and make arrangements. The bailiff will remain here until I return with some men to secure the house. Don't worry about Stella, your mother and the nurse will take care of her, but I need you both to stay here. Don't leave this house until I return and ... admit no one.'

With that, he was gone and at that moment the significance of what they were doing began to dawn on them.

'I fear we might be unequal to the task' said Aurora. 'How are we, two women, supposed to hold this great house? I fear Pascal will arrive at any moment and our lives will be in danger. That bailiff affords us little protection. I could knock him over myself.'

'Hah' laughed Elizabeth. 'That may be so, but legally he has authority to be here. He represents the law and Father believes we have a right to be here. With Benjamin's power of attorney, he is absolutely within his rights. Father is an experienced lawyer, so we should trust his judgement. Still .....' she said moving towards the fireplace ..... it wouldn't do any harm to keep one of these things handy' she said indicating to the poker.

'What does it all mean though?' said Aurora 'Am I supposed to live here from now on? Benjamin may not want to live here.'

'Of course he will' said Elizabeth as she poured them both a drink from a nearby decanter. 'I doubt whether the servants will bring us refreshments' she said 'so we'd better take care of ourselves'.

Moments later Elizabeth said, 'this is all happening so quickly'.

'Yes' said Aurora, 'Benjamin was here last night fighting with his brother, came home covered in blood and bruised, now his father's dead. Then Benjamin goes to York this morning .....' her voice trailed off as her thoughts were coming together.

Elizabeth picked up the theme ... 'and ... father's pistols are missing! You don't think ......'

'That Benjamin killed his father?' said Aurora 'don't be ridiculous. He wouldn't, he couldn't....... could he?'

Chapter 19

Elizabeth and Aurora hadn't stirred from the room when, half an hour later, the bailiff entered to tell them that two men were at the front door. They were solicitors, he told them, and he'd dealt with both of them in the past so knew they were genuine. They insisted on entering the house and had a copy of Gervase Vavasour's Will and a Deed which gave them a right to take the deceased's personal estate.

Aurora said 'no, they may not enter as we have strict instructions to allow no one to enter until our Father returns.'

'Yes ma'am' came the reply.

'Ask them to wait' said Elizabeth 'whatever their business is, it can wait.'

The bailiff left the room but, from the sound of raised voices that followed, clearly the solicitors were not going to comply. Moments later, they entered the room, pushing past the bailiff,

'We're here on urgent business that cannot be delayed one moment' said the first man. 'We have full authority' said the second.

'You were told to wait for attention' said the bailiff who followed them into the room looking out of breath.

'Our business cannot wait' said the first man. 'Who are you?' he asked looking at the ladies.

'This lady here' said the bailiff 'is the wife of Benjamin Vavasour and she has a valid power of attorney to claim this house on her husband's behalf'.

Elizabeth, speaking to the bailiff, said 'please remove these gentlemen, they can have no business with us and certainly none that cannot wait till our Father returns'.

'Indeed we have' said the first. 'I am Mr Jolson and my associate here is Mr Taylor. We've been instructed to act for Mr Gervase Vavasour's estate and are executors of his will.'

'More than that' said the second man, Mr Taylor, 'we have a deed here' he said waving a document in front of the bailiff 'to show that we have purchased the entire personal estate of Mr

Gervase Vavasour, deceased, and that being so we will not leave this house until we are in possession of that personal estate'.

'You will' said Aurora standing defiantly, 'have the courtesy to leave this room immediately. You were uninvited and are intruding. You will, I insist, wait in an adjoining room for the return of our Father who will deal with you in due course'.

The first man, Jolson, tried to speak but Elizabeth shut him up. 'You will do as we ask. Bailiff, escort these gentleman back to a room till we call for them. Unless you are going to defy the orders of a bailiff .....'. Both men acquiesced, though their blood was up and they were clearly prepared for a fight and relishing a heated discourse.

After they had left Elizabeth said, 'for heaven's sake I wish our Father hadn't left us. How are we supposed to hold a house that feels like it's under siege?'

More than two hours had now passed since their Father's departure and Elizabeth suggested they had a look round the house.

'I imagine we'll be staying here this evening' she told Aurora, 'so we better find our way about.'

They left the library and slowly moved from room to room, all of which they found in growing darkness and with no fires lit. Ascending the grand stair case, Elizabeth commented that the servants were conspicuous by their absence and that they would be obliged to call for them soon for candles. Moving down a long, cold corridor, she opened a door and gasped.

'Oh my God' she shrieked.

'What?' said Aurora peering into the room. What she saw was the body of Gervase Vavasour lying motionless on a bed. She recoiled for a moment, as if he was still alive, before relaxing.

'He's still here?' she whispered in disbelief. 'Don't they whisk bodies away after death?'

'I don't really know' said Elizabeth. 'We'd better go back down stairs'.

'Just a moment' said Aurora and she stepped inside the room and moved closer to the body. 'I feel the need to see for myself that he's dead'. She gingerly stepped closer as if she was expecting the body to move and looked at the expressionless face.

'It's the first time I've seen him without him shouting and telling me to get out the room' she said. 'How strange he looks.

Why could he not have looked so much at peace with the world whilst he was living'.

'Are there any ....' Elizabeth suddenly started as if remembering something ... 'gunshots to the body?'

'What?' exclaimed Aurora, 'I'm not going to look'.

'We must' said Elizabeth and she moved in closer, and she too was apprehensive about whether the body was actually dead too. She shook the body's arm, just to make sure. 'There now, he's definitely dead' she said and went to lift the sheet covering him and squinted underneath.

'You can't .....' pleaded Aurora, 'it isn't right'.

'No, you're right. Still .... I can just have a little peek ..... no .....I can't see anything, and I cannot bring myself to disturb his clothing'. With that, they moved back from the body and left the room. Walking towards them in the corridor was the butler who seemed furious at their presence near his master's room.

Chapter 20

Elizabeth headed off his enquiries by demanding .... 'Please light the fires and arrange for candles'.

'Ma'am!' was the only response she got.

'Do it', she demanded.

They returned to the library to continue waiting and after some time the butler came in to attend them. He lit the candles and brought in a young boy to make up the fire for them. He did all this in silence, a kind of passive resistance. He would do what he *had* to, but no more, after which he left the room.

As he went Elizabeth got up and went out straight after to him remembering to ask him something else.

Voices in the hallway drew Aurora outside into the hallway and there, to her great surprise and delight, stood in the doorway being challenged by the bailiff was Gentle George dressed in his army uniform.

'George!' shouted Aurora, 'what are you doing here?'

The bailiff relinquished his blockage of the front door and George was permitted to enter.

'Your father sent me. I'm to stay here whilst he makes arrangements. I only got back in England a few hours ago and I understand there's some crisis you are dealing with. He asked me to help and here I am. What will you have me do?'

'I hardly know' said Aurora, 'but we may well be in need of protection from Pascal Vavasour, my brother-in-law. He'll be here at some point and I have no doubt that he'll attempt to evict us from this place and I don't think ......' she rolled her eyes in the direction of the bailiff and whispered ... 'I don't think we have sufficient defences against him'.

'I am at your disposal' he said.

She guided him into the library and seated him by the fire.

'My father-in-law is dead' she told him. 'We've just seen him upstairs.'

'The body is still here?' he asked surprised.

'Yes', she answered.

'And where is your husband?' he asked.

'I don't know' answered Aurora. 'He went to York early this morning, before news came through of his father's death, and no one knows where he is. We can't contact him. My father, having Benjamin's power of attorney, advised me to act quickly and secure the house on my husband's behalf.'

'He knows best' replied George. 'And who are the other two men I saw as I came in .....'

'They're solicitors. Apparently they are executors of Gervase Vavasour's will and claim he sold them his personal estate.'

'But why are they here now. Surely they can wait for the will to go through probate, this is extraordinary for solicitors to be present in a house before the burial has even taken place. That shows a remarkable lack of respect' he said. 'I think I shall go and talk to them'.

'Would you? Thank you George', she said and he left the room.

Aurora sat quietly for a few moments before Elizabeth rejoined her to say 'I've found out that the staff are entirely hostile to us. The kitchen staff refuse point blank to prepare any food or co-operate in any way. They say they will only take orders from Mr Vavasour - that is Pascal when he arrives - and refuse to have anything to do with us. Only the butler, whose authority they are likewise defying, will render us any assistance.'

'Perhaps when Benjamin gets here, they will change their minds' Aurora added.

'Yes but we don't know how long that will be!' said Elizabeth. 'I think the whole lot should be sacked!'

'Well' said Aurora, 'let's not cut off our noses to spite our faces. Father will know what to do and I don't believe we should make any changes before the burial is arranged. It may yet transpire that we are forced to leave this house, and it's far from settled that we may stay here'.

'This is a grand house Aurora' said Elizabeth.

'Yes it is' came the reply.

'A grand house to be living in. And all this is Benjamin's? What a wonderful future it will be for Stella to have all this one day ......'

The sisters sat talking amongst themselves for a good while during which time the butler, who seemed to be coming round to their presence, duly came in and out with various messages; that the upstairs fires were being lit and told them that sleeping quarters had been arranged for them. He also told them that their Father had arrived and was with George and the two solicitors who were still at the premises.

'Do you think we should join them?' Elizabeth asked Aurora.

'What for?, said Elizabeth 'No I don't, 'they'll send for us if they want us.'

And so they continued alone in the library, getting used to their surroundings and resting. As darkness fell, the next visitor to the house needed no butler to announce him. It was Pascal, accompanied by his solicitor James Berry.

'God's socks! whispered Aurora with terror in her voice. 'It's him. Pascal! Someone must have got word to him and he's come back early'.

'Shhhh ...... keep back, don't let him see you' urged Elizabeth, 'let the men deal with him'.

From a chink in the library door the sisters saw and heard Pascal's raised voice shouting and hurling abuse at Benjamin who, he assumed, had taken possession of the house. He taunted the absent Benjamin with obscenities and cursed him at the top of his voice.

Most of the men in the house, and the servants George had brought with him were now in a rough circle around Pascal preventing him from moving and, when there was a pause in his shouting the calming voices of Duke and George suggested to him that they take him to see his deceased father. Pascal wanted to push through them and go himself but was locked down tightly by his custodians. He was escorted upstairs and through the house, to emerge back downstairs soon after. By this time his temper had run its course and it was possible for Duke to cajole him to join the others to discuss matters.

Once Pascal and Berry were inside the room the ladies, hearing raised voices again, went into the hallway and, seeing the door to the room slightly ajar, they approached so they could hear what was being said.

It was a cacophony of sharp voices talking over each other to start with before a solitary voice of authority emerged to command attention. It took a few minutes, but eventually Gentle George curbed the emotive and curse spewing Pascal by directing his solicitor to talk for him.

Pascal's fury on entering the house had been predicated on the assumption that Benjamin had seized the house whilst Pascal was absent. When he subsequently learned that, in fact, Benjamin was not on the premises, this took the wind out of his sails. Clearly he hadn't expected the Fairfax family to have obtained Benjamin's power of attorney and he, and his solicitor, quickly realised they had been comprehensively and conclusively outflanked.

'I've been speaking to Messrs Jolson and Taylor' said George 'for some time before you got here and I'm aware that they are the executors of Gervase Vavasour's will and have an agreement, signed by your father ...' he said looking directly at Pascal 'whereby all his personal estate is to be taken by them'.

'Yes' said Berry 'we know of the agreement and that they are executors of the estate. You should also be aware then that Gervase Vavasour wrote a will in the final few months of his life leaving everything to Pascal.'

'One moment' said Duke. 'The personal estate of Gervase Vavasour will have to be distinguished from that of his father Dionysus. There are a great many family heirlooms here that were not the personal property of Gervase.'

'We will not leave these premises without the personal estate' said Jolson adamantly.

'You will have to' insisted George. 'Duke, what is the best course of action to distinguish property?'

'There'll need to be a full inventory taken immediately. Only then can a proper evaluation be done.' He said, 'There'll need to be a lot of work done to identify particular pieces, wills and other documentation will have to be found. This will all take a long time. I suggest that, immediately after the burial has taken place, that a representative of Pascal, Benjamin and Gervase be appointed and that all of these representatives conduct a full inventory of the premises in each other's company.'

'Berry?' said George 'Is that agreeable?'

'Yes', he replied 'but who will watch the premises meantime.'

'Jolson?' asked George, 'Is that agreeable?'

'Yes, but we insist on staying here until it's done'.

'No' said George. 'The bailiff, or one of his deputies will remain here. That will suffice'.

'No' shouted Pascal, 'that will *not* do'.

'It *will* do' said George directing his reply to the solicitor who, in turn, urged Pascal to be more circumspect. 'Now to the issue of Gervase Vavasour's will, that is a matter than can wait for the due process of the probate court.'

'If you've seen the copy of the will Mr Jolson and Taylor have, you will know that Gervase disinherited Benjamin in his latest will, it's Pascal who is the main beneficiary.' said Berry. 'You, sir, have no right to be in this house at all, you should vacate it and make way for the rightful heir, Pascal.'

'Gentlemen' said Duke. 'I have been made aware that the will of Dionysus Vavasour, father of Gervase, left this estate in male entail to Benjamin and whatever is in Gervase's will, which I have yet to see, cannot overturn that. These are matters we can dispute later. I will just say this to you all ... we have amongst us .... what, some four lawyers? We are all well versed in our profession and .... ' he said slowly 'it should be abundantly clear to each and every one of us that Pascal can never inherit Vavasour Hall. We all know that in this country, at this time, Roman Catholics can inherit no land. Do you deny Mr Berry that Pascal, your client, is a Roman Catholic?'.

'I can neither deny or confirm that' said Berry in ridiculous evasion. Even Berry himself realised that his response was pathetic and wasn't surprised when it was ignored.

'There's no more to be done here today' said Duke.

'This is intolerable....!' said Pascal imploring Berry to say or do something and put up more of a fight. 'The will says I'm the chosen heir'.

'No' was the calm response from Berry, 'we are done here today. There will be other days .... And we *will* have our day in court, I can assure you of that,' he added resolutely.

Pascal rose to his feet and, in a fit of pique, kicked his chair away, stormed out of the room and left the house.

Chapter 21

Aurora and Elizabeth flashed a glance of surprise at each other on hearing the conversation and had to frantically scramble out of the way as Pascal pushed past them at great speed. They returned to their room as they could hear signs that the rest of the men were preparing to disperse.

'I'm beginning to see why father wanted you to take immediate possession' said Elizabeth closing the door, 'there'll be many disputes from the various interested parties and, as we've heard him say today, 'possession is nine tenths of the law'.

'Oh how I *wish* Benjamin hadn't taken off this morning' complained Aurora, 'why now, why today, after so many weeks of living quietly with us, why did he pick this day to disappear? Perhaps ...... he's arrived back home whilst we've been here today. He might be on his way over here right now ......'

'I don't know' said Elizabeth getting up to leave the room. 'I'm going off to find that wretched butler and get him to send out for some food for us. I will not be held hostage by sullen kitchen staff and we must eat'. With that she left the room.

Alone for the first time, Aurora took a proper look around her and found herself, quite grudgingly, liking her surroundings. There was nothing fashionable about that particular room, or indeed any of the others in the house, as the possessions were the collection of many generations of Vavasours over different centuries. Yet they co-existed in a harmony born of their quality and craftsmanship. The beauty of the wall hung tapestries wasn't diminished by their being of unequal sizes, rather it gave them an individuality and greater interest *because* they were different. Globes, walls lined with thousands of books and a desk, positioned centrally to show its great importance, and two well worn seats by the fire - all combined to tell a story of the importance of that room in the house. It was the room of business, of planning, of sorting out disputes but, at the same time, the presence of books gave it a quiet and comforting feel.

None of this she'd noticed on her previous two visits to the hall when the intense hostility of the occupants of the house had overwhelmed her powers of observation.

Into the room now appeared her father, looking tired.

'Come sit by the fire' she said.

'George is here with me' he said and, indeed, George followed him into the room a moment later. George looked utterly resplendent in his soldier's uniform and Aurora found herself drawn to watching him. Until she checked herself …. in case her interest in George was noticed …..

'We heard most of what you said, we were in the hall' Aurora told her father. 'I'm so sorry you both have been put to so much trouble. It's all my fault, I know it.'

'Regrets won't solve problems and you aren't to blame for the problems over this estate' Duke said. 'I've sent word your brother and Mason to find Benjamin in York. I know where he went to last time so I've told them where to look. I only hope he's not in the same condition as last time we found him'.

'George' said Duke turning to face him. 'Can I prevail upon you to stay with the ladies for a few days over the Christmas period until matters are sorted. Just in case Pascal makes a return visit?'

'Yes, of course' was the reply. 'Though I shall need a change of clothing …..'

'I'll get Catherine to sort that out' said Duke.

Elizabeth joined them and said 'I've sent out for some food as the staff refuse to serve us. Is the bailiff staying here too?'

'Yes he must' said Duke. 'He or his deputy will stay on the premises over night.'

'Oh er …… well now what have we here?' Elizabeth exclaimed as she ran over to the window, 'there are two carts loaded with goods leaving from the back of the house'.

George reacted immediately, sprang to his feet and ran out the room to alert the bailiff, but it was too late. Some of the servants had made off into the darkness with household goods piled high on a cart.

The bailiff was livid and, from that point on he knew no rest. Hour after hour he patrolled the house and surroundings anxiously watching for signs of movement. But he was fretting over a horse that had already bolted the stable. He spent some considerable time with those remaining staff warning them that nothing was to be moved in the house without his permission or he would have them thrown in jail. All his enquiries as to who had left the house with goods, however, drew a blank.

The Fairfaxes and Gentle George ate and retired for the night in their new, strange surroundings conscious that the dead body of Gervase was resting down the corridor from them.

It was, without doubt, the strangest Christmas morning any of them could remember. A slight warming overnight of the temperature had led to the first winter fall of snow, arriving just in time for Christmas day. Elizabeth, who had naturally inclined herself to the role of housekeeper, was first up. Before anyone else rose, she'd organised those staff who were willing to take orders, to make preparations to light fires and keep the house running smoothly.

There was nothing in the house to indicate that it was the festive season and it was clear there had been no female in charge of the establishment for many years.

Duke, who had returned back to Fairfax Manor, the family's home, that night came back the next day with Isabella, Stella and the nurse. Aurora, who had been anxious about leaving her daughter at such short notice and without having time to make plans, was enormously relieved and busied herself getting everyone settled whilst George went to the parish church to make arrangements for the burial of Gervase. He encountered unexpected hostility from the vicar but the curate, who made himself known to George, was given the task of making arrangements instead.

Isabella had the presence of mind to bring with her various trifles and gifts that had been prepared already at Fairfax Manor and so a make-shift happy Christmas Day was possible for those gathered, even if it was in a house bereft of festive spirit.

Immediately after Christmas, at the first opportunity, the burial took place of Gervase Vavasour. It was at night-time, after dark and without a funeral service and no one attended except for the Curate and grave diggers. With still no sign of Benjamin, there had been some apprehension that Pascal would intervene to halt proceedings but in the event he made no attempt. It was felt necessary to have the body properly taken care of quickly and the absence of family members made a funeral service unnecessary.

The removal of Gervase from the house lifted a cloud and as soon as the burial was completed, Elizabeth carried out her plan to dispense with those servants who had been idle, dissatisfied and not co-operated with them. All the kitchen staff were instructed to leave and the few remaining servants were given new duties to keep the house running until additional servants could be found.

Finally, almost a week after the death of Gervase Vavasour, as the new year of 1722 was beginning, there was news of Benjamin having been found. He was brought to Vavasour Hall by Nathan who had apprised him, during their journey, of his father's death.

When Aurora finally saw her husband she saw he was far from being grief-stricken over the loss, indeed his father's death hadn't affected him one jot. Neither did he show remorse at being absent at the time but did express gratitude to Duke for his actions in securing the house on his behalf.

No explanation was offered to Aurora for his absence but, when she asked her brother Nathan where he'd found him, he was more forthcoming with explanations. Speaking whilst Benjamin was in the nursery seeing Stella, he said, 'we were directed where to find him by Duke, who as you know found him last time.'

'Two Blue Pots?' she asked.

'Yes' said Nathan looking down to the floor, from which Aurora realised he *knew* the kind of places Benjamin frequented. Elizabeth, however, made no comment and so Aurora was relieved that the name meant nothing to her at least.

'Was he gambling? Drinking?' she asked tentatively.

'Yes' said Nathan. 'When I asked him where he got the money from to gamble with, he eventually told me that he'd pawned items. You recall he came to Vavasour Hall to challenge Pascal, the night before he disappeared?'

'Yes, he came home in a mess' said Aurora.

'Well, he took items from here. He also bribed servants to take goods the following day - he has one man in particular here who does all his bidding.'

'We heard the carts!' said Elizabeth. 'Hold on a moment, but that was after Gervase was dead. That means he would have to have known, what ..... for the last week, that his father was dead?'

'That's not all' said Nathan. 'He also stole from us. Father's pistols, mother's jewellery. That's just the items we know about. Anything of yours missing?'

'Err .... I don't know' said Aurora anxiously. 'We'd to leave the house in such a hurry and we haven't been back there yet, so I don't know. Oh Lord, what are we to do. I thought .... I really thought that after so many months of him staying away from his gambling friends and the fact that they dumped him unceremoniously last time, I really cannot believe that he went back to them again'.

Nathan, clutching Aurora's hand affectionately said, 'I'm worried what your future will be married to a gambler .... and a drunkard' Nathan said. 'He probably can't change, he's set on a course now.'

'Oh .... mother's jewels, father's pistols' said Aurora, fighting back the tears. 'The shame of it. How can I ever repay them?'

'If only he was a *successful* gambler!' Elizabeth muttered under her breath.

Chapter 22

Benjamin's arrival at Vavasour Hall was greeted with passivity from Aurora. A fundamental change in her feelings for Benjamin had come about almost imperceptibly, although the specific discoveries of his frequenting brothels and stealing from her family were the main catalysts of change in her.

Benjamin's unwillingness to discuss his absences and her growing disinterestedness in his well-being coincided, not just resulting in a breaking of the bond she believed existed between them; much more than that, there now existed an insurmountable barrier that ruptured their relationship. It was as deep and traumatic for her as going through the mourning process. Some relict of love was still there, like a fond memory, though it was now tinged with pity. He'd lost his hold on her. Aurora now, at last, finally saw him as others did: a weak man without a moral centre and bent on self-destruction.

She'd been joined in union with him by God and so leaving him was never an option for her, but in terms of her own feelings, she'd woken from a dream which had blinded her to the *real* Benjamin. The baby had supplanted Benjamin in her affections and what she wanted now was a secure privacy to surround baby Stella and give her a safe home; not the continual disappointments, risk taking and poor judgement of her husband.

His frequenting of brothels was a personal tragedy for her and that alone was enough to end her feelings for him, but the subsequent pawning of her family's possessions was of a different order. It was so utterly disrespectful to those who had done everything to help him.

It all felt like a really hard slap in the face to her and, for the first time in her life, she experienced a deep and sharp pang of humiliation and shame. It was impossible for her to maintain any affection for him now, and she now felt that her responsibilities to Benjamin only extended as far as seeing him cared for. An act she would have done for any injured animal. As her daughter's guardian, however, Aurora wouldn't abandon her duties as

Benjamin's wife. Her primary motivation now was to protect Stella's future as heir to Vavasour Hall.

Benjamin himself seemed not to notice his wife's changed affections, nor feel remorse at any aspect of his conduct. At the very moment when his father, his tormenter, was out of his life and he could look forward to starting a new life free of harassment, his past caught up with him and his future began to slip through his fingers. He began acting much as his father had, as if he had an almost 'divine right' to authority.

But the fingers of his father's legacy had a long, long reach. In effect and by his deliberate design, Gervase Vavasour lived on even after death. He'd deliberately empowered others to continue his son's harassment, long into the future. In fact, Benjamin would spend the rest of his life trying to move on from his father's death, but was never able to.

As regards the pawning of family possession, if there had been any apology to Aurora's family for the theft or any attempt to recompense them, then she hadn't heard of it. And her mother certainly would have told her as Isabella had no concept of discretion or of keeping secrets. As it stood then Aurora felt far more shame for his actions than Benjamin felt himself.

The only noticeable change in Benjamin's behaviour was his obvious relief at his father's death. Being the new master of Vavasour Hall fed his burgeoning self importance and he found it difficult to stifle a newly found predisposition for arrogance.

Aurora's subsequent discovery of missing watches and jewels passed without comment, she'd no need to ask him if he'd taken them because she already knew the answer. It was, she thought, quite breath-taking, that Benjamin could take the watch she wore every day, and which he himself had given her as a gift, and suppose she wouldn't notice its absence. She took to keeping secrets of her own and, in the case of her missing watch, managed to find out where it had been pawned and purchased it back again. She made no mention of it to her husband and, since he likewise never referred to it, she supposed he never made any attempt of his own to redeem the item.

She'd moved past the point of wanting to share every little piece of information and detail of their lives with Benjamin. The open sharing of every passing thought was over and she was now circumspect in her dealings with him. She was, in essence, beyond caring. She did, however, urge sister Elizabeth and George to keep any of their valuables under lock and key - as she'd heard of thefts in the area. Both acquiesced, knowing far more about Benjamin's situation than Aurora realised, but never made her aware of it.

When the time came for Duke to leave Vavasour Hall to return home, he requested that both George and Elizabeth be allowed to stay on. He told George that Elizabeth's fiancé or former fiancé, as she considered their engagement at an end, had fled the country.

'Whilst I don't believe Elizabeth has any real interest in William Knightley, I'd prefer her to remain as ignorant of what's happening with him as possible.'

'I'll make sure we see no newspapers here' said George 'and I'd never mention the South Seas company in her presence anyway'.

'Good' said Duke, 'I heard of a man the other day who lost everything when this so-called bubble collapsed. Such a tragic circumstance. He climbed into a boat on the River Thames, with 'is pockets loaded with stones, and plunged himself into the cold water. I don't want Elizabeth hearing such stories, and there are plenty more I'm afraid, so detain her here as long as you can please'.

'I've heard such stories too' said George. 'I heard Isaac Newton say he could calculate the movement of the stars, but not the madness of men ......'

'Hah! Maybe' said Duke wistfully, 'but you see tis a matter of honour. A man's responsible for his own affairs and, as there's shame in debt, then more so in these cases. Just a few months ago, speculation fever filled men's heads with dreams o' glory and easy fortunes. Tis very hard for 'em then to find themselves robbed of everything they possessed. And ..... then to face having to tell their loved ones that they are ruined. Tis very hard.'

'It is.' George agreed. 'Man's greed, however, is half to blame. Other half of blame lies with likes of Knightley who talked the price up and up beyond expectations to achieve.'

'Exactly so' said Duke 'But not a word to Elizabeth, she'd best start looking to herself' and forgetting about Knightley because he probably hasn't given her a single thought in all these months'.

As Duke left, Aurora shouted to him 'Thank you father, for everything!' and with that he departed.

George had started to wonder whether his stay at Vavasour Hall might be superfluous now that Benjamin was there but it quickly became apparent that Benjamin was no administrator. He seemed unwilling or incapable or applying himself to the business of running the estate. And yet there was much to do, not the least of which was to organise the collection of rents from the dozens of tenants. George by contrast was in his element, directing and organising staff and, almost instinctively, people were drawn to him as the focal point for all matters concerning the estate. Benjamin made no effort to prevent George taking charge. He seemed to want to wallow in the privilege of being a 'gentleman' without immersing himself in the business that went with it.

One of the first orders of business was to conduct an inventory of the estate to satisfy the lawyers, a task which took them three full days to carry out. Jolson, Taylor, Berry and George went off for hours taking stock but, when Benjamin was asked to review their findings, he argued over every item, saying it was all his grandfather's property. It was clear to George from this process that every little piece of the estate would be disputed as, for each item examined, Benjamin claimed as an heirloom so that Jolson and Taylor would be unable to take anything.

Benjamin's principal activity during the day time was hunting. Four days a week he was off going from one fox hunt to another and, for convenience, stayed overnight with the respective hosts organising the hunts. The few days he was at Vavasour Hall were spent, more and more as time went on, mooning about aimlessly, or he would wile away the hours drinking or playing billiards with his man servant.

Those evenings when he was at home he was always drinking. This resulted in the occupants of the house dividing into two camps, the ladies and little Stella being on one side and Benjamin, his man servant on the other. Gentle George, ever the arbitrator, was the only one who seemed to cross the divide. George actually spent most of his time with the ladies, but necessity of running the estate forced him to keep on cordial terms with Benjamin who he needed to engage in decision-making for the estate.

There was much business to oversee and this usually comprised of George telling Benjamin what he planned, or had done, and Benjamin nodding in agreement. There was never a single occasion where Benjamin disagreed with George's decisions, with the exception of the inventory.

It was quickly apparent to George that Benjamin had no capacity for business. Even when Benjamin was stone cold sober, it seemed he was too impatient to examine books and had difficulty forming opinions, having a mind that was in flux, unfixed and uniformed. Benjamin had no ability to manage the tenants, or even the servants and was hampered by having had no experience in dealing with men. When intoxicated, his shortcomings became more exaggerated. He was a man who became more aggressive after drinking; he would act disinterested in the tenants as well as being cold and ruthless to the servants. He became, in fact, an exact replica of his father.

All of which meant that George was kept extremely busy and was entirely free to manage the Vavasour estate much as he pleased. Indeed, as George's familiarity with the affairs of Vavasour Hall increased, it wasn't long before he arrived at the same conclusion that Duke had: that Gervase Vavasour's design to make over everything to his second son Pascal had been well advanced.

Vavasour knew full well that his Roman Catholic son was barred by law from inheriting the house and that Dionysus had made an unbreakable entail, so he circumnavigated a path around the entail which saw him cashing in every conceivable part of the estate. Selling off capital items enabled him to take control and divert monies to Pascal. By this means he would deny Benjamin's inheritance in favour of Pascal and it was only his premature death prevented conclusion of this plan.

George discovered how Gervase had spun a web deliberately designed to leave an entangled mess after his death, the estate being burdened with mortgages and bonds and, since Benjamin had been forced to be the co-signer of most of them, then he was bound to repay them.

Even the maintenance money Gervase had been forced to pay his son by the Archbishop of York was bound in this way and, in his will, Gervase explained the reason - that being, since his son

Benjamin had been the occasion of needing the loans then he should be the person to repay them.

Only his death had prevented Gervase from completing the last stage of his plan which would have seen him vacate the house and clear it of property, leaving it to fall into disrepair. His plan was ..... that Benjamin would inherit nothing but an empty decaying shell of a building, and an debt-laden estate that couldn't support it.

George was able to halt the destructive process Gervase had started to some extent, and then set about spending hours and hours working to turn the estate into a viable one able to support the hall.

A few weeks later, as fully expected, writs for law suits by Pascal and the solicitors Jolson and Taylor arrived. There were actually three suits: Pascal was suing Benjamin for possession Vavasour Hall and an income from the estate, then Jolson and Taylor were suing for possession of the personal estate of Gervase Vavasour and thirdly, Pascal and the two solicitors had combined together to sue the estate on other matters.

Aurora was present when George gave Benjamin news of the multiple legal cases commenced against him and witnessed Benjamin's utter defiance. He was entirely confident that all the cases would fail and said he relished the battles.

Aurora spoke to George afterwards, when Benjamin had left the house for his customary ride with a nearby hunt.

'It's all a front' she told George. 'At the very moment when he has everything he could ever want, he's now facing the battle of his life to hold on to it'.

'Well' said George philosophically, 'there's never been any doubt that Pascal was going to put up a fight, but he won't get the house or the land, that's for sure. But then maybe that's not his real objective. He knows the law prevents him inheriting the estate ....'

'Even if his father's will stipulated that he should?' asked Aurora.

'No he can't get it. But he may be counting on a probate court taking sympathy with his father's last wishes and coming up with a compromise.'

'Something .... of an equivalent value?' she asked.

'Yes, something like that. As for Jolson and Taylor' he added, 'I think they have a harder task to prove ownership of property. You see, I suppose it can be argued that pieces of furniture in the house belonged to Benjamin's grandfather Dionysus, but you can't use the same argument, say, for corn in the ground.'

'I suppose that has value ....' said Aurora.

'Of course, yes.' George added 'it's going to be a long road. These cases can sometimes run for years and years.'

'My father will know what to do' said Aurora. 'But how Benjamin will really cope with law suits coming at him from every direction I can't imagine'.

'He seems defiant' said George.

'No.' said Aurora with confidence. 'It's just bravura.' Later that day, Aurora saw exactly how Benjamin was going to cope with the challenge. After he returned from the hunt, he began drinking and, as the evening wore on, his excess of confidence sank with the sunset and the former arrogance swiftly deflated to despair. He crumbled under the strain and, finding every effort to talk to him rebuffed, she left him alone and hoped, with some solitude, that he might rally.

Aurora sought out Elizabeth and George for company where she found the suits were the main topic of conversation for them.

'It was inevitable that this day would come' said George. 'Nothing we could say or do was ever going to placate Pascal. And, as for Jolson and Taylor, Gervase could have given his personal estate to anyone. Just think about it! Why didn't he sign it over to Pascal? Why did he chose instead Jolson and Taylor?'

'Because ...... well, I don't know .... was money exchanged? Did they *pay* Gervase?' said Aurora.

'Of course they did' said George. 'Gervase has duped Jolson and Taylor every bit as much as he's tied Benjamin up in litigation.'

'So ..... he got money from Jolson and Taylor by entering a bond to give them his possessions and then .... I'm guessing now .... he gave that money to Pascal?' said Elizabeth.

'Yes' said George.

'Whereas' continued Elizabeth, 'if he'd bequeathed his personal estate directly to Pascal, he knew there would be a risk that Benjamin would get it instead?'

'And with Jolson and Taylor both being solicitors …. and sharp ones too I might add ….. he knew they would move heaven and earth in the fight to get their property' said George. 'So Pascal's had the money already, and now Benjamin has a suit against him being brought by two solicitors.'

'Bit like David and Goliath' said Aurora mournfully.

'Exactly what Gervase intended it should be' said George. 'But he also duped Jolson and Taylor too because most of the personal property here in the house, for example, belongs to many generations of Vavasours and, since the will of Dionysus Vavasour states the personal property is to pass down with the entailed estate, there" get very little. I've looked back through quite a few of the family wills and there are occasional mentions of specific pieces of furniture. Now where that happens we'll be able to have those items excluded.'

'Wouldn't Jolson and Taylor have been aware of that?' said Elizabeth.

'Not if Gervase told them everything was his. He had no motivation in disclosing that not all the furniture had been bought by him. I doubt whether they asked him for receipts! It would have lessened the money he got from them if he'd said only a small portion of the property was technically his. No, I'm afraid Gervase knew exactly what he was doing. He probably devoted all his efforts to finding ways to leave a tangled mess. He calculated that the solicitors would face a challenge after his death, and that, due to their professions and familiarity with law suits, they would pursue the matter to the bitter end. He did what was best for Pascal, but also set Benjamin up for potentially an endless battle over every aspect of the estate.'

'What a nightmare' said Elizabeth.

'All the worse because it was planned' said Aurora. 'I don't think Benjamin will be able to cope with the stress.'

'*You* can though' said Elizabeth affectionately, 'because you have us'.

'And Stella' added George. 'This is a battle for her future and she's too young to do it herself, so you must do it for her' he said looking at Aurora. 'I'd better go and look in on Benjamin now. He may need to talk'.

George left the room and Aurora spoke to Elizabeth, 'Well I couldn't get Benjamin to say two words to me earlier when I tried, but who knows, with George he'll probably be different. I'm afraid he *will* talk too now he's had a drink. They'll probably be talking all through the night. George has so much patience with him.'

There was a sound of rushing footsteps outside the room and they listened until eventually the door was flung open and George said,

'He's gone! Benjamin's gone. The servant's just told me he went out on his horse'.

'At this time of night, in the pitch dark' said Aurora alarmed. 'There's no moon light, and he's been drinking, how will he find his way? And where? There's thick, freezing fog outside.' The three exchanged worried looks and George determined to go and see if he could find him. He shouted to the servants down below to come and help him look and a general pandemonium ensued which saw people running about and across each other in different directions, back and forth. 'Check again upstairs' George shouted to someone, just in case ......'

'If he's gone off to York again' said Aurora angrily, 'I've got a good mind to saddle up a horse and go after him myself. All this running off with no word .... how would he like it if I did such a thing?'

'You know how men are ....' Elizabeth started to say.

Within minutes, there came urgent shouts of men's voices from a short distance away from the house. Aurora and Elizabeth knew immediately something was wrong. They rushed out the door but remained in the front doorway as it was hard to see outside with the fog being so thick. They could make nothing out, except dark figures moving back and forth. George was shouting to the servants who had gathered around him and giving directions to them.

'What's going on?' said Elizabeth straining her eyes to see.

'I'm not waiting here' said Aurora stepping outside. 'Hey there, what goes on? George, what's happened? Is it Benjamin?

Elizabeth caught up with her and both women moved closer the scene.

'Take Aurora inside right now' George shouted to Elizabeth and, as instructed, the ladies retreated indoors. The waiting was torture.

'Women are born to wait ….' said Elizabeth philosophically. 'Men jump straight into things and we …. we just wait …..'

Several minutes later, and with much activity outside, the group of men emerged from the fog carrying a figure laying out on an old door which had been requisitioned to serve as a stretcher.

'I've sent for the doctor' said George. 'Mind … let us through. It's Benjamin.'

'Is he alright?' asked aurora breathlessly.

'He's fell off his horse' said George. 'Let's get him inside out the cold'.

With that the men stumbled inside the doorway carrying Benjamin's considerable weight in addition to that of the door.

'You must take him straight upstairs' said Elizabeth.

The men doing the carrying, though they were nearly all elderly, made no complaint, even though the task was difficult, but after much effort and cursing, it was achieved and Benjamin was taken upstairs. He was lifted gently onto a bed but made no noise, no cry of pain. He wasn't conscious.

'We should not have managed him upstairs later without the men' said Elizabeth as she thanked the servants for helping. Aurora fussed over Benjamin while begging George for more information.

'Tell me what has happened?' she begged. 'I see no serious injury here …..'

'He was found just outside the house' he told her. 'I don't know how long he'd been there, but the horse gave up the alarm when it was seen wondering about with no rider.'

Not only had no one had observed the incident, but no one had missed Benjamin from the house. Those attending him thought he'd failed to secure the saddle properly and he had slipped off.

'The man who found him said he was lying at a very odd angle; made him think his back was broken. That's why we laid him out the way we did.'

'A broken back …..' gasped Aurora. 'Oh my God.'

'We won't know more until he wakes up' said George.
'We've checked and he's still breathing. We can do nothing more
till the doctor arrives.'
The injuries were indeed severe, not just the evident bleeding head
which was tended to. They all kept watch over him until the
doctor arrived, which took a considerable time.

There followed a general confusion, concerned whispers and
dashing back and forth followed by solemn voices expressing
despair at his condition.

After a long time ensconced with the patient, the doctor
emerged looking suitably grave. The prognosis was as specific as
his skills could make it; that Benjamin, though now semi-
conscious, appeared to have broken his back and had a head injury
too. He added that such extensive internal injuries were hard to
define and impossible to cure.

'I'm very sorry, but there is', he said with authority 'no
possibility of recovery. You can only make him comfortable and
let nature take its course.'

With that the doctor was gone, though with the promise of a
return in the morning.

George, Aurora and Elizabeth returned to the room where
Benjamin was lying, to see him.

'It's perhaps as well he has so much alcohol in his system'
whispered Elizabeth 'which may dull his pain'.

'Benjamin' said Aurora, 'can you hear me?' She took his
hand and felt some movement.

'Mmm ..... 'came the reply'.

'You've had a fall ... from your horse. You're going to be
just fine.' said Aurora.

'He's awake then?' said George. Then to Benjamin he said 'Is
there anything, anything at all we can get you?'

There was no answer.

Of course there was nothing they could do to help him and, it
was considered a blessing, when Benjamin seemed to drift back
into sleep again. George, after checking that he was still breathing,
motioned to the nurse to keep watching him and to let them know
if he woke up again. Then they left the room.

Aurora's heart was heavy. 'What *has* he done to himself!' she said angrily. 'This is no one's fault but his own. I am sorry to say it.'

'It was an accident' said Elizabeth. 'It's no one's fault'.

'Of course it wasn't an accident' insisted Aurora. 'He's been drinking all night. He wasn't in a fit state to get on a horse'.

'He was distressed by news of those court cases' said Elizabeth sympathetically.

'Yes' hissed Aurora, 'but by being so reckless with his life, what will that achieve? If ....' she said in a whisper 'God forbid that he should die, but if he does, it will change nothing. The burden just falls to me and Stella. And I don't want our daughter to have suffer because her father hadn't the courage to face difficulties. I sometimes think God is punishing me ....'.

'We're all tired', said George. 'Let's get some sleep. There's nothing more we can do for him. The nurse will let us know if there's any change. We should rest and look at the situation in the morning. It's better for him, Aurora, that he's sleeping. He can feel no pain right now.'

'Perhaps we can send for another doctor' said Aurora hopefully. 'A second opinion wouldn't hurt.'

'Yes, good' said George. 'Let's see how he is in the morning'.

With that they all left the room to retire. After walking a short distance down the corridor, Aurora decided to return. She wanted to stay with him.

Chapter 23

In the House of Commons, Nathan Fairfax and his brother-in-law John Mason took their seats ahead of an important debate. Such had been the clamour for seats that day that some members had 'bagged' their seats at six o'clock in the morning for a debate that wasn't due to start until three in the afternoon.

'There's such a crowd here today' said Mason to Nathan 'as we all have an interest in the debate about to happen'.

'Yes' said Fairfax sighing. 'The South Seas stock has fallen to such a point that many have been ruined by it. He will have the King's pleasure indeed if Wortley can manage to sort this almighty mess out'.

'Ah ...' said Mason nudging him sharply. 'Speak of the devil, look ..... he's heading our way.'

Moments later the Chief Minister, Sir Richard Wortley, who had just entered the chamber, rested his heavy frame on a seat immediately next to the men.

'Gentlemen' he said quietly, so as not to disturb the speech that was taking place, nor be overheard. 'I recall Nathan some time back seeing your delightful sisters at Leicester House'.

'Yes indeed sir' he replied.

'Well, you know, this government has so much business to do, so many problems to solve.'

'Yes sir' said Nathan, not sure what Wortley was leading to.

'I wasn't able to assist when you told me some time ago that your family had problems with Vavasour but I fear things are now getting out of hand Nathan.'

'Why is that sir?' he asked.

'Everywhere I go I'm hearing about Vavasour versus Vavasour - Pascal versus Benjamin - your brother-in-law I hear! It's being built up as Catholicism against Protestantism and the issue is dividing people. From the Archbishop of York to the Benedictine Monks who, I hear, have been solicited by Pascal for their support'.

'Really sir?' said Nathan surprised. 'That's news to me. The Archbishop did intervene to settle a maintenance issue between my brother-in-law and his father.'

'And likely to find in Benjamin's favour?'

'Well, we hope so sir'.

'And now I have it on good authority that Pascal has involved the Benedictine Monks and before too long we shall have two religious orders set against each other. It must stop Nathan. A major dispute such as this among leading families in Yorkshire will distract the government at a critical time.'

'Sir, our brother-in-law Benjamin Vavasour is lawfully entitled to inherit from his father' said Mason.

'Yes, he's his eldest son and heir and the estate is entailed on him' said Nathan.

'I know all that' said Wortley. 'But the named Catholic heir is trying to unseat his elder Protestant brother and that does not make for harmonious relations in the country. I would consider it a personal favour if you, and Mason here, could apply your minds to the problem and get it solved.'

'Yes sir' said both Fairfax and Mason.

'There are far bigger problems to sort out as this South Sea 'bubble' has damaged the government. My administration is getting the blame for the crisis and it's down to us to sort it out. We cannot have the distraction of a religious battle going on - even the King has heard about it. Find a way to stop it.'

'Yes sir' they both said like chastised schoolboys.

'Now' Wortley said rising to his feet. 'I have to go and make the speech of my life. The Directors of the South Sea Company are going to have to pay a heavy price for their greed. We shall have to seize their estates and see them punished.'

'What of William Knightley?' asked Mason. 'Is there any sign of him coming back to England?'

'Back to England?' Wortley said in astonishment. 'We don't ....' he whispered ... 'we don't want him back here. He'd fan the flames. Let him stay in jail wherever he is. We shall take the South Seas Company by the scruff of the neck, reform it, help those who have suffered most and .... above all else' he said with force ... 'never, never allow this to happen again.'

'Good luck sir' said Nathan.

'Remember …… get it sorted out' said Wortley departing.

Both men sank back into their seats and Wortley slowly made his way down the steps to his front bench seat, stopping every few yards to speak to various people. Then awaited the moment when parliamentary business moved on to the South Seas, when he rose to speak to a full house. He spoke with authority and calmness which had the desired effect of defusing the crisis and led to all those listening to him feeling he had grasped the matter and was bringing it under control.

'Benedictine Monks?' Mason scoffed. 'What next? Holy War?'

Chapter 24

Aurora, who had kept a separate bedroom at Vavasour Hall since arriving there, had left Benjamin during the night when he was looking peaceful and returned to her room. She was surprised when she woke the next morning having had a good night's sleep. She felt a huge degree of guilt at sleeping so well when her husband was in such a bad way, but his drunkenness having been the cause of his accident lessened her concern, perhaps more than it should have.

Leaving her room, she made the short journey along the corridor, when she was alarmed to see someone leaving Benjamin's room.

'I say there' she beckoned, 'who might you be'.

The figure, turning, she immediately recognised to be Obadiah Longshaft, Benjamin's solicitor.

'Sir ......' she beckoned ..... 'what are you doing in there?' she asked.

'Ahhhh ..... good morning Mrs Vavasour' he said in his usual friendly way.

He spoke, in a soft voice, to tell her that he'd received a message to call on Benjamin for the purpose of helping him write his will.

'Ah, so he's awake then? she said.

'I'm right sorry to see Benjamin taken badly' he said shaking his head. 'Don't often get called on to make wills out for men such as young as him'.

'Thank you' she replied and then asked, 'exactly who was it that sent for you?'

'John Gooding' he replied, 'one of your servants. You may check with him if you wish'.

'A will?' she said. 'And was this will written entirely in accordance with Benjamin's own wishes?'

'Of course' he replied. 'It was properly witnessed by John Gooding and .... oh .... your nurse. Her name is here somewhere

....' he said looking through the papers he had in his hand. On finding it, he showed Aurora where the witnesses had signed.'

'I see' she said.

'It's all in order' he assured her 'and you may ask those witnesses who'll confirm that it was read out to me by Benjamin who, I judge, is of sound mind though weak and frail in his person. It was entirely his own citation. I wrote it down, gave it back to him and he read it through before signing before those witnesses I mentioned'.

'Very well' said Aurora.

'Now you'll have to excuse me Mrs Vavasour' said Longshaft already walking away down the corridor, 'I have a client waiting for me. He stole a chalice from the chapel and is facing hanging. He's looking to me to save him, but God alone will help him now because I can't stop it! These will be his last days on earth, because justice must be done!' Good morning to you' he shouted as he disappeared down the stairs and Aurora watched him leave the house.

How shocking, how final, it seemed to hear talk of wills. Benjamin clearly was well aware that the prognosis was not good. She entered his room and found him lying flat on his back, just as they had left him the night before. His eyes were open and he looked towards the door as it opened. The nurse, on seeing Aurora, asked if she could be excused a little while to fetch some items from downstairs.

'You' said Aurora sharply, 'were supposed to tell us if there was any change in Master Benjamin's condition!'

'I'm sorry ma'am but .... you see I fell asleep in the early hours after you left. I was working all day yesterday. I couldn't help it. Then when I woke up I seen Master Benjamin was awake too and he asked to see John Gooding. And .... well ... since the whole house was in total quiet, with everyone asleep, I didn't see much point in waking everyone.'

'Go about your business' said Aurora 'and have a bed made up in the next room. Then we will get a servant to relieve you for some rest'

'Yes ma'am' came the reply.

Aurora then moved over to the bed where Benjamin was looking at her; looking every bit the broken man, both physically and mentally.

'Come here' he said to her in a hoarse and rasping voice. 'That was Obadiah Longshaft. I sent for him. I thought I should settle matters as I don't know how much time there is. I've made out my will leaving everything to Stella but I've made provision for you too and want you to raise Stella in this house. And …. If anything happens to Stella then it all goes to you.'

Aurora nodded and took his hand. 'I wish there was something I could do to help' she said, 'is there anything you want'. Are you in pain?'

'No I feel no pain. In fact, I can feel nothing at all', he said, 'I've done what I set my mind to do today, now I shall rest. The doctor says I'm to stay lying as still as I possibly can to see if the injury will heal itself. Aurora ….. I'm sorry …… but there are a great many debts on my estate' he said, 'but I've made arrangements for you to be able to sell part of the estate not entailed, to raise money to pay some of them. I just wish' he said glumly 'that I could have left my affairs in better order for you'.

'The doctor will be here soon' she told him 'and that's sufficient dwelling on things so gloomy'.

'There's no medicine that will cure me' Benjamin said, 'I am dying'.

'Nonsense' she said. 'You need attention and care and I'll see to it that you get both'. As she spoke, his eyelids looked heavier and heavier and so she watched as he drifted off into sleep, knowing that was probably the best thing for him at that time.

As she gazed on her husband Aurora wished he'd always been so honest and true with her, as he seemed that day. She'd seen him so many times in a helpless state but this time, she felt full of pity such that she thought she could have almost forgiven him anything. But, yet, such had been his behaviour that she couldn't bring herself to fully sympathise with him. It was pity tinged with resentment caused by his previous disappointing behaviour.

He had changed her. He had taken her childlike innocence and, in no more than the passing of one or two years, turned Aurora into a resentful woman who had lost the ability to trust. He made her doubt herself, made her less caring, less susceptible to believe whatever she was told. She wasn't as indifferent as her sister Elizabeth had become, but she was a changed woman to the one he had wooed in Matlock. The long hours he'd spent encouraging her affections there had evaporated once back home. Like an intoxicating holiday romance that was borne of foreign parts, and that could *only* flourish *because* of the artificial environment, it withered in the face of real life and the cold realities of home.

Aurora wondered if Benjamin could read her thoughts at that time and perhaps felt the same way but whether well or ill he wasn't given to deep thinking and wasn't capable of having such a discussion.

As she left the room, she passed the nurse in the corridor and told her 'I'll keep watch on Stella today as you're needed here'.

'Yes Ma'am' the weary nurse replied.

The following days saw Benjamin's spirits sink as he grew weaker and weaker and, within a week, he quietly stopped breathing.

His death did distress Aurora, but not perhaps to as great an extent as she imagined. She had, in many ways, already mourned over his loss whilst he'd been living, so now his actual death seemed less tragic. A broken spine compounded by other internal injuries meant he was never likely to recover and his death, when it came, was an unspoken relief to everyone. Tragic though it was as he was just 27 years of age.

Chapter 25

A formal funeral service was arranged for Benjamin which was in stark contrast to the hasty, night-time burial for Gervase Vavasour. Full mourning was observed with servants and attendants fitted out in black, church pews and two carriages were also draped in dull black cloth. Grand though the funeral was, it fell to the curate of the church to conduct the service, for there was a history of bad blood between the Vavasours and the local church and the Vicar himself refused to conduct the service. As a beacon of Christianity, the scars nurtured by the vicar were too deep and even he couldn't bring himself to set an example of forgiveness. So the young, inexperienced curate stepped into his shoes.

A lavish wake was put on for the mourners and most of the estate's tenants and employees attended. Those who stayed away, and there was a small number, had used the excuse of a Vavasour family dispute to demonstrate their allegiance by continuing to make their rent and tithe payments to Pascal. George, however, had picked the dissidents off one by one and he found that the more tenants he won over to his side, the more pressure it put on the remaining ones and the estate was almost back up to full strength.

All of the Fairfaxes were there, including Nathan and John Mason who had been tasked with quelling the religious quarrel by Wortley. An invite - an olive branch - extended to Pascal Vavasour hadn't been replied to, but to everyone's astonishment, he attended the service.

Back at Vavasour Hall, the large entrance hall had been suitably dressed to receive the guests for the wake. Ancient Elizabethan coats of armour stood guard inside the entrance way as guests piled in to a hall decorated and saturated with family crests and other symbols of heraldry. It was, as it had been in the time of Gervase Vavasour, with no changes - a sombre room designed to impress. If guests got no further than this large entrance hall, then they would leave with the impression that this was a family of historic importance, of ancient origins - part of the very fabric of

England. Not one single opportunity was missed to send a subliminal message. We *are* England. It would certainly have been a room to intimidate tenants and lower ranking visitors.

'Gentle George' moved around the room full of guests looking very uneasy. The arrival of both Pascal and his friend Stanhope in the hall had him on edge. He spoke to Duke, 'We should expect trouble from those two'.

'Stanhope was never sent an invite' said Duke.

'He probably calculated that, at such an event no one would challenge him' said George.

'Perhaps they'll have respect for the occasion' said Duke hopefully.

'No' said George, 'absolutely not'. And with that he positioned himself in close proximity to the perceived threat. Surprisingly, after some time had passed the unusually well behaved Pascal left the house, after which there was a palpable sigh of relief amongst the Fairfaxes.

'Wonder why Stanhope didn't leave with him?' observed Duke.

George thought for a moment and, still looking at Stanhope, told Duke 'there's always someone waiting in the wings to take advantage of situations. Stanhope has made full use of both Vavasour brothers; Benjamin didn't see it and neither does Pascal. They can't see how artful he is. How he ingratiates himself with them for his own advantage. He used the same tactics with his own family. He became so close to his father that he persuaded him his elder brother wasn't worthy to inherit his property.'

'Like Pascal then?' added Duke.

'Well ....' continued George 'Pascal certainly played the tune his father wanted to hear. Embracing Catholicism, being the loyal, obedient son. Perhaps Stanhope was guiding him. Why can't people distinguish between flattery and guile ....'

'Because' said Duke smiling, 'we are all susceptible to flattery. We like it and it can be hard to know what's behind someone's motives, it isn't always obvious'.

'I can't say I've seen that too often in the army' said George. 'But my brother has commented on it often ....'

'Yes' said Duke grinning 'I should say Stanhope's got enough guile and subterfuge to make an excellent politician'.

'Shame my brother beat him to the post then' said George laughing. 'Politicians ... worse of all shallow scoundrels ..... um .... except for Nathan of course' he added quickly.

Stanhope gave a quick glance round the room and, in a moment while others were distracted by Pascal's departure, he seized the opportunity to confront Aurora.

'My dear Mrs Vavasour' he said in a mocking tone. 'I do commiserate with you in your loss.'

'Thank you' said Aurora. She'd heard such similar sentiments throughout the day.

'And yet' he continued '.... I realise that this isn't the appropriate time, but nonetheless I feel it incumbent on me to tell you that Benjamin owed me a great deal of money against which I have a court-registered bond. That puts me right at the top of his priority creditors. And .... I'm really *very, very* sorry to say that necessity now forces me to call in that debt for immediate repayment. By which ....' he whispered in her ear ... ' I do hope to force you into bankruptcy!'

'Begone you viper' hissed Elizabeth who had crept up behind him and momentarily startled him.

Standing up and speaking louder for others to hear, he said 'my condolences to you Mrs Vavasour!' And, with that he moved away and left the building.

'What did he say?' asked George who had moved like lightening towards Aurora when he saw Stanhope.

'Ohhh,' she said exasperated. 'That Benjamin owed him money on a bond, that he will call it in and have me bankrupt,' she replied.

'So that's it', said George who turned to go after Stanhope.

'No' said Elizabeth blocking his way. 'Not today George. This is not a day to go after Stanhope.'

'I knew they had a reason for being here' said George angrily 'and all the polite formalities they went through was for this .... just to distress you Aurora. They planned it between them.'

'Oddly enough I'm not distressed at all' said Aurora. 'Perhaps familiarity with an evil spirit somehow renders its nasty threats more commonplace and less shocking'.

'George?' said Aurora. 'Please, don't tell Nathan. I believe everything Stanhope does is targeted at my brother. He took advantage of Benjamin's weakness to get at me but he can't touch Nathan, so I do believe I am seen as the next best thing.'

'If you say so' said George 'but I think he should know'.

'No not this time' said Aurora. 'I won't give Stanhope any satisfaction. If Nathan isn't aware of his threats, then they can't hurt him'.

The wake wound down after this incident but, it was only after the funeral that Aurora began to really feel like Benjamin had gone out of her life. His legacy, however, for good or bad would continue to dominate her life until the day she died and his home being the inheritance of her daughter Stella would likewise become her lifelong obsession - by necessity.

Chapter 26

George Mason, having retired from the army, became a constant presence at Vavasour Hall. Indeed the original invitation for him to stay for a few days was never thought of again and, without anyone realising it, he became a permanent resident at the hall and made himself indispensible to Aurora personally and also to the running of the wider estate. Everyone depended on him being there.

His calm air of authority pervaded all negotiations with tenants and diffused many situations which, in more volatile hands, could have erupted into arguments and law suits. He even made inroads into pacifying Pascal who, though never on friendly terms with Aurora, could at least bring himself to deal with George on occasions.

For Aurora the months after Benjamin's death were a transition to a new life that had begun before her husband's death. Even whilst he had still been living she'd begun distancing herself from him and thinking on the future, but through her daughter's eyes. What did *Stella* want, what did *Stella* need. Not Benjamin.

Probate of her husband's will dragged on and on and, over the next year, there was a constant stream of visits to York to visit the courts and also to see the Archbishop. Aurora had been named as defendant now, in place of her dead husband, in all the litigation and there had been scant respect for her widowhood. Legal papers were served on her even before Benjamin's funeral had taken place.

The Archbishop, who had helped Benjamin and Aurora secure maintenance from Gervase Vavasour, was every bit as keen to help again in the battle to prevent Pascal claiming the estate. It was thought he was already predisposed to find in Aurora's favour, especially when he was heard to comment that 'whatever must be done to stop these Papists, will be'.

George accompanied Aurora everywhere and talked her through, and calmed her down, during every twist and turn of proceedings. He was liked by the Fairfax family and, almost without anyone noticing, he assumed the role that Duke, her father, had begun. Elizabeth too joined them, but not always, on their journeys.

On one particular visit to York, all three of them made the journey and decided to stay in town for the night and enjoy a visit to the Assembly Rooms. It was the first social occasion since Benjamin's death and it was looked forward to with anticipation. As it was a Friday, there would be music and dancing; Monday's Assemblies being less enjoyable for the ladies as they were reserved for card games for the men.

To Aurora's great delight, the evening was particularly enjoyed by her sister Elizabeth. George had introduced the sisters to one of his friends, Captain Jeremiah Wadebridge, a Royal Naval commander who was ashore on leave. Elizabeth happily danced the evening away with Wadebridge and Aurora sensed her sister's delight with the captain. Elizabeth's eyes betrayed her pleasure in Wadebridge's company and a determination to enjoy herself.

'Oh, you've no idea how good it makes me feel to see Elizabeth smile again' said Aurora to George. 'Just look at her! I'm so glad we all came to town. I haven't seen her enjoy herself this much for months, nay years.'

'He's a good man' said George. 'I've known him since childhood. And ...' he whispered quietly .... 'I do know he is unmarried and therefore highly eligible'.

'Really?' said Aurora laughing. 'I might set my cap at him myself then ....'

'No you won't' said George with great authority. 'You're spoken for!'

Aurora was so astonished by his comment that she was speechless, though she knew his meaning straight away. That she was spoken for ..... because he thought of her as 'his'.

'*If* I really was spoken for ....' said Aurora looking round the room, 'then I'm sure I'd have someone to dance with but as you see .... I haven't!'

George took the hint, took her hand and they were away ..... dancing. Two couples behind Elizabeth and Captain Wadebridge.

It was a strange, totally understated conversation that seemed to seal their fate. His confidence; her acceptance; their humour and happy acquiescence. It was all so effortless and, if she'd chosen to make a comparison, which she didn't at that moment, so incredibly different to Vavasour's frantic haste and subsequent dithering.

At some point as they were twirling around the ballroom it occurred to Aurora that she'd never danced with Benjamin. What must surely be part of every couple's courtship simply hadn't happened to them and, although she'd no wish to think of Benjamin at that time, the contrast with George was so glaring that it couldn't pass without registering somewhere at the back of her mind.

The evening was almost at an end when Elizabeth, who brought her dancing partner to join their group to make a foursome, noticed someone they knew across the room.

'Look, there's Mary' she said to Aurora. 'We better pay our respects'.

'Come with us' Aurora said to George and Captain Wadebridge 'and meet our cousin'. Both men duly followed to greet cousin Mary. The duchess was a portly lady, heavily made-up with white leaden powder on her face and painted red lips. Her magnificent gown reeked of wealth and was of a fashion more suitable to court than a provisional assembly at York. She was seated in stately splendour and with some fawning attendants, but responded with pleasure when she saw the group approaching.

'George' said Aurora, 'this is our cousin Mary, the Duchess of Buckingham. And this' she said indicating in George's direction 'is General George Mason, formerly a commander of British Forces in Spain'.

'Good evening ma'am' said George politely.

'And this' said Elizabeth 'is Captain Jeremiah Wadebridge' of the Royal Navy, presently in command of the Coverdine, one of His Majesty's finest ships of the fleet.

'Pleased to meet you all' said Mary smiling. 'I'm so old, don't you know, that I find it a strain to make new acquaintances but I know from experience that I never regret the effort' she said. 'My, we are in fine company this evening! I haven't been to one of these Assemblies in years' she continued 'but I just happened to be in York for a few days with some business to settle and, with little to occupy my time, I thought I'd come along for some diversion. Now, gentleman' she said looking at George and

Captain Wadebridge 'I do have some personal business to discuss with Aurora and Elizabeth, would you excuse us for just two minutes?'

'Of course' came the courteous replies.

Then, when they were out of earshot, Mary said, 'I must apologise to you both, and to your sister Catherine, for the failure of the annuities that were granted to you. It was out of my hands. I've apologised to your father, Duke, and he's still engaged in work for me, but I haven't had the opportunity to apologise to you both in person. I hope you know that if there had been any way to have continued them I would have, but it's all out of my hands now. The courts have taken control of my estate and finances and they will not countenance annuities when there are such creditors to pay. I'm so very sorry. You know' .... she said in earnest 'truly, if there's anything I can ever do for you I hope you'll ask. I have no funds, of course, but I do maintain plenty of contacts and if I can ever put them at your disposal, as some of my nearest relations, I will do so.'

'Thank you' said Elizabeth.

'Actually' said Aurora 'there is something you might be able to help us with. Or .... maybe it's too much to ask .....' she hesitated.

'Anything!' said Mary.

'Well .....' continued Aurora. 'We've heard some rumours that our brother Nathaniel might be in the running to be Speaker of the House of Commons'.

'Oh, wonderful' said Mary 'I'm very pleased for him'.

'Ah well .....' added Elizabeth 'they're only rumours, nothing definite. And you know it's such a coveted position with enormous prestige.'

'It is indeed.'

'So, if there was to be some way you could use your influence to put in a good word for him ..... in the right ears' said Elizabeth smiling, 'that would be a favour to us'.

'Consider it done' said Mary. 'I return to London soon and, within a few days, I shall get to work on it.' She smiled broadly and said 'oh I do like it when I can do something useful! And I love to help my friends and relations. Now, off you go and have fun. Return to those handsome young men behind you who are waiting for you'.

And with that, Aurora and Elizabeth left Mary and returned to their party. Captain Wadebridge said, 'I'm afraid I'm overwhelmed ladies. The Duchess of Buckingham, no less! I am only a humble sailor, and certainly not used to mixing in such exalted circles'.

'Here, here. Same goes for me' said George. They all laughed.

Later in the evening when Aurora was alone with George she told him of the conversation with Mary and their request for assistance for Nathan. Then they all departed from the Assembly and, to Aurora's enormous pleasure, Elizabeth and Captain Wadebridge had already made plans to see each other again.

Chapter 27

As Sir Richard Wortley had indicated, Pascal Vavasour was pulling out all the stops to garner support for his claim to Vavasour Hall and the estate. His father had been a patron of the Benedictine Monk Order at York and Pascal himself had been sent for a Catholic education at Lambspring College at Hildesheim in Hanover where his tutelage came under the same jurisdiction of the same Order.

Nathaniel Fairfax and John Mason's attempts to keep the dispute between Pascal and, now, Aurora as heir to her husband's estate out of Parliament and the Law Courts had been successful to a certain degree. The Archbishop of York's deliberations were considered of lesser profile but Pascal had made full use of his contacts to pressurise the Archbishop by showing he had the backing of the religious order. As Wortley had feared, it was a case which fed into deep rooted religious prejudices and polarised public opinion in a Yorkshire which still, in 1723, had a few who could remember the Civil War. A larger number, who were too young to remember the war, had grown up surrounded by the country-wide destruction left in the war's wake. They had also inherited - by word of mouth from their parents - their utter hatred for certain families associated with puritans, Catholics, royalist or parliamentarian causes, as the case may be. And .... there could be few families who so represented the extremes in the civil war in Yorkshire as the Parliamentarian Fairfaxes and the Royalist, Catholic Vavasours.

By the following spring, the Archbishop of York was finally ready to make his decision known to both parties and summoned both Pascal and Aurora, who attended with George and her brother Nathan, to hear his conclusion.

He declared that, in his judgement, the estate of Dionysus Vavasour (the grandfather) took precedence over that of Gervase (the father) and the entail was unbreakable. Vavasour Hall should, and would, descend to Stella, Benjamin's daughter.

However, the will of Gervase Vavasour was to make provision for his second son Pascal and, in the interest of fairness, the Archbishop decreed that the Vavasour Hall estate should pay a £200 per year annuity to support Pascal for the rest of his days.

George, who had suspected that this result was Pascal's motive all along in bringing the case, glanced over to see Pascal's reaction and immediately deduced that it was true. Pascal was grinning with satisfaction and, clearly, had known all along that there was never any realistic chance that the estate would be his, since his brother had been married with a daughter.

Aurora sat quietly, not wishing to give a reaction in front of the Archbishop but, as soon as she was alone with Nathan and George she gave vent to her feelings. 'I shall not pay it' she said. 'His father bled the estate dry during his lifetime in order to give Pascal as much money as he could. He already has a house and has received a substantial sum. He has a lot more money than I do' she fumed.

'There's no choice' said George softly. 'The Archbishop's decision is binding on both parties and we agreed that in advance.'

'He did what he thought was fair' added Nathan. 'And, that's not all, you must backdate it to the day Gervase died'.

'So, the wretched man has won then' she said with despair.

'Yes and no' said Nathan. 'Pascal, you might say has lost because his wish to have this estate taken away from you and given to him has failed. The courts, however, couldn't ignore the last will and testament of his father who clearly wanted his estate to go to Pascal in preference to Benjamin......'

'Yes' said George. 'So you see this is a compromise. Your right, and Stella's to occupy Vavasour Hall is now beyond question as I always thought it was, but Pascal too has a right to be taken care of as his father wished. It may not be to our liking but it's a reasonable compromise'.

'How much do I have to pay him?' she asked.

'Two hundred pounds a year' said Nathan. 'Father negotiated the figure, down I should say from a much higher initial sum as there was some argument about what the estate could fund. It's the same sum of money that was granted to you and Benjamin by Gervase Vavasour for your maintenance'.

'But I don't have that kind of money. That money was covered by loans on the estate, not from the estate income.' she said.

'We'll sort that out later' said George. 'I'll try to negotiate some sort of compromise with the court and, in any event, we'll appeal for extra time to pay'.

'But Benjamin left so many debts .....'

'One step at a time' said George reassuringly.

Aurora, in the face of both George and brother Nathan insisting the right thing had been done, found herself reconciling to the development.

'I just don't like the idea of him getting one over on me!' she said.

'He didn't' urged Nathan. 'And the case is now over and done with. Wortley will be pleased' added Nathan in a quiet aside to George.

'Yes, well. I should thank both of you.' said Aurora. 'I really don't know what I'd have done without your help, and father's. Actually I'm surprised he didn't join us here today, must have had something else to do that was more important.'

The business being completed, all three left York and made the return journey to Vavasour Hall. When they returned, however, they found Elizabeth in a flood of tears.

'I've just received some terrible news' she told them, holding a note in her trembling hand. 'Mother's dead!'

Chapter 28

The death of Isabella Fairfax was an unexpected shock which stunned them all. It was the first experience of real grief Aurora and her siblings had felt and was difficult to deal with. Next to the loss of a loved parent, the bad news of the annuity to Pascal paled into insignificance.

Accompanied by George, the three siblings Aurora, Elizabeth and Nathan set off a few hours later to make the journey to Tadcaster to see their father. He greeted them with sadness visibly etched on his face. Although their presence couldn't fill the void now left in Duke's life, they could at the very least fill the empty house and offer such comfort as their father might need.

When he was able to talk about it, which in good time he did, it emerged that Isabella had died from a dreadful asthmatic attack and, although it would have been comforting to say that she didn't suffer, it would also not have been entirely true. Because she did. The death was all the more shocking because it hadn't been anticipated. She wasn't an elderly relation who had reached the end of a full life and whose end was inevitable and so it was the lack of expectation that enhanced the shock. This was different; although Isabella had suffered a variety of minor ailments, of which her mild asthma was not thought the most serious. Yet it had taken her from them.

Once more Aurora, Elizabeth and Nathan found themselves required to attend a funeral service though this was the first when they had experienced tangible grief and distress. Funerals taking place in spring seem worse than at any time of year. At the very moment when buds are forming, hedgerows and trees are greening up and nature is bringing the earth back to life and preparing for a new growing season, a burial ... an ending ... seems to contrast so starkly with all that is beginning again.

Aurora's feelings at her mother's funeral put those at her husband's death, if she needed to compare them, into perspective. It was, she thought, so hard to see the person who brought you into the world, depart it.

The siblings and George stayed with Duke for some time afterwards but, within a few days, he began to talk of resuming work and needing to keep himself busy. With the good will of friends and neighbours and tender care of his children, little by little his faith in life began to be restored to him until, at last, there was a general feeling that it was time for them to depart and return home.

The contrast between the strain of losing her mother and Ben's complete disinterest when he lost his father was stark, and Aurora noted it with sadness.

Although Duke asked George about the outcome of Pascal's claim on Aurora's estate, George told him that the Archbishop was still making his decision. On the coach journey to Tadcaster, a decision had been made that now was not the right time to tell him what had actually happened in case it added to Duke's distress.

Once back at Vavasour Hall, to a place Aurora now considered her true home, and Stella's home, her own practical difficulties quickly resurfaced and began to crowd in on her. The money for Pascal's annuity had to be found as well as the back payments, the money to pay Benjamin's creditors had to be found, taxes, death duties and a whole range of other expenses had to be paid and there was insufficient funds to do so. And, all the while, there was that threat from Stanhope; his claim to have entered a bond with Benjamin which he would call in.

The only good news at this time was that Elizabeth's relationship with Captain Wadebridge was flourishing. Wadebridge was very different to William Knightley, Elizabeth's former fiancé. Like Aurora, it seemed that Elizabeth had chosen a less flamboyant partner the second time around. Both women, whether consciously or not, had chosen men of good standing, well respected, thoughtful and caring - in every respect the opposite of their first choices.

In Elizabeth's case the courtship was cut short by Wadebridge's return to sea but, on the eve of his departure, the couple had reached an understanding. On his return from tour of duty, they would make plans to marry.

For George and Aurora, their budding romance was blossoming but was then stymied by the urgent need to focus all their energies on keeping Vavasour Hall going, against the onslaught of difficulties.

One unusually dark morning in early June Aurora was sitting alone in the library next to a small fire and was listening to a fierce storm that had got up. Gusts of wind blowing down the chimney caused the fire to hiss and shrink, disturbing her reading. She rose from her chair and walked over to the window which was rattling in the gale. The rain, whipped up by the wind, thrashed into the panes making it difficult to see out.

The view from this particular window was usually her favourite in the house. It looked down to the serpentine lake and she found the view of water, with its ever changing landscape, soothing, but today it was barely visible. She felt safe and cosy to be indoors in such a storm.

She held in her hand a letter just arrived from Nathan and she was mulling over the words she'd just read when a noise from behind her took her attention. It was George entering the room.

'Stella's's upstairs playing in the nursery' said George. Then, on getting no response, he asked 'Is there anything the matter?'

'Well, yes, I think there is a problem, a new one ....' she said. 'Or perhaps I should say a continuation of an old one ...'

'Problems are my speciality ....' said George optimistically.

'One day, one will occur that you can't solve' she said smiling.

'Try me!' he said.

'Well, it's Nathan. I've just had a letter from him in London. It's about the position of Speaker in the Commons ....'

'Yes' he nodded.

'Well, he writes to tell me that he has been shortlisted for the post ...'

'Ahh, that's good news then, isn't it?' said George.

'He also writes to tell me that, whilst in London, he ran into our old friend Stanhope ... that worthless man again ... who seems to be most unhappy that Nathan is being considered....'

'I should have thought he would have been very happy about it' said George. 'After all if Nathan gets the job, he'll relinquish his seat at Yorkshire and Stanhope will be free to pursue it'.

'Yes, "if" the corporation want him, that is. In any case, Nathan and Stanhope had a confrontation in one of the London clubs and Nathan writes to tell me that Stanhope threatened to force me into bankruptcy .....'

'He threatened that before at Benjamin's funeral...' said George

'Yes he did, but now he thinks if he pursues it that will ruin Nathan's chances of becoming speaker. A speaker of the House of Commons whose sister is a bankrupt?'

'What does that man want?' said George exasperated. 'Does he want to be MP for York or not? Or, is it that he just wants to stop Nathan getting on?'

'I think the latter' said Aurora. 'For some reason he has an implacable hatred for Nathan and will stop at nothing to undermine him.'

'Well, he threatened to force your bankruptcy before Nathan was being considered for the post. Is he just going to keep using the same threat over and over again, every time something happens that he doesn't like. It's ridiculous.'

'But I don't want anything I do to harm Nathan' said Aurora plaintively.

'Yes I know' said George sympathetically. 'But this has got to stop. We cannot bow down to blackmail from Stanhope, because that is what it is' said George.

'You're right, of course' said Aurora. 'He's a wicked, wicked man and, if he'll probably pursue his bond whatever we do. Unless .... I wonder, does such a bond even exist?'

'Yes, I've seen a copy of it amongst Benjamin's papers, it does indeed exist.' nodded George.

'So what shall I tell Nathan?' asked Aurora.

'What does he say about it in his letter?

'That he would withdraw his candidacy if he thought it would stop Stanhope, but that he too thinks Stanhope would likely proceed anyway.'

'He doesn't know, does he, that Stanhope made the same threat at Benjamin's funeral'.

'No' said Aurora, 'I didn't tell him.'

'Well, there's your answer. Nathan knows that Stanhope is his perennial enemy and will use any and all means available to him. Then I think we should all brace ourselves for a bumpy ride. We should expect Stanhope will bring you to bankruptcy ... and ...

he will make sure that those deciding on Nathan's suitability for the post are made aware of it - thinking it will ruin his chances. He will do his worse no matter what we do. So, let him do it. Then ... he can go to the devil' said George.

Ethel Fledd

Chapter 29

Aurora wrote back to her brother urging him to pursue the post of Speaker at all costs. She told him that, with George's help, she was prepared for whatever Stanhope did next. In fact, it was George who helped Aurora draft the letter and it was carefully crafted to let Nathan know that there was a high probability that Aurora would be brought to bankruptcy anyway, even without Stanhope's intervention and that being the case, Stanhope's threats would make no difference. This was no exaggeration. The truth of the matter was, that the Vavasour estate had been deliberately sabotaged by Gervase. Aurora had inherited a problem that was impossible to solve, it was designed to be impossible to rectify. George had brought the estate back from the precipice of a cliff, but the debts run up voluntarily by Benjamin and deliberately by Gervase, had made it an impossible square to circle.

'He looks for a weak chink in the armour ...' George said of Stanhope. 'Not that you're weak ....' he added swiftly ... 'I only mean that the financial position that you have been forced into means you are vulnerable at present ...'

'And he's bound to take advantage .... 'isn't he?' said Aurora. 'I don't know how I shall cope with the shame of being declared bankrupt. Now they will certainly take the house ......'.

'No' said George firmly. 'That, they cannot now do. Only Stella can evict you from this house and .... I think she might be a tad young to do that at the moment', he said smiling. 'When she's 21, of course, that's a different matter. It will all be hers anyway. So, things will get tough .... really, really, difficult. There will be difficult creditors - who I shall deal with, control of money may be taken from us .... but I'll be with you, every step of the way. We'll get through this together!'

George gave Aurora a hug and they both seemed comforted by the conversation.

A few weeks later, during which every day had been thought as being "the" day when bankruptcy must be faced, there was simultaneous development on both counts: the speaker's post and the threatened bond.

Nathan wrote to tell them that he had been offered the post of Deputy Speaker. This news left everyone baffled as to whether Stanhope had managed to influence the selection or not. It was, of course, never going to be any easy task to discover if he had been instrumental in influencing anyone as such details would never have been divulged in any eventuality.

The person who was given the coveted post of first speaker was someone, Nathan freely acknowledged, whose connections were far more powerful than his and, since those connections were vital at this time to advancement, he seemed not too surprised that one of Wortley's Norfolk friends got the top job. Nathan was actually happy at his appointment, secure in the knowledge now that when the first post should become vacant in the future, he was extremely well placed to be considered.

Aurora and George, in the circumstances, felt reasonably satisfied that Stanhope had either failed to sufficiently influence the right people or that he had just been full of bluster. Perhaps too the Duchess of Buckingham had used her influence to secure him the post - it was impossible to know for sure. The outcome, nevertheless, satisfied Nathan.

From the timing of the next event, it was thought Stanhope had failed to influence the decision, because it was only after Nathan's appointment was published in the newspapers that Stanhope made his move.

So it happened then, that just a few days after it was learned that Nathan had been successful, a writ was served on Aurora for redemption of Stanhope's bond. This was, as Stanhope knew perfectly well, sufficient to push the Vavasour estate over the edge and into bankruptcy.

George examined the detail but no amount of close scrutiny could change the fact that the large bond of £5,000 couldn't be repaid. It was impossible.

The reality of Aurora facing bankruptcy over her deceased husband's estate had now began to dawn on them. It was real. Stanhope had done his worse and had played his ace card.

The only surprise had been his timing. He could have brought the action at any time but, thought George, he likely did so now when he heard that Nathan had been successful, at least in part, with a speaker's post.

Duke was consulted but the arithmetic wasn't in doubt. He concurred that the process, now started, would have to run its course and the only thing for Aurora to do was to get used to the idea of being declared a bankrupt, because it was now a reality. The only questions to be asked now were …. what would the courts do and how to mitigate the effects of whatever they did. Certain facts couldn't be altered though, that Aurora had a right to be at Vavasour Hall and that Stella was the legal heir. The courts would not expel the legal heir, an infant, and her guardian from the home they were legally entitled to inherit. Aurora was her mother and guardian, and they unquestionably had the highest claim to occupancy of the house and income from the estate.

George had now almost completely replaced Duke in directing Aurora's affairs, though her father did frequently visit and give his valuable legal advice to guide them.

One result of them having to constantly work through difficulties was that George and Aurora grew closer. Considering the perilous state of her finances and imminent bankruptcy, Aurora was impressed with George's steady, unshakable affection for her. He was like an anchor in a storm. It would have been so easy, she thought to herself, for him to walk away. Her circumstances were now desperate financially and there were many men who wouldn't have wanted to become involved at all in such a mess, but George took it all, took all things, in his stride.

The legal proceedings were a long, long saga running right through the winter months. Mainly they consisted of a frantic flurry of activity when the courts wanted information, followed by a long, very much longer, lulls of inactivity and waiting.

The idea of being declared bankrupt, a thought which had so horrified them initially, grew so familiar to them over the months that by the time the process came to its inevitable end, there was no longer any fear associated with it.

In other respects life continued unabated and, almost a year after they had first met, the long awaited wedding of her sister Elizabeth and Captain Wadebridge was fast approaching.

In order for the wedding to take place at the church on the Vavasour estate, which was where Elizabeth wanted it to be, the services of 'Gentle George' were once again required in order to smooth things over with the vicar. The vicar harboured a deep grudge against the Vavasour family and had only permitted the burials of Gervase and Benjamin at the church on condition that his curate oversaw the rituals. It was thought his influence was behind the burial plots being placed at the outer perimeter of the churchyard too. In an area almost obscured from view underneath some heavily overgrown weeping willows. Now Elizabeth wanted to be married there, George arranged to visit the vicar in person to see if he could persuade him to carry out the service himself.

The falling out between the squire's house and the vicar dated back to when Gervase Vavasour's wife Celine, had been alive. Equal to her husband in arrogance and impatience of others, she'd cruelly slandered the vicar, resulting in the two sides going to court. To everyone's surprise the vicar won the case, but since then there had been mutual hostility between those living at the 'big' house and the church.

The slander concerned allegations made by Celine, Benjamin's mother, who told the vicar's own curate, in front of a group of parishioners, that the vicar was a crook and a common thief who belonged in a circus. Most damning of all, she claimed that he pocketed the sacrament money; money that was given in charity for the use of the poor of the parish.

The young curate was completely shocked at this conversation. He, being entirely dependent on the patronage of the vicar, was fearful that such allegations would rub off on him too and he determined to intervene to settle the matter. His youth and inexperience in the ways of the world and the manner grand ladies had in expressing themselves, conspired to make an issue of what might, to a less impressionable mind, have been dismissed as nonsense.

The curate decided that he must tell the vicar directly what had been told and seek an explanation. Naturally, the vicar on hearing what was said responded with anger. He presented the young curate with a tally book showing the distribution of the sacrament money, just to satisfy the young man's curiosity and then his next step was to commence legal proceedings against the lady in question.

The slander was probably nothing more than unguarded comments deliberately exaggerated. In the way of gossips who are prone to demonize an unpopular 'target' to make their point abundantly clear. It makes a far greater impact on a listener to say a husband beat his wife senseless, as opposed to saying a husband gave his wife a good ticking off!

It seems, on this occasion, that the young curate took the comments he heard literally. And such comments from a leading family in the community against the vicar of their own patronage were unfortunate to say the least.

When the case did come to court it wasn't only found in the vicar's favour but he was awarded substantial damages. The several judges hearing the case felt such comments about the sacrament money were enormously damaging to a vicar of Christ and undermined his position with his congregation. They could potentially have turned the entire parish against the vicar and made it difficult for him to ever find employment again. The Vavasours were consequently forced to pay a hefty fine and, when they appealed against the damages, the result was that the damages were doubled.

The vicar had fared very well after the case. He had enough money to live on for the rest of his days and his success in the courts convinced his parishioners that he had been innocent all along. The vicar subsequently outlived nearly all the Vavasours, except for Pascal, and must privately have thought God was truly on his side!

George actually found the vicar very accommodating and friendly; perfectly willing to have a fresh start now that George and the Fairfaxes were at Vavasour Hall. It was a friendly and lengthy meeting at the end of which the vicar half jokingly asked if it was to be a double wedding; if George and Aurora might marry too. George smiled at the comment but, then wondered at it being a rather good idea.

Ethel Fledd

Chapter 30

Up to this point George hadn't considered *how* his living at Vavasour Hall might be looked on. Could it be seen as an impropriety in the neighbourhood? The thought made him uneasy. Whilst he had no desire to move away, indeed he couldn't think of separating himself from Aurora and the estate without some pain, what if he had unwittingly exposed Aurora to censure. It was essential to speak to her. If the issue was now of concern to him, then it might be a subject that had distressed Aurora without him realising.

After mulling the issue over for a few days, he spoke to Aurora. It was a quiet evening as Elizabeth was out with Captain Wadebridge and they'd just finished dinner,

'I went to see the vicar a couple of days ago ....' he started to say.

'Yes I know, you told me. It went well and Elizabeth is happy now. She wanted to be married there and have a reception here afterwards - which I couldn't be more pleased about.'

'Of course' continued George. 'But, he said something else that I've been thinking about ..... he suggested we make it a double wedding ....'

'Really?' said Aurora laughing. 'And what did you say to him?'

'Well that's the thing,' he said thoughtfully, 'has me living here caused a problem for you'?

'In what way?' she asked.

'Well, I just wondered if you'd been concerned ..... you know, about having an unmarried man living in your house .... it occurs to me that I may have unwittingly exposed you to vulgar comments .... I in no way want to cause a rupture to our happy arrangements here, but must know if it has been of concern to you.'

Aurora laughed, 'What? With me *and* my sister? *and* Stella; *and* Nurse. You might just as well say you've exposed Miss Nursey to vulgar comments! It's hardly just been you and me. Of course not. Besides, you're family. My sister Catherine is married to your brother.'

'Well, I wouldn't quite put it like that' he said with great meaning. 'Still ….. thank goodness for that' he sighed with relief, 'it suddenly occurred to me that I had been selfish and not considered your reputation.'

'Huh' said Aurora indignantly, 'I don't care tu'ppence for my reputation. Besides I don't think double weddings are a good idea - they seem to diminish both couples by forcing them to share their special day ....'

The couple exchanged smiles of intelligence. George, then sensed that though the idea of a double wedding wasn't welcome, that the idea of *a* wedding, of them marrying, might be thought of favourably. So he pursued the matter, 'so ….. it's got me thinking ….. that, well, may it's not such a bad idea ...'

'George Mason' Aurora said still laughing, 'if that was a marriage proposal it was the most pathetic one I've ever heard.'

He grinned broadly and took her hand, 'I won't go down on one knee' he said, 'but, you do know I love you....'

Aurora said the words that George hadn't quite got the temerity to say, 'George, will you marry me?' He looked shocked for a moment and then kissed her. It wasn't a big, dramatic moment as such times are for other couples. There was already a meeting of minds between them and, in truth, it felt like that they were already married. A simple ceremony was all that was needed to seal the circle.

The prospect of marrying George brought into the open some thoughts that had lain dormant in Aurora. Like a remembrance of a dream that is half forgotten on wakening, she was now free to allow herself to openly recall feelings he had stirred in her. It made her head swim a little. 'Had she *really* asked him' she thought to herself. It was of no matter, decorum and manners had been thrown to the wind, but that all seemed unnecessary with two people who were so intuitively connected.

Moments later, George, was still looking preoccupied. There was clearly still something else on his mind because instead of looking happy and joyous, as Aurora felt, he seemed intense.

'What?' asked Aurora plaintively.

'Elizabeth's wedding is .... what .... in a month's time? To take place here.'

'Yes' she nodded.

'Then I think we should be married before then. And away from here!'

'Why?' said Aurora looking puzzled. 'Though I am happy to marry you anywhere'.

'Well, you see .... it needs to be planned carefully. I probably need to speak to Duke about things.'

'You don't need my father's permission to marry me' said Aurora.

'No, it's not that' he continued. 'We can marry any time but you're going through bankruptcy proceedings at the moment.'

'So?'

'Well, if we marry now then I will be included in those proceedings. As your husband my name will take precedence in the writs and other legal documents .... and, I too would be declared bankrupt. Which, for myself I wouldn't mind, but the house I inherited from my parents, which your sister Catherine and my brother John live in, could be seized by the courts....'

'Oh I see. Should we wait till the end of the bankruptcy process then?' asked Aurora.

'No, I don't want to wait that long' he said. It was a casual comment which made Aurora smile.

'Then what are we to do?' she asked.

'Well, I will check with Duke, but I think we should get married over at Tadcaster. He will help with that. Then no one from Vavasour Hall need know about it. Not the servants, not Pascal, not the solicitors and not the courts'.

'Oh no .....' gasped Aurora. 'Not again!'

'What?' said George in surprise.

'My first marriage to Benjamin was a big secret for fear of upsetting his father. Now this one too must be?'

'Then we will have to wait for the bankruptcy process to end. I can't risk losing my property and rendering Catherine and John homeless!'

'No, of course you can't' said Aurora. 'And I don't want to wait that long anyway' she said. 'It's just a feeling of déjà vu. It'll pass!'

Ethel Fledd

Chapter 31

The arrangements were made and the wedding took place. George and Aurora were attended only by Elizabeth, Duke and young Stella and, as weddings go, it was as quiet as could be. There was fanfare, no peal of bells, no wedding supper and gathering of friends. It felt, however, to Aurora all the more solemn and memorable *because* it was without distraction, noise and the presence of people. Her eldest sister's wedding had, she thought, almost been spoiled by the intrusion of relations; where *their* welfare was worried about by the bride and groom; that *they* should have a good time and be happy. On this occasion they had only each other to worry about.

After the short ceremony, Duke was taken home and then they all returned to Vavasour Hall where plans for Elizabeth's wedding the next day were being finalised.

Aurora, having reluctantly removed her wedding ring, went through the process of preparing for Elizabeth's wedding with delight. It was as if, though Elizabeth's big day, it was in some way George and Aurora's too. It was a wedding celebration that involved them all and they got to enjoy the formalities of Elizabeth's event 'almost' as if it was theirs too. Every word the vicar said to the couple was *felt* by George and Aurora as also referring to them. And George found it difficult to resist the impulse to 'kiss the bride' at the appropriate time. Instead just gazed at Aurora, a gaze which said and promised 'later' our time will come.

A reception after the ceremony being at Aurora's home was, like at the church, equally enjoyed by both couples and all marvelled at the splendour of Vavasour Hall which hadn't seen such merriment for decades.

Needless to say Pascal received no invitation to the event and it all passed off with everyone in good humour. Immediately after the wedding party was over, Elizabeth and Captain Wadebridge left for the West Indies where Wadebridge was to be stationed for a six month tour of duty.

Alas, there was no romantic or exotic honeymoon for George and Aurora. Her second marriage was so completely different to her first that Aurora began to wonder if everyone *really* went through the same thing when they married. How could the experience vary so markedly, she thought. With George, it felt like a blissful contentment, the likes of which she'd never experienced for one moment during the whole time she knew Benjamin. His 'gentleness' had the power to quieten her mind and make troubles float away. This wasn't just because of the new intimacy between them, it was more to do with his temperament - the same temperament she'd, a few years earlier, thought so repellent, turned out to be the making of her.

Their early married days were a continuation of the processing of endless court papers and managing the estate. There was a constant flow of information, messengers (of which Gentle George was the busiest), letters of instruction from her father, correspondence from other solicitors and courts and a great deal of work in order to comply with the court's requests for information. Filing claims, digging through boxes for indentures, deeds and mortgages and such like consumed much time.

Proceedings were long and protracted and dragged on month after month, and, for most of that time Aurora was convinced it could mean them losing Vavasour Hall. Yet the knowledge that daughter Stella was the heir to the estate reminded her why she must continue the process.

The six months of Elizabeth's absence flew by in a busy blur for Aurora, such was her happiness with George. Even the distressing thought of bankruptcy didn't penetrate the marital contentment. It had been going on for so long now, it felt like 'old news'. It was merely another step in the marathon business of salvaging the estate from the mess left by Gervase.

Elizabeth, who had now returned from the West Indies, returned to Vavasour Hall, and lived there much as she did before she was married. With her new husband away so much at sea, it was thought better for her to stay there in his absence. Captain Wadebridge returned for a few days when he could and spent all of his leave time there. They would, they said, at some point take up a separate residence - perhaps when Wadebridge left the navy or reached retirement. In the meantime Elizabeth had no desire to be living alone.   Finally, the day came when the bankruptcy order was official. It was a hardship which had to be borne as it was a fait accompli. Indeed it had taken so long to go through the process that when notices were published in The Gazette that the Vavasours were bankrupt, young Stella had just celebrated her fifth birthday.

Ethel Fledd

Chapter 32

Post-bankruptcy, the courts eventually decided, as expected, that Aurora could remain at Vavasour Hall as Stella's mother and legal guardian ensuring her welfare and that she would be allowed to sell one of the small manors on the estate in order to clear the debts and, whatever was left over, would be for Stella's benefit.

George had prompted Aurora to suggest this course of action to the courts during the bankruptcy process as her first husband's will, which made specific reference to his debts, made provision for this.

After the long process of identifying and surveying the particular acres and properties that were to be sold, the day at last arrived when all was ready to seek a buyer.

A prospective purchaser appeared through the enquiries of William Severn, who had originally been appointed as solicitor representing Stella's interests. He had visited the numerous coffee houses in the district and posted notices in them all about the sale of the manor and all was proceeding well until the buyer unexpectedly withdrew from the sale at the eleventh hour. It really was the eleventh hour too and almost to the last second of the sale when the devastating news came through. Even the courts had been advised of the imminent sale, as they were overseeing the estate since the bankruptcy.

Then, quite unexpectedly, William Severn thought of purchasing the manor for himself, that he would buy it with his life savings and use one of the properties on it for his family residence. He suggested the idea to Aurora who readily agreed. The fall through of the previous sale had left everyone feeling that "anyone" buying the manor would be better than no one.

Still, and for as long as the protracted bankruptcy process went on, Aurora concealed her status as a married woman, rather than as a widow. As a married woman, in eighteenth century England at that time, she could conduct no business on her own, only her husband could. A widowed woman of course was entirely free to manage her own affairs as she had to, but not a married one. And

Aurora had successfully kept George's name detached from the various court cases that were still running for a considerable time.

So the deception continued and George being ever present at Vavasour Hall was explained away by his role in running the family's affairs. He was, after all, a family relation and what could be more natural for him to assist the ladies at the hall. William Severn, of course, was completely ignorant of Aurora's changed status. He had only ever dealt with her throughout their business dealings which stretched over many months and, at long last, the sale to him of the manor moved to completion.

It went through. Although not realising the ideal hoped for amount, the sale did enable Aurora to clear the estate of mortgages and all other debts. Creditors were paid and there was even something left over which was to be held over for Stella's use when she was older. The courts too withheld some of the funds, a surety against any future creditors who might emerge. At long, long last the stressful financial burden that she'd inherited from her dissolute husband and his vengeful father, was lifted and the estate was, not only working well, but the income from tenant farmers and property owners was sufficient to support Vavasour Hall. The Vavasour estate was now in a position to be discharged from bankruptcy.

Then somehow ..... somewhere ..... someone leaked news of George and Aurora being married to William Severn. Whilst being tempted to put the blame at Pascal or Stanhope's doors - given their past animosity to the Fairfaxes - on this occasion they couldn't trace the informant. And once Severn knew the situation, they were too busy trying to assuage him to really care how the information had come out.

As Severn had already handed over his money and the transaction was completed, the fact that he had discovered their marriage seemed too late to do them any harm, but for Severn the validity of the sale now called his ownership of his home into question and he was incandescent with rage.

Arriving unannounced at Vavasour Hall one day, he challenged George who, since the revelation of Aurora's new status, was now the only person he could do business with.

'Whilst I understand your reasons, I am desolate that you have put my family's financial future in doubt,' he pleaded. 'As your wife was married at the time of our conveyance, nothing in law can pass between us that was without your knowledge and, that being in writing.'

Severn was facing a large fine to rectify the problem, if indeed it could be rectified and, in sheer exasperation, said to George, 'I cannot suffer such supine indolence to render me silent' which words, for a lawyer, were as strong as his tightly disciplined mind would allow him to utter.

'I truly understand' said George , 'but what are we to do?'

Severn went away unhappy and, as time wore on, the placid nature of 'Gentle' George wore thin on him. He pleaded for help but George, either deliberately, or otherwise placated him whilst assuring him that he would do everything to help him, yet failed to give Severn any documentation that would satisfy him.

Eventually Severn, in sheer desperation, threatened to take Aurora and George to court to strengthen his title and it was only then that George was prompted into action and a way was found to regularize the situation.

Once the sale of the nearby manor had gone through and Severn had been given documents to placate him, that was more or less the end of Aurora's legal difficulties. She had, with help from George and her family, retained Vavasour Hall, put her finances back in order and paved the way for her daughter to have a clear and free inheritance. The claims of Jolson and Taylor had likewise been settled though they were disappointed that their claim for the entire personal estate failed. Only Jolson lived long enough to receive any benefit from his claim and he received but a small portion of what he believed himself owed.

It was only with the end of the legal trials and tribulations that George and Aurora began peaceably living at Vavasour Hall with long visits from Elizabeth and Captain Wadebridge and their growing family, as Elizabeth had given birth to a son. These were to be the happiest and the most peaceful years that Aurora was to know.

Peaceful, that is in terms of the absence of litigation, though increasingly fraught from a new and unexpected quarter.

Chapter 33

Throughout their marriage, as the years moved on, George and Aurora grew even closer than they'd been before. Theirs was a union that went beyond the physical, to the spiritual. Often times they could almost read each other's thoughts before they became words - a mere flinch of an eye movement or a shadow of an expression was enough to tell the other what feelings were about to be formed. It was as if they were one, in every way. George was her other self.

Thus they lived contentedly through the next fifteen years. They were good years which saw the Masons of Vavasour Hall, with Aurora's daughter Stella, enjoy freedom from money worries, freedom from law suits .... but not quite freedom from all strife. There was one among them who was set to disturb the harmony. Young Stella, who now had become a young woman, was as far from being settled and content as her parents were as it's possible for anyone to be.

Stella, the heiress of Vavasour Hall grew into a difficult teenager. It didn't happen overnight; the petulance of a child, which had seemed amusing when she was younger, remained with her into adolescence when her ability to express herself sharply increased but ..... she was no longer amusing.

'She'll grow out of it' George would say, 'and we shall have to be patient'.

But a procession of governesses through the years had been unable to curb the child's aggression or mould her character into a pleasing disposition. Stella was constantly hostile to her mother, who had been Mrs Mason for as long as she could remember and George - the only father she'd known.

Quite why Stella turned out to be such a difficult child was unfathomable to Aurora; Stella had been shielded from knowledge of her real father's dissolute lifestyle and had been treated with absolute kindness by George. Yet it was perhaps the fact that she hadn't known her father that led to her imagination creating an heroic image of him which was very wide of the mark. Though too young to be aware of her father's death at the time, Stella later became tormented by thoughts of his death, seeming to think that her mother had been the cause of it and, at the same time, it seemed to invoke in her a dread of the future.

She sought out people who'd known her father, usually tenants on the estate who, mindful of their precarious position as tenants, told her nothing but kind things about him. She thus managed to reinforce her own thoughts about her father and could favourably re-write his life's story in her mind.

Stella believed her father was everything that George was not; which in a way was true. But she had a misguided view of what her father had been. In her imagination she'd built him up into a hero and, against that standard, everyone else failed. George had taken his place. George shouldn't be there.

The only way George could rationalize Stella's challenging behaviour was to see it in terms of her inheritance and the power it gave her. Whilst ever Stella had been too young to know she was an heiress there had been no difficulties, it was only later when that realization dawned on her that she began to be affected by it.

Perhaps it was to be expected that a young woman's head could be so turned. Many who are exposed to power find it enchanting, especially if that power gives them control over other people. It can be hard for mature people to deal with, let alone a teenager. Stella tried to wield that power as a weapon, in the full knowledge that she could do so with impunity. That same arrogance that her father had acquired on becoming master of Vavasour Hall, springing from the knowledge that the parents were powerless to prevent inheritance, was visited on Stella. She became unruly and ungovernable.

Stella knew full well that her place at Vavasour Hall was cast iron secure but, at the same time, came to realise that George's position was not, indeed even her own mother's situation was vulnerable and that they only held the hall by virtue of being her guardians. George, in particular, Stella saw as the weakest of all, that he was only there by virtue of having married her mother. If anything happened to her mother, George had no power to remain there. She not only knew it but made sure George felt it.

At one point an attempt was made to send Stella to stay with another family; this was a common practice among large, wealthy households at the time and was seen as a way of encouraging social skills in young adults and, of course, introducing them to a different circle of friends. It could even be a way of finding husbands for woman of the right age and Stella, at almost 18, was now approaching the right age to be seeking a husband.

All attempts to place Stella out, however, had failed as she'd point blank refused to leave Vavasour Hall. She bitterly argued with her mother, saying that she and George were only there as her guardians and that if they sent her away then they gave up their own right to live there.

Seeing this approach was failing, George and Aurora tried a different tactic and began taking Stella with them to York for the Assemblies. A husband must be found quickly to take on the burden! This course of action entirely met with Stella's approval and she eagerly awaited the next visit as soon as the previous one was over.

George, Aurora and Elizabeth, who frequently attended with them, all conspired to get Stella introduced to suitable young men at the dances and, though none entirely met with Stella's approval, they were hopeful that the right one would be found .... eventually.

Chapter 34

Week after week, the journey to York was undertaken and Stella seemed to blossom in the new society she was immersed in. Friendships formed with girls of her own age too, which Aurora encouraged.

Over a period of months Stella became more involved in the lives of her friends and asked to spend more time with them. As George and Aurora already knew the families of the girls she associated with, they happily agreed to Stella staying in town on occasional nights where her particular friend Anne Waterhouse's family had a town house.

This then was how it began. Parents with the best of motives for a daughter; though, yes, for their own peace of mind too. Stella being socialized into society under Aurora's watchful eye. All that was needed was for the right man to come along, for Stella to fall in love with him and all would be well.

For a few lucky people their lives go exactly to plan; for many others their lives go roughly to plan; but there always has, and always will be, a great many people who either do not have a plan or find it impossible to keep to one. Stella was destined to defy any and every plan anyone ever had for her. Those who are wilful are remarkably tenacious at resisting any attempts to direct them. Especially if that direction is intended for their own good.

The first hint that something was amiss about Stella came from Nathaniel who, on a visit to Vavasour Hall to see his sister and brother-in-law mentioned something that had been brought to his attention. On a visit to the Burgesses Hall, he had called in at the Crown & Anchor Inn and saw Mr Wentworth the owner.

'I know him' said Aurora, 'he helped us on the night Stanhope's men were spoiling for a fight'.

'Yes', said Nathan. 'That's the thing, you see. Wentworth told me that Charles Stanhope came to his hostelry a few days ago and that he was in company with a young woman. Apparently she was half his age....'

'I don't think Stanhope's married is he?' said George.

'No' said Nathan. 'Not to my knowledge. Anyway, the reason I mention it is because, though Wentworth couldn't be absolutely sure, but he seemed to think that the young woman might have been Stella.'

'What?' said Aurora in disbelief. 'That's impossible'.

'Is it?' said George. 'Can he be certain it was Stella?'

'No I don't think he can' said Nathan. 'He seemed to think it was her, but I said it couldn't possibly be. What would Stella be doing out on her own, with him of all people, in the centre of York? It doesn't make sense.'

'When *exactly* was this' asked George frowning.

'Could it have been her? Just let me think now, I saw Wentworth in York last Tuesday night and he said Stanhope came into the inn I think on the previous Friday or Saturday .... yes, I'm sure that's right.'

Aurora looked at George. It was a knowing look. It was a worried look. 'Yes, she was staying at Anne's last weekend' said Aurora, 'Stella has a friend in town. We know the parents quite well and she's been staying with them some weekends.'

'I can't believe they would let Stella out alone, in the company of a man twice her age, without an escort, without our knowledge! No' said George. 'Let's hope we're mistaken.'

'I'll have to speak to Stella' said Aurora.

'And say what?' said George. 'This needs handling delicately. What if we're wrong. It might be totally innocent and we risk aggravating Stella for nothing.'

'What should we do then?' said Aurora, 'go and see Anne's parents?'

'If you like I could do that' said Nathan. 'I'm on my way back to York right now.'

'I'm coming with you' said Aurora determinedly. 'George, please, would you mind keeping an eye on Stella while we're out. Don't let her leave the house till I return'.

With that, Nathan and Aurora left Vavasour Hall and headed for York. During the journey they planned what they were going to say and arrived at the Waterhouse residence just before dark.

They were greeted with civility from Mrs Waterhouse and Aurora was full of apologies.

'We're sorry to drop in unannounced, my dear Mrs Waterhouse, I think you know my brother Nathan?'

'Yes of course, hello Nathan, both of you come in and sit down' said Mrs Waterhouse beckoning them over to the fire in her drawing room. 'This is an unexpected pleasure'.

"Well we were in town and I thought we really should drop by, just for a very short few minutes, to thank you for taking such good care of Stella.'

'Ohh, that's no problem at all. She's good company for Anne and the two of them get on so well.'

'I'm glad to hear it. It's good for young people to spend time together. But .... I wonder, don't they get under your feet being here all the time? What do they do with themselves? They must wear you out?'

'Not at all I can assure you.' She said. 'When Stella first came to stay with us at the odd weekend the two girls would spend hour after hour in Anne's room. Heaven knows what they find to gossip about, but they do you know.'

'And ..... they never leave the house?' Aurora asked gingerly.

'Well, of late, I've allowed them to visit Dorothy Carter's daughters, just round the corner from here on Sandy Lane. They are all such great friends, and I don't see there's any harm in it.'

'No, of course not.' Said Aurora. 'Still .... I think it's a great imposition on you. Perhaps we could return the favour by inviting Anne to visit us at Vavasour Hall this weekend. Then we can return the hospitality?'

'Oh you're very kind. I will give Anne the good news.'

'We'll send the carriage for her'.

With that, Stella and Nathan left the Waterhouse residence and climbed back into their carriage.

'That should, at least' said Aurora, 'give me some time to think'.

'Do you think it was Stella then?' asked Nathan.

'I do', said Aurora glumly. 'Those young girls are covering for each other. Stella is using the movement from one house to another to cover her absence.'

'Which her friend Anne must know all about', said Nathan.

'Let's get them away from York this weekend then, 'said Aurora, 'and see if we can nip this in the bud.'

'But why Stanhope?' puzzled Nathan. 'The man's old enough to be her father. What do you think's going on there? '

'I don't know' said Aurora. 'But, if you think about it, Charles Stanhope is the one person, probably the only person, in the world who thought well of Benjamin. He could impress Stella with stories of her father that no one else can. She's so young, so impressionable. We all know that opinions can be caught like the common cold. One of her friends remarks how handsome Stanhope is, and that then becomes Stella's opinion. He tells her how wonderful her father was, that reinforces Stella's opinion and so on ... oh God, I wonder what stories he's told her about us? It would be so easy to turn her head, if he'd had a mind to.'

'But more?' he said, 'do you think they could be having a relationship?'

'I hope not' said Aurora emphatically, 'there certainly haven't been opportunities for them to spend that much time together. I wonder, would Stanhope stoop that low to injure the Fairfaxes?'

'He certainly would' said Nathan.

'I recall he once stood over Stella's cot, and called her a 'Filthy, filthy Fairfax'. Though he was roaring drunk at the time and probably doesn't remember. But I certainly do.'

They continued the journey back to Vavasour Hall where Aurora left the coach and Nathan set off back to York. George was given the details and agreed on the course of action Aurora had set in place.

Stella was given the news that Anne Waterhouse was visiting her at the weekend but seemed seriously displeased at the prospect. She complained bitterly that there was nothing for them to do at Vavasour Hall and that she was far better off going to York, but to no avail, Aurora made it clear to her that there would be no deviation in the plan.

The weekend came and went and poor Anne Waterhouse looked miserable for most of the time. Though the same age as Stella, Anne was younger in maturity and it was her youth that had been taken of advantage of to engineer Stella's time away from the Waterhouse family. Stella, with a face like thunder, seemed to want nothing to do with the young girl and when the time came for Anne to leave, she looked visibly relieved.

Chapter 35

Now Aurora really was alarmed. Yes, she'd outflanked her daughter but only for one weekend. Should she directly challenge Stella, or hope that she would forget Stanhope - if indeed there was a relationship in bud there.

She chose, after talking to George, the latter option. Excuses were made for the family not going to York during the course of the next week: the roads were impassable, the assemblies had been cancelled and even a cholera outbreak. As time went on it became difficult to think of new excuses but, by such means, Stella was prevented from going to town for almost two months during which time her moods darkened, there were fits of extreme temper and she was impossible to live with.

At one point George, who was having the greatest difficulty dealing with Stella, told Aurora that he wished Stanhope *would* take her off their hands, so that they may have some peace. George was nearing the end of his tether and Aurora found herself, unusually, adopting the role of peacemaker in the house. It was a position she didn't like to be in.

'I have seen plenty of parents who, after producing children, then go on to despise them, but I never thought myself capable of being one of them' she told George.

'Well ... look at Gervase Vavasour' he said, 'and his behaviour to Benjamin, his eldest son. He acted as if he hated him. It does happen.'

'But I feel as if it shouldn't. I feel I have failed as a mother if I cannot love my own daughter, my own flesh and blood'.

'That is no failing on your part' said George sympathetically, 'Stella's own character makes her hard to love. If she cannot garner her own mother's love, then I fear she'll go through life finding it hard to find anyone willingly caring for her.'

'But still, I blame myself ....'

'No' said George. 'These years of difficulty we've had with her she's been a minor and under our protection. All the difficulties we have gone through, all the endless legal battles, all

191

the hardship and struggles we've endured, it's all for her benefit because all of this estate will be hers one day. That's why I find her disrespect to you so hard to endure. I don't much care if she disrespects me. Perhaps as her step-father I should expect as much. But I cannot abide her being rude to you. Which she is.'

'I hope' said Aurora, 'she'll be better behaved tomorrow because Elizabeth is coming to stay for a few days.'

'Elizabeth knows full well what Stella is like and won't be moved by her tantrums' said George.

'Yes but these last two months she's got much, much worse. I wonder if we can keep her from going to York much longer.'

'We can take her to York' said George 'for the next Assembly. But she'll go with us straight there, when we take Elizabeth at the weekend, and she'll come straight back home again'.

Aurora told Stella that they were all going to York at the weekend when Aunt Elizabeth visits and the news lifted her spirits straight away. Stella spent hour after hour in her room readying herself for the night out, though was angry when her pleas to stay in town with Anne Waterhouse were rejected. Still her excitement at the visit made her so happy and sociable that Aurora began to think she'd been wrong to hold her back from being in town.

Elizabeth, now with a growing family of her own, had left Captain Wadebridge and her children at Vavasour Hall to join Aurora, George and Stella for the night out. Inside the Assembly Rooms the three adults enjoyed the evening, whilst keeping Stella under a loose surveillance while she talked to friends and had the occasional dance.

Then, without warning, George shot to his feet and drew their attention to the dance floor where Stella was smiling flirtatiously at her dance partner, Charles Stanhope.

'Well if we were in any doubts about the rumour of Stella meeting up with Charles Stanhope, this is the proof. This is retaliation for us not bringing her here for so long. The girl has no shame.' said George.

'She knows full well that the mere mention of the Stanhope name is likely to infuriate you .....'' said Elizabeth. 'It's an act of defiance.'

'Yes, but she refuses to grow out of this phase she's going through' said Aurora. 'It really is too much'.

'They're only dancing' said Elizabeth. 'Goodness they make an odd couple; he's absolutely murdering this waltz. .....Look, look' she said excitedly, 'he's just trod on Mrs Waterhouse's gown. Bet he's torn it! What a booby!' Then turning to Elizabeth, said 'Stella probably doesn't even know who he is'.

'She knows exactly what she's doing' said George, 'and she knows exactly who he is'.

'Well,' said Elizabeth 'I shouldn't let her see she's disconcerted you George. Sit down. That's probably the plan. I should defy her expectations completely and invite her to bring her partner over to join us'.

'Hah' laughed Aurora. 'Now she wouldn't be expecting that!'

'No ..... she wouldn't' said George thoughtfully.

Moments later Stella returned to the group looking triumphant and cast a side look from face to face. Elizabeth had been right, she was expecting to have caused a fuss and was surprised by the absence of one.

'I think you should bring your friend over to meet us' said George to Stella casually.

'Oh?' she said puzzled. 'I ... er .... well' we'll see ....' she said mumbling.

Aurora smiled to herself and made a mental note that Stella could be wrong-footed by unexpected behaviour.

Chapter 36

As the evening came to an end and the assembly began to break up, the guests walked back to their coaches and the Fairfaxes came face to face with Anne Waterhouse and her family. Aurora greeted them all warmly but Stella made a particular point of cold-shouldering Anne which left the adults in the group feeling slightly uncomfortable, so the greetings were cut short. George and Aurora gave each other a knowing look of intelligence and a few minutes later they were leaving York heading for home. In the coach Aurora told Stella 'We called in to see Mrs Waterhouse a while back'.

'Oh?' said Stella in an uninterested tone.

'Yes we did. She told us all about you visiting Dorothy Carter's daughters.'

Stella stared ahead, struck dumb, as if waiting on tenterhooks for the next words. 'Yes, we'll be sure to pay them a visit soon' said George, giving Stella a knowing look.

That brief conversation and meaningful look was all that was needed for Stella to know that her secret assignations had been discovered. She felt a blush of consciousness tinge her cheeks but made no reaction to this revelation and continued the journey, listless, knowing that the slightest conversation on this subject would bring the matter into full scrutiny. It then took a few minutes for her thoughts to catch up with events. 'No wonder' she thought, 'they were not surprised at me dancing with Stanhope, they already knew!'

The following day the peace of Vavasour Hall was utterly shattered when Stella's reaction to her uncovered subterfuge became evident. At some point during the day, though no one could tell precisely when it was, Stella had left the house. When she failed to appear for dinner, Aurora went to her room and found an envelope on the clock on the mantelpiece addressed to her. She noticed the fire in the room was cold, as if the room hadn't been occupied for a considerable time. She read the note which said:
Dear Mama,

I am gone to stay with grandpa at Tadcaster for a few days. A friend is taking me, and you are not to worry. I was in such a rush to catch the ride, that I hadn't time to tell you. Stella
PS: I will write again

Aurora read the letter through twice and, now with heavy laboured breathing, felt a surge of panic overwhelm her. She took the letter straight to George.

'What a letter to write! What can it mean?' she said distraught. 'Who is she gone with? When did she go? I must ask Elizabeth if she knows anything.'

George was about to speak but checked himself just in time, knowing what he was thinking would alarm Aurora even more. 'This cannot be right' he thought to himself. 'Duke is in London, he isn't even at Tadcaster'.

'She'd the presence of mind to leave you a note' he said, trying to calm Aurora. 'And she's gone with a friend .... we'll just have to find out which of her friends is missing. We'll find her. We know how thoughtless and inconsiderate she can be ..... and this is a fine example of both.'

'Oh God' said Aurora in desperation. 'Where *has* she gone?'

'If she's gone to see your father, then he'll take care of her' he urged.

There followed several hours of stress as enquiries were made of everyone within the house or nearby but not one single clue could be found as to where she'd gone. George took the carriage and sped off to York to see if any of Stella's friends there knew of her whereabouts and, finding no information from them, made a long return journey via Tadcaster, just in case Stella might be there. He thought she may have made the journey, not realising that her grandfather was away at London. On arrival at Tadcaster, however, he could find no sign of her. Messages were left with neighbours to look out for her and to take her in if she turned up and get a message to Vavasour Hall.

All to no avail. There was not a sighting of her anywhere. Then, as darkness grew, and Aurora grew more and more worried, a search was made of Stella's room where it was discovered that certain items had been taken. A bag, a few clothes and toiletries were deemed to be missing. It hadn't been as hasty a departure as they'd been led to believe!

The two sisters were alone in Stella's room and were talking,

'I saw nothing' said Elizabeth 'not one clue that she might take off like this.'

'Unless ....' said Aurora thoughtfully, 'do you think her dancing with Stanhope last night has anything to do with it?'

'I don't see how' said Elizabeth. 'I'm sure that was just an act of defiance. She was trying to be provocative.....'

'But *why* does she feel the need to do these things?'

'Why do any of us do stupid things when we're young. It's part of being young. She's a young woman, but she's also a child too. She's in no-man's land at the moment.'

'I wonder .....' said Aurora. 'Is she keeping secrets from us?'

'Well' said Elizabeth smiling 'she wouldn't be a normal 20 year old if she *didn't* have secrets would she?'

'No ......' said Aurora, remembering very clearly her own secrets at age 22. 'If you recall, I kept a big secret from my family years ago.'

'Yes' said Elizabeth smiling, 'I do remember very well. But, no .... don't go thinking the worse, the note only said she'd gone to her grandfather's.'

'We've all done it though, haven't we Elizabeth! We've fallen for the wrong sort of men in our first loves. I certainly did it, you too.'

'Yes .... The more unsuitable they are, the more dangerous, the more attractive they seem. It's all mother nature's fault .....'

'Is it?' said Aurora, 'or is it just mothers ..... mothers and poets all tells us there can never be anything as sweet as that first love. We're told ..... "love is not love which alters when it alteration finds .... it is the star to every wand'ring bark" ..... we're encouraged to think there is only one, only one right person, destined to be our soul mate and that we can never love the same way twice .....'

'No, I don't think you do love all people in exactly the same way; for me the second relationship is far superior to the first. All nonsense, isn't it' said Elizabeth. 'It's all designed to keep us tied to the first person that comes along.

'I wonder .... if she kept a diary?' said Aurora as she rummaged through drawers in search, before announcing 'no, there's nothing'. There was nothing else in the room which told them anything further and they stayed until it was felt that everywhere had been checked.

All enquiries they made drew a blank on where she may have gone. Aurora didn't sleep that night, she couldn't put her head on a pillow to sleep without knowing that her daughter was safe and so she paced back and forth, hour after hour, worrying and distressed but feeling powerless to do anything.

The coming of morning made no difference to the situation. Still there was no news of her and both George and Elizabeth tried everything in their power to calm Aurora down. At one point they'd to physically prevent her from leaving the house as she was intent on scouring the countryside, convinced her daughter was lying in a ditch with no one to care for her.

And so the angst and fear continued, day after day until, at long, long last a letter arrived from Stella.

'At least we know she's still alive' said George pragmatically. 'Let's hope the contents make things intelligible and excusable which, at present, defy all understanding.'

'Where is she and what does she say'? said Elizabeth, who'd extended her stay due to the crisis.

'... She's in ..... London!'

'London?' said George astonished. 'How did she get there? Is she with Duke?'

'Oh no ..... no ..... no such luck. She's .... she's .... oh God, she's married!'

'What?' cried Elizabeth.

'She got married a few days ago at the Fleet.

'Stupid, stupid girl' said George. 'Who did she marry?'

'I don't know' said Aurora breathlessly, 'Oh ... here it is .... she signs herself ..... Mrs ..... Charles Stanhope'.

The name was met with universal grief and silence. 'Stanhope, of all people' said George sadly, in disbelief.

'You don't think .....' said Elizabeth trembling .... 'that he forced her to marry him ... that he *kidnapped* her!'

'No I don't,' said George, 'I regret to say that Stella probably believed she knew exactly what she was doing. It was planned ..... she had time to take some belongings. Besides, there was nothing in the note she left that suggested any sort of coercion. Quite the contrary.'

'I don't understand' said Aurora, 'I thought I knew my daughter until lately. I never thought she would do something like this. How could she hate us so much that she has done this deliberately? Where has it come from. What could have overcome her powers of judgement so as to forget herself?'

'What else does she say' asked Elizabeth, 'anything else?'

'That she will be "visiting" us in a few days time.' Note that, "visiting" us?

'Well she can hardly walk back into this house and expect to reside here with an unwelcome husband in tow can she?' said George in some sarcasm.

'I wouldn't put anything past that little minx' said Elizabeth.

'She's probably coming back for her things' said George 'and, if she doesn't apologise to you Aurora for all the stress she's caused, then I will have nothing more to do with her. She has no right to treat us this way.'

'I don't know' said Aurora fighting back the tears 'what will happen, but at least I know she's alive and well. For days I had feared something terrible had happened to her. You see, it's my job as her mother to protect her.'

Unknown to Aurora, George and Elizabeth flashed a glance of disbelief at each other.

'She doesn't deserve you' said George. 'Truly, I sincerely mean it. It's all one way. *You* do the caring, *you* do the worrying, *you* provide for her and she...... just *takes* ..... with no gratitude'.

'She's coming home soon' said Aurora with relief. 'We may not like what she's done but at least no harm has come to her'.

'A Fleet marriage? George, really!' said Elizabeth when Aurora had moved out of earshot. 'Hardly an auspicious start to your married life.'

'That great gangling creature's too old for her' replied George. 'Has she done this just to aggravate us? What a troubled soul that girl has. I don't understand how someone can turn out so wicked when they've come from a kind, loving home. We've bred a viper in our midst! I've never seen Aurora do anything to Stella except be kind and this is how she's repaid. Perhaps we've been too kind, too generous with her. I'm not her real father and so have never felt able to discipline her too well, for fear of upsetting Aurora. Maybe that's what we've done wrong, a good beating may have done Stella some good. But this .... to run off and marry a man twice her age, just to spite us? I confess I do not understand'.

'Could it possibly be real love?' said Elizabeth.

'If it is, then the next thing I'm ready to believe is that mules can fly!' said George. 'Everything Stanhope does is aimed at damaging the Fairfax family, Stella is just another toy to play with and she's too damned foolish to realise his game. It's incredible. I find it amazing the lengths people will go to in their hatred of others. I don't think, thank goodness, that I've ever experienced that level of hatred, I've known quite a few people that I've disliked but never to the point that it's taken over my life. People like Gervase Vavasour and Charles Stanhope I truly believe have a touch of madness about them.'

'Do you think she'll bring Stanhope with her. Stella, when she comes here?' asked Elizabeth.

'Huh' said George gruffly, 'she's stupid enough to do just that...... yes, the letter said "we'll" be visiting .....'

'So ......' said Elizabeth grinning with mischief, 'why don't you force matters into the open?'

'How so?'

'By getting Nathan here!' Elizabeth said furtively. 'Stella has proved herself aggressive, yes, petulant, yes. And, she thinks she knows exactly how you and Aurora will respond in any given situation.'

'Yes .....?' agreed George.

'So. It's Nathan that's behind Stanhope's hatred, let's bring them face to face.'

'That's a bit risky' said George. 'This is Aurora and her daughter we're talking about. I don't want Aurora hurt'.

'And her daughter being married to Stanhope isn't hurting?' she said. 'I think it's worth bringing Nathan here. It could flush Stanhope's real motives out. If he's been playing at being a doting, loving husband then Stella seeing him here, with a room full of Fairfaxes, might be an epiphany. She needs to know the Stanhope that we all know, not what he's flattered her into believing he is. Let's open her eyes to him because we know he won't be able to maintain the façade of a besotted and loving husband for long ....'

'Would Nathan want to get involved?' asked George. 'He has recently married and is beginning a new life. He holds an important position in government now and may not want to do anything that might jeopardise that'.

'Oh yes he will want to be here, he knows Stanhope better than all of us, he knows what he is capable of. He is outraged that Stanhope, after forcing Aurora into liquidation, has now persuaded Stella to marry him. You must tell him at once.'

'Mmmm' said George thoughtfully, 'I will send word to Nathan tonight, it's very short notice but I'll see if he can come'.

'For my part George, I shall have to be taking my leave of you all. We will be leaving in the morning,' said Elizabeth. 'We have to go back home and, now that Stella has been found, I think we should depart and let you sort things out.'

And with that, Elizabeth and her family departed Vavasour Hall the next day.

Chapter 37

The anticipation for Stella's visit finally gave way to the actual day and, by this time, Aurora was beside herself with excitement. In the happy prospect of seeing her daughter again, it seemed that all thoughts of how Stella had left them were forgotten, and even excused.

Nathan's arrival, to Aurora's surprise and delight was, she thought, so well timed. She was, of course, quite ignorant of the part George played in bringing him there.

Aurora's excitement peaked but began to fall as time ticked by and the expected hour came and went. Then finally, arriving almost two hours later than expected and when thoughts had turned to them not going to turn up, a coach arrived from which Stella alighted looking exceedingly pleased with herself.

Nathan quietly commented to George, 'Everyone knows it's unpardonably rude to be early for a visit, almost as bad as being late. Detracts from the hostess who is the centre of attention, so we shouldn't be surprised they failed to make it here on time. Wouldn't have made a grand enough entrance if they'd been on time, would it?'

Following her out of the coach was the thin, gaunt figure of Stanhope, looking every bit as smug as his new wife. On setting his feet on the ground Stanhope adopted an exaggerated regal posture, with shoulders thrown back high and, looking from left to right, nodded in pleasure at the property and was evidently congratulating himself on his prospects.

He was entering Vavasour Hall with the future heiress of that estate and, in his eyes, his humiliation of the Fairfax family was utterly complete. At least it would be when he saw their reaction, for a victory is not so great or joyful until the defeated are seen to be ignominiously humbled with loss of face. For Stanhope he had to 'see' the Fairfaxes pained, to see them suffer would heighten his own satisfaction.

And so, deliberately slowly, they made their stately progress into the hall ready to face those they had triumphed over. Their altered status had puffed up Mr and Mrs Stanhope whilst conversely made Aurora timid and unsure of herself. Stella and Aurora took the lead in instigating greetings; Stella joyous at the shock of her being a married woman whilst Aurora was just glad to see her daughter and know she was well.

For George, and Nathan in particular, however, the occasion was met with very different feelings. They felt no such intimidation and were like coiled springs pegged back on a hook, ready to let go at a moment's notice.

It was to be a full ten minutes into the gathering before anyone other than Aurora and Stella spoke. The questions had all been asked, the answers - such as Stella gave - were all given and all readily accepted by Aurora and still Stanhope had said and done nothing but nod.

'Something must be done' George thought to himself. 'He's going to leave this house a paragon of virtue if he isn't challenged. He must be teased out of his complacency'. George's army training had taught him how to handle certain types of men and, although he had a reputation for being 'gentle', he knew full well that, with some men - usually of the lowest rank, gentleness and reasoning never gleaned satisfactory results and could, to some, be seen as weakness. Severe discipline and authority was necessary for those who were incapable of responding to anything else. Stanhope was such a man.

So, in language Aurora had never heard George use before, he began his assault:

'And where do you plan on living Stella'? asked George bluntly.

'Why here, of course' she said nonchalantly. 'Where else would I live'.

'And you?' said George looking directly at Stanhope.

'With my wife naturally' came the insipid response.

'Over my dead body!' said George.

'If needs be!' came the instant retort.

'You think you could take me on then?' said George.

'Makes no odds to me. I could take both of you on .... at the same time if you like .....' Stanhope felt in his pocket for a handkerchief to mop beads of sweat that had formed on his brow. He then gave an arrogant sneer at Nathan.

'What yew la'ffing at you blockhead ......' said Nathan, piling on the provocation.

Provoking Stanhope was child's play. Stanhope lunged forward as if to strike Nathan but, quick as lightening, Stella put herself between them and they both pulled back.

As George and Nathan both knew full well, Stanhope was a man who didn't have the capacity to let a slight go. He couldn't stop himself responding to the merest hint of criticism, so they kept piling it on till he buckled,

'Oh ..... dear' said Stella feverishly. 'Charles means long term, not straight away ....'

'No I don't' said Stanhope arrogantly, looking at George, 'and if you want to settle it man to man, then I'm ready!'

'No, wait,' intervened Nathan. 'I'm the one with a score to settle with you Stanhope and nothing would give me greater pleasure than to call you out in a duel!'

'Stop this!' interceded Aurora. 'There will be no duels. Stella' she said pleading to her daughter, 'you must have known this would happen bringing *that* man here. Did you really think we could *ever* be reconciled to this abomination? Is this what you wanted? Do you want your ..... husband .... if indeed you truly are married ..... to be killed in a duel?'

'No, of course not' said Stella stumbling for words. 'I ..... no .... this is not what I planned at all. I think we better go ....'

'Why?' said Stanhope sneering, 'it's just getting interesting! And *I* would not be the one to get killed I can assure you ...'

Aurora, who had not immediately realised what was going on, slowly began to realise what George and Nathan were doing ..... and why.

George could hold back no longer and, getting close up to Stanhope, said in a calm steady voice 'I don't much like your method of getting wives. You're nothing but a common thief, snatching a babe from its mother's arms. You're pathetic'.

Stanhope reacted with fury. He was taking the bate!

George was now ready to capitalise on his opponent's growing agitation and started to lay it on thick.

'I know exactly what kind of man you are' he said walking away and turning his back on Stanhope. 'The army has its share of men like you ..... men who run away at the first sign of battle ....

those who change sides … those who go with whoever offers more money ... men who rape and plunder ... common thieves. Men' .... he said with emphasis .... 'who were bought by the King's Shilling. You're nothing but a treacherous coward that steals away under cover of darkness and hides hoping not to be caught. That's what you are.'

Stella was desperately trying to restrain Stanhope who was trying to reach Nathan and taunting him to fight …..

'What would it take to buy you off now' George continued, '..... not much I bet. A few pounds should do it. Nay, this small change I have here in my pocket would suffice I'll be bound .... you haven't the guts to duel with any man. I, however, would gladly give my life if the world could be rid of you. What are we waiting for ... let's do it right now.'

'Stop it!' cried Stella in distress. 'I will not permit this'.

'*You?* ..... *You* …… will not permit this?' said Stanhope laughing in his rage. 'And who do you think you are to say no to me, dearest wife ..... chattel ..... filthy Fairfax!'

'What?' cried Stella.

'Yes, that's right' said Aurora now in a growing temper. 'You've said those words before haven't you Stanhope? When you were at our house, when I was married to Stella's father, Benjamin Vavasour. You stood over Stella's crib and called her a filthy, filthy Fairfax and … you said she'd grow up to be the queen of the sluts! Yes, Stella ….. you!' she said looking at her daughter before looking back at Stanhope, 'and now ... look at you ... you've really got your ultimate revenge against this family ... because Stella's is too young, too naive and .... too stupid to know what kind of person you are.'

'Stop this!' said Stella in tears. She was frozen to the spot, incredulous at what her mother was saying .... 'You said what?' she said looking at Stanhope.

'You *dare* to come amongst us' Aurora told Stanhope ….. 'and fancy yourself on an equal footing, after forming an improper attachment and conducting such a despicable elopement of a child, taking her from her family and friends…. deceiving her as to your intentions. We should bring charges of abduction against you. You took an ill-tempered, spoilt and impressionable young girl and have now made it impossible for her family to take her back. You are more vile …. more detestable …. and more wretchedly ugly than any man living. You belong in a midden and I pray to live long enough to see you turn to dust and may your soul thereafter burn in hellfire for all eternity.'

'Mother!' gasped Stella in disbelief.

'Now get out!' yelled Aurora. 'Stanhope. Go. And you too Stella …. I can do no more for you. I want you to go now too!'

George watched, in some astonishment and satisfaction, as his wife finally snapped at Stella's folly and he made no attempt to intervene, he'd done what he intended. He knew Aurora well enough to know that this moment was a turning point, that Aurora wouldn't be able to forgive Stella for bringing such a viper into their home.

Stella, who had entered her former home with all the false heroism and bravura of youth, felt her natural over-confidence vanish in an instant. Faced by a solid phalanx of anger from her closest relations, she withered inside. Confused and surprised by her mother's words, she turned to go and, but Stanhope was riled up and shouting. So she pushed passed him and left him in the room alone.

'You won't be living here long, I shall see you out of Vavasour Hall' Stanhope shouted. 'You see if I don't.'

Nathan signalled to two servants who'd been placed near the doorway - in case of trouble - the men escorted Stanhope out the door and he was bundled into the coach. Nathan signalled to the coachman to depart and it pulled away at great speed, violently shaking the inhabitants as it bounced hard on the cobble stones. The sound of the couple arguing inside the coach, with Stella in floods of tears, could be heard for some time as they disappeared off the estate.

'So much for the blissful union of newly-weds' said Nathan on moving outside to hear them. 'Poor Stella'.

'Poor Stella my foot' said George, then turning to Aurora he said 'we had to draw him out ….. my dear I couldn't tell you in advance, I needed you to be yourself …… and not part of it. Nathan and I knew what we were doing'.

'I know' she replied. 'I could see that, and it worked, Stella has had her eyes opened today. But he ….. the man ….' She said despairingly, 'appears to have no concept of his impropriety. Nay, that is too soft a word to use in relation to him. He is bereft of integrity and now Stella, in her foolishness, must share in the shame. There is no point of return from what has happened here today and I feel I no longer have a daughter…...'

It was hard to give words to all the emotions that had been played out that day and what was now needed was time for reflection, albeit unpleasant reflections. The day's hard words would have to be weighed in a calmer time of reason to arrive at a more balanced judgement.

Nathan indicated his need to depart and, as an aside, said to George 'Thank goodness he didn't hold me to a duel. I'm so short sighted I probably wouldn't have been able to hit him!'

George winked at Nathan, but now was not the time to talk things over. Aurora had just undergone a traumatic confrontation with her daughter but after a little quiet reflection she was satisfied as to the cause of her agitation.

'I do have some regret' she said after a few moments, 'I really shouldn't have called him ugly, but I *was* provoked!'. George smiled and said 'I'm glad that's the only word you regret using'.

It was such a moment of fundamental change. Aurora was no longer distressed and worried about Stella in terms of her safety, her fear of what "might" have happened to Stella was less an evil than what "actually" had happened to her. Stanhope had troubled her family for too long, had brought her to bankruptcy, tried to destroy her brother's career several times, had threatened her family for so many years and had now bewitched her daughter. It was too much.

Aurora now felt that if her daughter had willingly married Stanhope, then so be it. That was the end of the matter. She felt foolish that she'd spent so much time worrying and grieving over what had happened to her daughter, and yet all the time Stella was laughing up her sleeve.

She reasoned with herself and regulated her thoughts by this process. She knew how stubborn her daughter was, that she would never concede that her marriage was anything less than idyllic and so the dye was cast. This was the moment that Aurora consciously chose to distance herself from her daughter in favour of George and her own Fairfax family.

Little did she know then, that this was to be the last time she would see Stella. That their final words to each other in this world were the harshest imaginable.

Ethel Fledd

Chapter 38

With all connection between mother and daughter ended, it seems likely that Stella, under Stanhope's direction, went through a similar process of hardening her attitude to her mother. Three months later, in spring, legal papers were served on Aurora and George by Stella and Charles Stanhope for immediate possession of Vavasour Hall.

Aurora took the news very badly. After everything she'd gone through for Stella's benefit and, having lived peaceably for so many years without litigation, it gave her a heavy heart to think it was going to start all over again. Worse yet, that it should be her very own daughter who was instigating them. An action that, if her daughter was successful, may well result in George and Aurora losing their home.

Then, to prove the phrase that 'when sorrows come, they come not single spies, but in battalions' another, new, major problem occurred on the estate which demanded immediate attention.

After returning from a visit to York, George and Aurora's carriage went past a group of men gathered on the side of the road. They were close to Vavasour Hall and on the estate's land and so George wondered what was going on. As they passed the group by, George commented they he knew the men, that they were all their tenants,

'Woah' he shouted to the coachman, 'hold back a while'. Then he pushed his head out of the window and, on seeing him, the men moved towards him to talk.

'What's going on?' he asked.

'Sir' said one of the group, 'there's a problem with the water supply.'

'What kind of problem?' asked George.

'We have no water for the cattle on the common land, nor for the fields or cottages. Water wheels have all stopped and there's no water to Vavasour Hall either'.

'How can that be?' asked George. 'Follow us to the great house and we'll get this sorted out' he said. Then the carriage moved away with the men following behind. 'I'll find out what's wrong' George told Aurora, 'You go inside'.

The men arrived a few minutes later and George beckoned them all into the hall where they could talk out of the wind, and he immediately heard what they thought the cause of the problem was.

'We seen some workers over last few days working on the river bank, just t'other side o'serpentine lake' one said pointing. And we didn't think nowt of it, they weren't local people so we didn't pay much attention. But now they've done, we can see what they were doin. They've blocked the river with boulders. Water has been pooled into side field and nowt flows downstream'.

'But isn't that over on Pascal Vavasour's land then?' asked George.

'Aye, sir, it is'.

'I wonder he's not concerned about it too then' said George thoughtfully.

'Aye sir, well, maybe he ain't concerned about it 'cos he might be the one that dun it, sir' a voice from the back said, and there was a murmur of agreement and nodding heads.

'But you say you didn't recognise any of the men? None of them were his?'

'No sir, but it stands to reason, he's the only one on the entire estate who's got water, more water than he knows what to do with, and the rest of us 'ave nowt. Our crops and animals will die, sir, if this ain't sorted out quickly.'

George pondered a moment. 'Right men, here's what we'll do. Give me an hour to go and fetch the local Justice of the Peace, then meet me back here. If we can't find out who's done this, then we'll take the obstruction out ourselves so the water can flow but ..... mind not a word of this gets back to Vavasour .....'

The men gave up a loud cheer.

'Bring ropes, horses and as many men back with you as you can muster. We'll only get one chance to do this, so we need to act quickly. But remember to tell no one connected with Pascal Vavasour!'

George instinctively knew who was behind the disruption. Following on so swiftly after Stanhope's visit, who else could it be.

Ethel Fledd

Chapter 39

As arranged, over an hour later the men returned in a great number and George met up with them. He had already brought the local Justice to examine the dammed up river and told him what the consequences were. The Justice confirmed that no one had sought permission to divert the river and, since the estate depended on it, that George was within his rights to restore it to its proper path.

The assembled men went over to where the river bank had been blockaded and began the heavy work of clearing the obstructions. Horses were put to work and ropes strung around the boulders. Though hard work, it was made lighter by the great numbers that had turned up; with the exception of a few elderly men, almost every single one of the Vavasour estate's tenants, their sons and friends had been enlisted to help and were happy to do so.

Little by little the water pushed its way back to its familiar pathway and there were cheers and hoorays with each bit of success they had.

It took many hours to complete and, as they were nearly finished, George observed a solitary figure riding towards them. It was Pascal Vavasour.

'Hey there' he shouted, waving a pistol in his hand. 'What are you doing on my land?'

'Pascal' shouted George identifying himself. 'Come here'.

Pascal approached, looking somewhat intimidated by the large group of men giving him cold, evil looks.

'What goes on here?' he said.

'It would appear that someone has trespassed on estate land, dammed up the water and flooded your field. Water has been diverted away from the rest of the estate. Perhaps your friend Stanhope?' George suggested.

'My friend?' said Pascal, as if he'd never heard of Stanhope. 'I know nothing about this. See look, it's my field that's been flooded. I've been away for a few days, and I come back to find all this has happened'.

George called over one of the men, whispered in his ear and the man rode off at speed. He listened to Pascal's fake protestations of innocence which, of course, were entirely for the benefit of the Justice of the Peace. He knew full well that Pascal was complicit in the crime and that as Stanhope's closest friend he had colluded with him. Of course he would deny involvement.

'You will therefore be very pleased that we've rectified the problem then' said George. 'I'm sure too that you'll keep a look out for strangers coming on to your land and doing this again'.

'Um .... of course' said Pascal.

'So you didn't see the men who built the obstruction then?' asked the Justice.

'Why no, of course I didn't, I should've stopped them if I had' said Pascal.

'But your house, sir, is only over yonder. I wonder that you didn't see the work being done?' the Justice persisted.

'No .... I .... I have been away for a few days, sir, I .... er .... I've only just returned .....'

'Please let me know if you see any illegal activity like this again and it will be dealt with. At least' he added, 'it's easier to unblock the river than it must have been to block it in the first place!'

With that the Justice and the men began to disperse and move away. Pascal tugged at his horse and returned to his house.

Chapter 40

George returned to Vavasour Hall where he found Duke had arrived to see them. He's been waiting for some time, having travelled directly from London when he heard about Stella being missing. Aurora had already told him of Stella's visit, Stanhope's threats and the impending law suit.

Aurora's mood was despondent and she told Duke that she felt certain that, once more, their living at Vavasour Hall was at risk, since she only held her position there as guardian to the heiress Stella. With Stella now married, she believed Stanhope now held the destiny of Vavasour Hall entirely in his hands.

'But what of Stella' asked Duke. 'Where is she now?'

'She's moved into Stanhope's residence and severed all connection with her family and friends.'

'I suppose it could hardly have been otherwise' said Duke sanguinely 'as the law suit continues'.

Aurora got up, kissed her father on the cheek and then left the room to lie down, saying she must be excused but she was over tired.

When she'd gone, George and Duke had a frank discussion about the water incident and the prospects of the legal case Stella had brought.

'This case is entirely Stanhope's of course' said Duke. 'We all know his vindictive nature and his animosity to the Fairfax family. The law suit may be in Stella's name but he's behind it alright. He knows full well that Stella is her father's heir and that Aurora only holds this house during Stella's minority.'

'I've spoken to Severn who bought the separate manor and he's perfectly willing to throw his weight in on our side. '

'What of Pascal Vavasour? What of him ....?' asked Duke.

'We'll get no support from him, quite the contrary. As someone with an interest in the estate he may also have papers will be served on him, as well as Severn, in the next few days.

'I wouldn't be surprised if Stanhope doesn't want to oust both of them from the estate too.'

'I should be on my guard against Pascal' said Duke warily, 'now that he is aware, he make seize the opportunity to approach Stanhope himself and offer his support to him - in return for an increase in his annuity, or some other such sweetener.'

'Yes,' said George, 'I'm aware he could do that.'
A knock at the door, followed by the entrance of a servant carrying a tray, brought a note.

'It's from Stella' said George taking it. 'Addressed to Aurora'.

He didn't hesitate to open it and read it out to Duke.

'I know Aurora won't mind' he said, 'but we need to know what is says right now, whilst you're here with us so you can advise us'.

Reading through it, he said, 'No, there's no mention of anything relating to the case but .... here .... look, she says she is expecting a baby.'

'I wonder she took the trouble to write to her mother to say such a thing when she's taking her to court at the same time. Foolish girl.' said Duke. 'Now we shall have Stanhope's offspring at Vavasour Hall! Stanhope has done what he needed to, to secure his claim on the estate. I imagine Stella will soon, after giving birth, find herself with an absent husband. He will have no reason to stay constant to her once an heir is secured.'

Duke's candid comment took George by surprise as the infant would be Duke's grandchild, but conversation between men, without ladies present, was always more direct. George found it refreshing to be able to discuss matters with a clear thinking lawyer than with Aurora, who had so many emotional ties to the house, her daughter, even her dead husband, that dispassionate conversation was impossible.

After calling for his coach to be brought to the front of the house ready for his imminent departure, Duke stood pensively looking into the fire. 'So let's think this through logically' he said. 'The situation is this; Aurora holds the estate in trust as guardian during her daughter's minority, Stella is not yet of full age, therefore Aurora can stay here until Stella is 21. But, as a married woman, Stella has freely chosen to live elsewhere with her husband. So, how does that leave Aurora's position to be living here ...... and could Stella and Stanhope successfully take Vavasour Hall from her mother.?'

'If she was 21, then yes' said George.

'But she isn't 21 is she?' Duke said with significance. 'Exactly how old is she, 20?'

'Just turned 20' said George.

'Then we need to act fast before she does turn 21 years of age. Right, I must be going' said Duke. 'That's it, the matter is solved.'

'What?' said George, 'solved how?'

Walking out the room, Duke turned to George and said 'all the answers you need ..... are in the will ..... the will of Dionysus Vavasour!'

With that, he was gone, leaving George completely baffled.

Chapter 41

The next day, George - who had spent hours musing over the will as directed and then consulting with the solicitor - was busy about his usual business; most of his days were filled with managing everyone else's activities - a word of instruction here, encouragement there, solving estate problems and above all controlling the finances.

This day, after speaking to his steward, and on returning from a cursory inspection of the stables, he went for a walk away from the house and over in the direction of the river bank. This wasn't part of his daily routine but yesterday's discovery of sabotage had shattered his assumption that it was a place that needed no surveillance, so he now felt it necessary to give a cursory inspection to the scene. He reflected on the previous day's herculean activities of his men and felt a certain pride and satisfaction.

As expected, he saw the river had been restored to its proper path and a subsidiary filtered into the serpentine lake adjacent to Vavasour Hall. All was as it should be.

After a few minutes of reflection, he saw the figure of Pascal on horseback moving slowly in front of him. Pascal had probably been watching over the same scene and, George had been in hopes of speaking to him ....

'Wait Pascal' shouted George. 'A word with you please'.

Pascal paused, stayed seated on his horse and waited for George to approach him.

'I've been reading your grandfather's will' said George.

Looking somewhat incredulous, Pascal responded with complete disinterest, ''Should have thought you'd have more urgent matters to attend to. Like finding out who did this' he said pointing towards the river 'and making sure it doesn't happen again.'

'Oh, I know who was behind that' said George in a matter of fact way. 'I think there's something you should know. Step down a moment if you please'.

Pascal obliged and descended to the ground, 'And what might that be' he sneered impatiently.

'You will know, of course, that Stanhope has gone through a clandestine marriage with young Stella.'

'I do believe I've heard that' he said.

'And ... I doubt not that you also know that Stanhope and Stella are suing us for Vavasour Hall?'

'Is that so?' Pascal said carelessly.

'That is so' said George. 'And that being the case, there may be implications for the annuity that you receive from the estate'.

'My annuity' said Pascal defensively, 'is supported by the courts and will be paid, come what may.'

'So then it matters not to you who wins this case?.

'I have no interest in it' he said coldly.

'And ...... you had no involvement in this incident here yesterday?' asked George directly.

'I didn't' Pascal replied arrogantly. 'And there isn't a man in the world who could say I did either'.

The verbal combat continued a while until George decided he was gaining ground.

'That is good' said George. 'Because .... You see .... I shall tell you how things are. Just in case you might at any point in the future get tempted to side with Stanhope against us ... again .....'

'Again .... What do you mean ... I told you ....' Pascal tried to interrupt.

'T'was no difficult matter for me to send a man to ask your servant if you had been away while the river was blocked. He learned that you hadn't been away, so then you *must* have seen what was happening. You knew full well about it. So let's have no more of your protestations of innocence .....'

'What I do or don't do is entirely my business not yours!' said Pascal angrily.

'It is .... when you meddle with the Vavasour estate!' said George.

'Which was my home .... not yours!'

'Listen.' George said veering the conversation back in the direction he wanted, 'You need to remember this, that in your grandfather's will, Dionysus Vavasour made it a condition that if the heir to the entailed estate was to marry before they reached the age of 21 years, it must be with the consent of their parents.'

'And?' said Pascal looking blank. 'What of it?'

'Stella was ..... 20 ..... when she married Stanhope!' said George.

Pascal paused, trying to keep up with the conversation .... 'but she is still the heir?'

'She is. But .... *because* she foolishly married before her majority, she cannot now inherit Vavasour Hall until after her mother's death which, God willing, will be many years hence. The will stipulates that an heir marrying without parental consent under full age, shall be entitled to a bare maintenance only. In that eventuality, the right to reside at Vavasour Hall, to receive the rents and tithes, all remain with the parent, or in this case Aurora the surviving parent, for the term of her natural life. Stella's foolishness, encouraged no doubt by Stanhope's haste and direction, has led to her forfeiting the estate for the foreseeable future. And ... that means ... your friend Stanhope has made a gross miscalculation, hasn't he?'

Pascal realised the significance of what George had said but didn't wish to show it.

'What is that matter to me?' he said nonchalantly.

'Well, if you were thinking .... Indeed, already have .... joined forces with Stanhope - then, my friend you are on a high road to ..... nowhere! And ... if, by and by, you make an enemy of me, I shall devote the rest of my days to making your life a living hell, a continual battle ground with non-stop litigation, starting with that annuity .....'

Pascal, his silence conceding the limitation of his power, mounted his horse and rode off.

Chapter 42

Back home, George relayed some, but not all, of the details of the day's events to Aurora who was not at all surprised to learn of Pascal's involvement. The next day, with the water supply to the house and estate returning to normal, George went back over to the river's edge to examine the repaired banks and observed Pascal coming towards him.

This time it was Pascal who sought him out, from which George immediately detected a change in mood from the previous day and Pascal greeted him, if not warmly, then at least civilly.

'Good morning Pascal'

'Good morning' came the reply 'come on over to the house'.

So to George's surprise he was invited into Pascal's home where he lived alone and was shown into a small comfortable sitting room. Pascal was unmarried, and with just a couple of servants managed his living arrangements very simply.

'What can I do for you?' asked George.

'I've been thinking about what you said yesterday' said Pascal thoughtfully. 'I'm truly shocked about Stella, I was always under the impression that Stella would never do such a thing ... that she would never marry without her mother's consent.'

George was listening and assessing Pascal. Obviously, he thought to himself, he's been thinking about the fact that Stanhope has no case against us and he's decided to switch allegiance.

'I wasn't involved, you know' he said. 'If Stanhope was behind the obstruction to the river, he didn't tell me'.

'Yes, well you can see how it looks Pascal. Yours was the only property that still had water, the rest of us didn't'.

'No I wasn't involved' he insisted. 'If you think about it, why would he tell me? He knows full well that I have an interest in the estate and that by marrying Stella, the future owner, that his interests would directly clash with mine. No. No, it's no wonder he would not divulge those plans to me! I'm really shocked.'

George then saw how Pascal's mind was turning to the potential practical consequences to them all. 'And what of the estate then' he said, 'what might be the implications for you, for Aurora .... and for me if Stanhope should succeed?'

'Well depends on how the land lies between us' said George. 'If Stanhope is going to continually look for ways to attack this estate, then it would be better if all those with an interest in it stuck together'.

'I should be happy to do that' conceded Pascal. 'I suppose from my point of view it matters not who the owner is, so long as I continue to get my annuity paid'.

'And you think Stanhope would honour it?' said George with incredulity. 'At least with myself and Aurora you know it's guaranteed. Do you think your financial future would be secure in Stanhope's hands?' said George.

'So .... Better the devil you know! ....' said Pascal grinning.

'Just so. And if you wish to pass on the content of our conversation yesterday to your friend Stanhope, then the case might be stopped. It's no matter to us if it continues until he is bankrupted by legal fees as we shall ask the courts to pay our fees.'

After his visit, George left Pascal's house knowing that there was, at least, one less enemy to deal for now.

Later that evening Aurora joined her husband in the library, the couple sitting either side of the fire, just as she'd seen Gervase Vavasour and Pascal doing when she'd first visited the house. Deep soul-searching wasn't a common past-time in the eighteenth century, but Aurora had strong feelings,

'What will we do' she said, 'if we are forced to leave Vavasour Hall? I have such a feeling about this place, like fate meant us to be here. I think my spirit will stay here, long after the flesh and bones are gone. Where else should we go if we're forced to leave?'

'You've always known that once Stella reaches 21 that Vavasour Hall would be hers and she may have thrown us out to the hedgerows. In the present climate she is hardly likely to ask us to continue living here is she?'

'And we wouldn't want to anyway' said Aurora. 'I think it's time for us to start thinking about where we're to live in the future?'

'There's always my home. Catherine and John spend most of their time in London and have no need of a country residence, it's there for us at any time so there's no need to worry. We'll be fine.'

'But' said Aurora, 'I have grown to love this place. I really would not want to leave it ....'

'It's just a house' said George 'there are plenty of others and, one thing I do know, we'll be leaving this estate in a far better shape that we found it.'

'You know' said Aurora. 'I really can't imagine Stella being mistress here. She's just a child herself .... and .... expecting a baby, just imagine that'.

'Not such a child then is she?' said George. 'I think she will have a very hard life with Stanhope. He's used her wickedly and, once he has the Vavasour estate, he will have no more interest in her. I don't believe he will be a good husband to her, not for one moment.'

'So long as she doesn't come back to us in the future. I don't want her to see us as a refuge if Stanhope treats her badly. By her own actions, she has most likely lost us our family home. Now, if he treats her badly, then she has no one else to blame and I will not take her back. I have nothing more I can give her. She's taken everything from us. I will not see us impoverished even more on her account'.

'It won't come to that', said George.

'It might' Aurora insisted.

'No, it won't.' said George confidently. When I told you about my meeting with Pascal earlier, I omitted to mention something .... something very important. I thought I'd save it to this evening.'

'What?' asked Aurora curiously.

'Duke said something to me before he left earlier. He directed me to the will of Dionysus Vavasour.'

'Benjamin's grandfather, yes, what of it?'

'Well, Stella and Stanhope may have been well acquainted with Benjamin's will, they may also have been very well acquainted with Gervase Vavasour's will, but I don't think they would've taken the trouble to go back as far as the will of Dionysus.'

'Did Father find something that would help us in that will? asked Aurora.

'Yes' said George looking pleased with himself. 'It seems that entailed heirs to this estate should not marry without parental consent ....'

'But Benjamin didn't have consent .....' said Aurora.

'No he didn't, but then he was past the age of his majority. He was, what, 24 or 25 years old when he married.'

'Yes that's right' said Aurora. 'What of it?'

'And Stella is precisely how old .....?'

'She is 20 years and 6 months' said Aurora.

'Well the will of Dionysus says that any heir marrying under the age of 21 years *must* have parental consent, or .... and this is the interesting part .... or their parent, or surviving parent, will retain the right to occupy the house and receive all the rents, profits, tithes etc for their lifetime.'

'What?' said Aurora in astonishment. 'So Stella has forfeited her right to inherit everything, just by marrying without my permission?'

'Oh no, she is still the heiress of Vavasour Hall, it's just that she has forfeited that right during the course of your life time. That's right'.

'Oh my God' said Aurora sighing heavily. She threw her arms around George and embraced him. 'Why didn't you tell me this sooner?'

'Tis ironic, but if the foolish girl had waited a few months, she could have married, even without your consent, and inherited it all straight away. But .... she didn't wait .... or he coerced her'.

'Oh I can't believe it. So we can stay here?' gasped Aurora.

'We certainly can. But it was Duke who discovered it, not me. And he only mentioned it this afternoon. You know how lawyers are ... with their love of details. We were thinking things through this afternoon, when you were resting, and it suddenly occurred to him.....'

'Yes he knows the documents inside out' said Aurora. 'He spent a lot of time helping me in the early days over Benjamin's estate'.

'That's right' said George, 'and it's entirely down to him. I can't take the credit for this. He pointed me in the right direction.'

'So' .... said Aurora furtively and lowering her pitch '*they* don't know then, do they?' she said referring to Stella and Stanhope.

'No obviously not. Wouldn't have brought the case if they had any idea'.

'We should tell them straight away ....' said Aurora.

'Should we?' pondered George. 'Or should we leave it a while ....'

'But if we tell them straight away they'll stop the case! Of course we should tell them'

'I think they will find out soon enough, now Pascal is aware of the situation. Let him tell them, I'm in no rush .... I don't know a great deal about Stanhope's finances, but I don't think he's a match for us. What fortune he gained from his father has been gambled away'.

'But Stella ....' said Aurora wistfully. 'Her fate is tied to his, if we hurt him, we hurt her'.

'Not necessarily', said George. 'The will does stipulate that although this estate defaults to you if Stella marries without consent under age, it does also state that there is a requirement to provide basic maintenance to her in the meantime'.

'Whatever we give her, he will take' said Aurora.

'We can set something up .... perhaps a bond ... whereby money is provided for Stella's sole support. It will be legally binding, so she can support herself without any recourse to him. He will have no claim on it or access to it and if she cares anything about herself and the child she's going to have, she'll keep quiet about it'.

'I like the sound of that' said Aurora. 'My God, he will be furious' she said trying to suppress a laugh.

'As they say' said George 'what goes around, comes around and Stanhope's had it coming for a long while.'

Ethel Fledd

Chapter 43

Aurora's relief, after this conversation with George, was palpable. Charles Stanhope, having been given sufficient rope, had comprehensively hung himself. Not only that but he had unwittingly given George and Aurora a life-time of security at Vavasour Hall. In return, he was now saddled with a young bride, who he had probably no real regard for, and whose temper and unpleasant disposition would guarantee him a troublesome future.

The absence of Stella in the house was initially so very noticeable to both of them but, with the passage of several months, Aurora found herself enjoying freedom from worrying about her all the time. Someone else was now responsible for her, she was someone else's problem and Vavasour Hall was a far more peaceful home without her.

Every now and then Aurora would make a comment as she wondered how Stella's pregnancy was progressing but George took pains not to encourage these conversations too much. He felt it was better for Aurora to have some distance from her daughter and, in truth, he was enjoying Stella's absence the greatest.

Stella was gone and there had been no letter from her or word about her from anyone until early the following year when a servant arrived at Vavasour Hall with a note. Aurora, who was alone at the time, took the note eager to know what it said and read it straight away.

'Ma'am' interrupted the butler when he could see Aurora had almost finished reading, 'the servant that brought this note is down stairs in the kitchen, with the bairn and has indicated that it's to be left here'.

The note said that Stella had died shortly after given birth to a girl. The baby downstairs was hers. Stanhope had wanted nothing to do with it and told the servant to deliver it to Aurora as he would not care for it. Aurora swept downstairs instantly to see the child and cradled it in her arms. Distress at her daughter's death was tempered by the sight of the live, wriggling, chuckling little baby and there was never a moment's doubt that she would take it into her care. She quizzed the servant for several minutes before letting the young woman go and the door was closed.

It was a miracle. She and George had no children of their own, and yet here was a God-given miracle, her own flesh and blood, and just handed to her to raise. It seemed too good to be true.

Within a few hours George arrived back home to be greeted by the astonishing sight of his wife cradling a baby. News of Stella's death was met with due sadness but it was difficult to stay subdued for long with the new arrival. All attention was now on the child who caused a pleasant fuss and delight in the house until a crib was sorted out.

After settling the baby, George asked Aurora 'I wonder what this means. Has Stanhope washed his hands of us now? I suppose we'll have to travel over to attend her funeral?'

'No, that has already taken place' said Aurora. 'With no one from her family there!'

'He must know I think' said George 'that his legal case against us is now lost. He must know about the stipulation in Dionysus's will.'

'But doesn't Stella's ….. death ….. my goodness, I little thought when I woke up this morning that I would be saying those words …. Stella dead! ….. Doesn't the death put an end to his case against us any way?' said Aurora.

'No not at all. Stella's child is the next heir. I would have thought he'd keep the child, so he can retain his claim on the estate, said George perplexed.'

'I think sending the child to us is his way of throwing the towel in' said Aurora, not really paying much attention to the conversation.

'Mmm' pondered George, 'I suppose if he did discover that the house will remain in your hands during your life time he may think the game is over. You're younger than he is and likely, I hope, to outlive him. And, in the mean time, he doesn't want the inconvenience and expense of raising her ….'

'I'm just glad we've got her' said Aurora smiling. 'Now can we put an end to the legal case hanging over us? She said.

'Soon …..' said George, 'just want to see what Stanhope does next, then I'll end it'.

The weeks passed by quickly with Stella's daughter, who had no name at this point, keeping everyone busy. It was felt necessary to urgently arrange for a baptism to take place and it was decided to name her Isabella, after Aurora's mother. The families of sisters Elizabeth and Catherine, together with Nathan visited for the ceremony. George's brother John too attended and Isabella was welcomed into the world as Isabella Mason with George and Aurora as her de facto parents.

The baby grew, fattened out nicely and, within a few months, a relaxed domestic routine evolved and Vavasour Hall became something it hadn't been for decades: a happy family home.

The law suit against them, which George had been fully expecting to be called off dragged on, from which George deduced correctly that Pascal hadn't bothered to inform his friend of developments. When George was satisfied that Stanhope had been put to the maximum trouble and cost, he presented his evidence and the case was ended immediately.

Nothing had been heard of, or about, Stanhope after Stella's death nor had there been any reaction to the abandonment of the court case either and life moved on as usual. There had been some fears by both George and Aurora that Stanhope would use his daughter's presence at Vavasour as an excuse to make himself a nuisance by calling there, but that fear proved unfounded.

News on the eventual fate of Stanhope actually came some months later from Duke who, on visiting them, told them of an incident he had recently heard of.

'Are you at all acquainted with James Craggs?' Duke asked George.

'No' he replied. 'Although ….. I have heard that there's a Craggs standing for the election at York. Is it the same one?'

'Yes' said Duke, 'James Craggs. I've known him for years. He was in parliament some years ago and the corporation were trying to persuade him to stand again. But …. he faced some stiff competition from our friend Charles Stanhope.'

'Stanhopes held York for many years didn't they?' asked Aurora.

'Yes, for decades, Charles Stanhope's father was MP right up till his death…… and Charles fancied he could fill his boots …..'

'Yes' said Aurora, 'and we know what a bad loser he is!'

'Well, that's so' said Duke. 'Certain members of the Corporation were dead set against Stanhope's selection and when Stanhope got wind of that he weren't too happy about it.'

'He's always unhappy about something' said George. 'Just not one of those souls destined to go through life with much happiness. He certainly doesn't spread it around'.

'Nay, and he won't have chance to spread anything about now. He's dead as a door nail!'

'What?' cried Aurora in astonishment. 'Really?'

'Is that so?' asked George. 'How did he die?'

'He was shot! In a duel. Fighting with Craggs.'

'Huh, why am I not surprised by that?' said George sarcastically. 'So, Craggs kill him?'

'Yes, Stanhope died from a single shot, died instantly' said Duke. 'It was over the contest for the parliamentary seat for York. They got into some sort of argument and Stanhope challenged Craggs to a duel. Apparently they were both shot; but thankfully Craggs still lives, though badly injured. If he pulls through, which I'm told he probably will, then I think the corporation will be mightily relieved and he'll get their blessing to stand as MP'.

'Well, well' said George thoughtfully. 'Praise be to God for our deliverance.'

'Poor little Eleanor' said Aurora. 'Now both her parents are dead. Thank heavens she's too young to know what's going on. Still, she need never know about him now as we'll raise her as our own'.

They continued talking about his death for some time until it was time for Duke to depart. As he was leaving he said, 'Let's hope this is the end of your sorrows. This closes a painful chapter in your life and you can start thinking of yourselves now. Nathan too. He'll be mighty glad Stanhope's out of the way.'

Chapter 44

Aurora rose early the next morning and took her favourite walk from the house towards the lake where a thin mist shrouded the water like a thin veil. Above her head in the trees, she heard a blackbird singing and, as it suddenly flew away, its departure sent clouds of blossom drifting down onto her head.

She was deep in thought, prompted by the news of Stanhope's death. This lakeside was Aurora's private world; a place where she could clear her mind of the vexations of daily life; a place where opinions could be formed, decisions made and cares and worries could be buried.

It was only now that she, at last, could give way to an overwhelming sense of relief. Relief that he could never again triumph, or threaten to triumph, over her family. That they were safe from his relentless pursuit of ruining their happiness or prospects.

One by one then, the protagonists in her life had died off: Gervase Vavasour, the vindictive father in law; Benjamin Vavasour, the dissolute husband; and then lastly Charles Stanhope, who hated all connected with the name Fairfax and many others who crossed his path. All those who had contrived to make Aurora's life difficult had departed the world.

To that list she could have added Stella Stanhope/Vavasour the troublesome daughter but she couldn't quite bring herself to put Stella in the same group as the others. So much of her life had been spent with Stella that she felt some failing on her own part that she hadn't been able to protect her …. even though that meant protecting Stella from herself. Nothing she could have done, however, would have prevented her daughter's fate of dying in childbirth but yet she was left with the unsettling feeling that she *should have* done more.

Still ….. what she was left with now was all goodness. Perhaps, she thought, Its true after all that the meek shall inherit the earth..... "if" but only if they can outlive their adversaries!

On this particular morning, she felt her blessings warmly. Perhaps at last she could live in peace. Yes, her daughter was dead, but having infant Eleanor to care for felt like she'd been given a second chance to experience happiness. Married now to a man she loved and respected and with the support of her wider family, it was all so different to the swirling torrent of hatred and revenge she'd been forced to raise her own daughter in.

Aurora also had the pleasure, and it was still a pleasure despite the passing of years, to be living at Vavasour Hall. Aurora felt, what many do who have lived through troubled times - if they are fortunate - that she'd gone through the worst and could look forward to happier days.

Since George and Aurora had no children of their own, Eleanor effectively became their daughter and they raised her in the formative years. The little girl became the centre of their life. 'This time it will be different' Aurora told herself. The sins of the father may have passed to Stella, but with Eleanor it would be different. Eleanor's spirit of fun infected them all and, in many ways, they lived *through* her. What a difference one happy individual made to the home - from the moment she woke up until she fell asleep she ran, she played, she laughed and she brought the best out in everyone.

There was no interference, indeed no contact whatsoever, from the wider Stanhope family concerning Eleanor, which made George suspect that Charles Stanhope hadn't made them aware of Eleanor's existence, and the Masons were happy to keep it that way.

In time, therefore, the name Stanhope was forgotten by those with an interest in the history of Vavasour Hall. Those who had known of him, chose not to talk about Charles Stanhope and he was quickly forgotten as nothing but a bad memory.

And what of the future ....

For George and Aurora there followed many happy years which sped by quickly. Their years of misfortune and dreadful drama were behind them and, in many ways, were easy to chronicle. The years of contentment they enjoyed were less dramatic being a harmonious existence where the little pleasantries and events of everyday life, passed by without much notice and their only desire was for their continuance.

There were many times when George and Aurora would walk from the house to look out towards the lake, watching Eleanor playing with the dogs. All living in the moment and enjoying their play. They wished such moments would last, that they could continue into eternity. The stress and suffering that they had endured was now for the benefit of Eleanor, so that she could enjoy the same contentment that they had found, though without the struggle. This was their reward; for all the years of litigation and fighting, just to see little Eleanor living care-free.

If only …… life really was that simple. If only ….. the future was reliably known. Tragedy has a cruel way of striking those, especially those, who are giving it no thought. To catch us unaware.

Epilogue

Media vita in morte sumus
In the midst of life we are in death

This, then, brings us to the closing end of Aurora's personal story.

It would have been so nice to have contrived a happy ending where she lived out her days in her Yorkshire home in domestic bliss. Having outlived her adversaries, how apt it would have been to say …. and so, she lived happy ever after.

This story, however, has been based on real life and, sadly, in real life not everyone gets the happy ending they perhaps deserve.

This small epilogue tells the story of what became of the characters in this story ….. how their futures unfurled in real life.

- o - o — o

Aurora

Aurora enjoyed fifteen years of marriage to George during which she discovered what real love and contentment was. After the great difficulties of bringing up Stella, it was a joy to raise Eleanor, a child blessed with a fun-loving and easy temperament.

Vavasour Hall, a place she'd grown to love, were her happiest, until a sudden short illness brought an abrupt end to her life. She took to her bed as she declined and George was with her constantly throughout the final days. In her last moments he looked at her eyes which were still beautiful and, like the lights of a star, he watched her soul depart and the lights dim and fade.

Moments later, George walked over to the window in the bedroom and looked up at the sky. For several months there'd been a comet visible in the night sky outside this window and he'd taken to looking out at it late in the evenings. That night, he

239

wondered if its presence was an omen, a message from God that it was time for him to take his northern star back to the heavens. 'Please God' he said to himself 'let the spirit of Aurora as it leaves her pass to young Eleanor - that Aurora might live on through her'. George knew he would never remarry, he knew that he had lost the love of his life.

Eleanor

Grand-daughter Eleanor was just eight years of age when Aurora died and she was now left in the care of George. As Aurora's illness had become apparent, Eleanor had been sent to live with Nathan's family, to spare her seeing her grandmother's decline.

After giving the matter great thought, George decided that it would be better for Eleanor to be raised as part of a large family rather than with him, as a solitary individual. Aurora's siblings were consulted and there were plenty of offers all around. Elizabeth, Catherine and Nathaniel were all eager to take Eleanor into their homes. But in the end it was decided that Eleanor would stay with Nathaniel's family where she'd been settled for some time and there she remained until she married many years later.

Vacated of family members, Vavasour Hall was then rented out for some years until such time as Eleanor was old enough to take up occupation. Eleanor eventually married a cousin. Whether the match was engineered by her relations or not is unclear but, in the fullness of time, young Eleanor married Elizabeth's son Edward, her first cousin. Vavasour Hall thereby stayed in the family and Aurora's descendants kept it for many generations to come.

George

George, still a comparatively young man when Aurora died, returned to military service as, by this time, Britain was once more at war with Spain. The colonies, as always in a war with a fellow European colonial power, were at the forefront of hostilities. George went to the West Indies as Captain of an independent company and was sadly killed, by the Spanish, en route to defend the island of Jamaica. His vessel was captured and all aboard, including women and children, were slaughtered.

Nathan

Nathan brought Eleanor up in his family home and was widely thought to have brought about the marriage of Aurora's grand-daughter to Elizabeth's son. Nathan continued his parliamentary career and remained in government until his eventual death. He played an important part in successive Whig administrations.

Duke

Duke never remarried and carried on his legal career, continuing to divide his time between London and York. He became embroiled in a bad investment when he was duped by the infamous Lady Ivy, a forger, and spent his final years trying, unsuccessfully, to recover funds.

Pascal

Pascal lived to a great age, having outlived them all, and when he died without heirs, left his estate to a friend and, in a mean gesture, left a poultry sum of a few shillings to his great-niece at Vavasour Hall. His will, and interest in the Vavasour estate, was contested by Aurora's descendants.

Elizabeth

In the years ahead, Aurora's grand-daughter Eleanor married Edward Wadebridge (Elizabeth's son), thereby uniting the descent of two of the northern stars. Edward forged out a career in the navy. Many a night when he was a sea, and dependant on the North Star to guide him, he would think and smile in remembrance of his mother and aunt ..... two of the Northern Stars ..... as they lived on in his thoughts. His naval career prevented him from spending too much time living in Yorkshire which was too far from the sea-faring port of Hampshire where he needed to be, but, in his later years, he handed the house over to his son who spent his whole life living there.

Edward Wadebridge achieved greatness in his lifetime and became one of Britain's finest Admirals, saving Britain from invasion by the French at the Battle of Quiberon Bay.
It was said his heroics fired the imagination of future admirals, such as Nelson, who was an admirer of both his naval tactics and

his philosophy of not shooting at the enemy till the whites of their eyes could be seen. The Northern Stars would have been so proud.

*The character of Aurora Fairfax
was inspired by the true story of
Frances of Scarthingwell Hall, Yorkshire*

*Some names, places, events and some details
have been changed*

Further reading:

Frances of Scarthingwell
By
Karen Proudler

ISBN: 978-0-9566831-9-9